Peter and Mary Have a Row

DAMIEN OWENS

FLAME
Hodder & Stoughton

Copyright © 2002 by Damien Owens

First published in Great Britain in 2002 by Hodder and Stoughton
A division of Hodder Headline

The right of Damien Owens to be identified as the Author
of the Work has been asserted by him in accordance with the
Copyright, Designs and Patents Act 1988.

A Flame Paperback

1 3 5 7 9 10 8 6 4 2

A CIP catalogue record for this title is
available from the British Library

ISBN 0 340 79285 X

Typeset in Fournier by Palimpsest Book Production Limited,
Polmont, Stirlingshire
Printed and bound in Great Britain by
Mackays of Chatham, Chatham, Kent

Hodder and Stoughton
A division of Hodder Headline
338 Euston Road
London NW1 3BH

For Shane, Ciara and Conor

I would like to thank my agent, Faith O'Grady, and my editor, Philippa Pride, for all their help and support.

1

'Ah, don't be like that, Mary. It got good reviews.'

'Peter—'

'And not just from the *Sun*. Lookit: "All the thrills and excitement you've come to expect from the Bond movies, and then some." That's *Premiere* magazine, that's reliable, that is.'

'You said to me—'

'Just give it a whirl, like.'

'— let's get a video. We—'

'You might enjoy it, you don't know.'

'We'll get whatever you want, you said. That's what you *said*. You looked me in the eye and you said, "We'll get whatever you want."'

'Yeah, but—'

'And now this. Now . . . this.'

He went into one of his routines. First, he allowed his bottom lip to hang and his eyes to drop. Then he slowly lowered his head, nodding ever so slightly. He even had the nerve to breathe a gentle sigh. Mary felt herself developing a thousand-yard stare. She was gripping her own film so hard that the case was bending. He seemed to notice.

'OK. Fine. OK. We'll get yours. We'll get' – he turned the cover towards him – '*Fargo*. All right? Bye-bye Pierce Brosnan, hello . . . Steve Buscomi.'

'Buscemi.'

'Yeah. Him. He was always the best of the Buscemi boys, anyway,' he said. 'I knew them well, the whole family. From Carrickmacross they were, originally. Now Seamie Buscemi would give you a pain in your ear listening to him, and Jamesie's only a liar and gobshite. But I've nothing against the Steve fella. Not a bad lad. C'mon. We'll get this and go.'

He did that smile he did, with the raised eyebrow. She once heard him refer to it as his 'winning smile'. Well, he wouldn't win with it this time. He wouldn't even scrape a draw. She walked past him to the counter without a word.

'Is there something wrong?' Peter asked as they drove away from the video shop.

'No. Nothing,' Mary said.

He nodded. 'You sure?'

'Yup.'

'You seem a wee bit . . . tense.'

'No.'

'You're not?'

'No.'

'Because if—'

'I'm fine.'

'All right then,' he said, slapping the steering wheel with both hands. 'Right, I've got a good one. David had it at work. Are you ready? Ready? Right. Paddy Englishman, Paddy Irishman and Paddy Scotsman are on a desert island. And on the whole island, there's only one—'

'Leave it, Peter.'

'Eh?'

'Just . . . leave it.'

'Trust me, you haven't heard it.'

'I don't want to hear it.'

'How do you know?'

'Because,' she said slowly and quietly, 'it's the twenty-first fucking century. Paddy Englishman, Paddy Irishman and Paddy Scotsman have no business here.'

He clearly didn't know how to respond. There was silence for a moment. Then he made a noise at the back of his throat, switched on the radio and skipped through several stations before he was able to find something that he wanted to sing along with.

Back at home, they went through the pre-video ritual in silence. Mary made the drinks, while Peter faffed around, adjusting cushions and lighting.

'Hang on a minute,' he called out to the kitchen after a while. 'Where's the poofy gone?'

She took a few deep breaths before replying. 'It's in the bin,' she said. 'And that's where it's staying.'

He skipped into the kitchen, where she was calmly stirring her coffee. 'But the poofy! You know I love that poofy.'

She stopped stirring. And then started again, in the opposite direction. 'First of all, it's a pouffe and *you* know *that*. Calling it a poofy is not even remotely funny and I've asked you not

3

to do it and you still do it and I can't understand why. Second of all, it's the cheapest-looking piece of shit, piece of crap, shitty, crappy, awful, horrible, *shitty* item of furniture I have ever seen. It makes me feel like I'm in a seventies sitcom and I've asked you a million times, from the very day you bought it, to please throw it out but you didn't so I did and now it's gone and I'm glad.'

She avoided his eye as she spoke, staring hard at the revolving spoon. When she looked up again, he was gone. She picked up the drinks – decaf, no milk for her, milky tea for him – and followed him into the living room. He was installed on the couch, legs stretched, feet planted flat on the carpet. He was peering at the latter with a forlorn expression. As she set the mugs down on the coffee table, she braced herself for a row.

Instead, Peter pulled his legs in and said, 'I've done something wrong, haven't I? If I have, I want to know. What is it?'

Mary lowered herself into an armchair, feeling suddenly ashamed and confused. She wanted to tell him that he hadn't done anything. And he really hadn't, as far as she could tell. But she stalled. She found she couldn't absolve him, somehow. It felt like . . . lying.

'Don't mind me,' she said, as a compromise. 'I had a bad day in the shop. Just put the video on.'

'If you're sure you're all right?'

'I'm sure.'

'OK then.'

He got up and stuck the video in the slot. When he returned to his seat, he took to staring at his unelevated feet again.

'There's no chance then that I could—'
'It's staying in the bin, Peter.'
'Right. Right you are.'

Almost as soon as *Fargo* started, Mary realised she had made a mistake in choosing it. Not because it was disappointing in itself (it wasn't), but because its characters had funny accents.

'Where's this set again?' Peter asked.

'Minnesota,' she told him, making a conscious effort to sound pleasant.

'Mad accent, isn't it?' he said, and she knew immediately that there'd be trouble. Sure enough, the film was only twenty minutes old before he started up.

'Reaaalll good, yah?' he chirped, apropos of nothing. 'Reaaalll good there.'

It wasn't a bad attempt at Minnesotan, she had to admit, considering there were broad Monaghan vowels to be overcome.

'Peter?'

'Yah?'

'Are you going to do that voice the whole way through the movie, because if you are, I'm going to bed right now.'

She hoped that her threat would sound playful, casual. It came out mean. He made a small submissive noise and went quiet. But she knew he was still practising it in his head, honing it, filing it away for another occasion. She even caught his lips moving once or twice and had literally to bite her tongue, afraid that no matter how carefully she chose her words, her tone would choose itself.

Mary knew that when inexplicably stressed, some people tried to jimmy the back door to good humour by doing something they called 'thinking pleasant thoughts'. As far as she could tell, this usually involved protracted meditation on sunshine and puppies and the like. When she felt her own mental temperature rise and didn't know why, however, Mary would always think deliberately *un*pleasant thoughts. She'd hike back through the recent past and poke the uglier memories with a stick, hoping one would squeal. Once the offending incident was discovered, she figured, she'd be free. And it usually worked. She would sit at the kitchen table or behind the counter in the shop, close her eyes, and after a while she would have her answer. She'd realise that her day-long annoyance had stemmed from dealing with a particularly rude customer or from forgetting to pick up her dry-cleaning. Thus, the mystery solved, she could congratulate herself on her positive approach to life and refusal to be a hostage to little things. The fog would lift and she'd be back to her usual self.

This time, however, the strategy was failing her. In truth, she hadn't had an unusually bad day at work. It had been quite good, in fact. Some kids had been in, asking about Radiohead tickets. Mary had not only been able to give them details about the concert and the support acts, she'd also told them the name of the new album, which wasn't even coming out until September. She'd read all about it on the Internet. They were impressed. She could tell. After work, she'd walked home in good spirits and heartily enjoyed the leftover chilli she heated up for herself on arrival. The TV news had been no more depressing than usual, reporting perfectly normal levels of murder, robbery, child-abuse, road death and corruption. She had a bowl of mint-choc ice cream in front of it, and then did the newspaper crossword in good, perhaps even record time.

Sitting there, waiting for Peter to come back from his bi-annual run, she distinctly remembered feeling quite contented. What the hell had gone wrong? Whatever it was, she shouldn't be taking it out on him.

'Peter?' she said quietly.

He made a small grunt of response, never shifting his gaze from the screen. Typical, she thought. He tries to talk me out of a film and then gets lost in it himself.

'I'm really sorry,' she said in the most serious voice she could muster.

He turned to face her. 'What for?'

'You know. I've been a bitch all night.'

He nodded. 'So long as you're OK.'

'I'll be fine, really. I don't know what's been bugging me.'

'You know, if I find anything bugging my Mary, I'll take it outside and kick its hole in.'

This was supposed to be chivalry. She tried to feel grateful. He was doing his best. And she was glad to have said something. Always apologise when you're wrong, her mother taught her early on. It was the best advice she'd ever heard.

'I can usually work it out,' she said. 'You know? If some wee thing has been playing on my mind, I can usually work out what it is and . . . cure myself. But not today. Not several times lately, in fact. I feel funny about it. It's like I've got a stone in my shoe, or something. An uncomfortable feeling . . . it's not like me.'

She let her voice trail away, wary of lapsing into Californian psycho-speak, and looked to her husband for a response.

7

Damien Owens

He seemed to mull it over for a moment. She waited. And waited. Then he shrugged dismissively, groped around for the remote and rewound the tape back to where it had been when she started to apologise.

2

'I'm a big *Star Wars* fan,' said the orange-coloured man with the spiky hair, 'and my favourite character is Han Solo, because he's a cool hero . . . like myself. Which *Star Wars* character do you identify with and why? This is for number two.'

The blonde in the yellow mini-dress peered out from beneath her stringy fringe and smiled. 'Well, Darren,' she said, 'I think that would have to be Darth Vader.'

Darren pulled a face. 'Why?'

'Because I look great in black leather and I'll take any excuse to breathe heavily.'

The studio audience responded with applause and whistles. Alone in his murky sitting room, Finbarr Grealey shook his head sadly and felt around the sofa for his bag of Murray Mints.

'Hoor,' he mumbled, popping a sweet into his wrinkled maw. The problem with this sort of bird, Finbarr reckoned, was that they were always trying to get discovered. Probably sings or acts or something. A vigilant producer, a phone call, next thing you know it's on *Top of the Pops*, miming its little heart out.

'A tough choice,' Darren said, feigning concern, 'but I think it'll have to be number one.'

Finbarr grimaced and squirmed. 'Gobshite! Number *one*?'

He sucked his sweet in disbelief as numbers two and three bade their farewell.

'Yeah, go on, fuck off. Back to the sunbeds and pulling off sales reps at the weekend. Better luck next time.'

Number one was the bit of posh they sometimes snuck in among the beauticians and aerobics instructors. Legal secretary, or so she said. Miranda. Not bad, he supposed. Might look good in jodhpurs, something appropriate like that. He made a mental note to watch next week, to see how they got along on their date. Not that he couldn't have guessed. Your man was getting nothing off that one. Not a prayer. Tight as a snake's arse. You only had to look at her. Still, he seemed fairly pleased with himself when the dividing screen went back. He stared openly at Miranda's chest for a full second and then put his hand on her ass. Finbarr was surprised to note that she didn't remove it. Hmmm. Perhaps there was some hope for spiky after all. Then again, he mused, maybe that was how young people said hello these days – by putting their hands on each other's asses. Maybe that was how they'd always done it. Finbarr had long since given up on the assumption that things didn't happen just because they didn't happen to *him*.

Date-choosing time then. Miranda plucked at an envelope and swished it open.

Finbarr crossed his fingers. 'Horse-riding! Horse-riding!' he pleaded.

'Hey, cool!' Miranda gushed. 'A fly-fishing weekend!'

Finbarr groaned and hit the power button on the remote. He glanced up at the clock.

Pub time.

Finbarr tried decorating once. Some time in the late seventies, it was. He'd been solemnly making a corned beef sandwich in the kitchen, at one with the universe, when he had a sudden, overpowering urge to get rid of the wallpaper. He wasn't sure what he wanted as a replacement, he just knew that the incumbent must go. Immediately. It was a curious sensation, and not an entirely pleasant one. He put it down to constipation at first – Finbarr was cursed with sullen, moody bowels – and drank several glasses of Andrew's before he realised that it was the real thing. The urge to purge lasted long enough for him to strip approximately two-thirds of the poky kitchen's grey and brown diamond-patterned wallpaper. He stopped very suddenly, in mid-scrape in fact, and stared dumbly at the bread knife he was using on the wall. What for? he asked himself. Why? Who's going to see it? He downed tool right there, leaving a ribbon of half-stripped wallpaper hanging loose. Then he spent an uncomfortable half-hour on the toilet, vowing to be more cautious about sudden brainwaves in future.

And so, décor-wise, the house stayed almost exactly as it had been in 1972, the year when his parents bookended the summer with their respective deaths, leaving him home alone for the first time. The bathroom, in particular, suffered greatly from neglect and with its various drips and slime patches now provided a reasonable facsimile of a cave. Although Finbarr had

11

long since ceased to notice much less care about the house-wide gloom, he couldn't fail to notice the lack of space. He was cruelly reminded every time he tried to enter his armpit of a bedroom, for example, when the door struck the end of the bed before it was even halfway open. It did so now, forcing him to gain access, as usual, by swinging his left leg round first, then following through with the rest of his quivering frame.

'Jesus,' he gasped as his groin squeezed past the bulbous doorknob. 'Me bollocks.'

He could have moved into his parents' room, of course, which was marginally bigger. But he didn't like to go in there. It gave him the screaming willies.

Finbarr's bed was narrow and quite short but it took up most of his room. At the headboard end, it was flanked on one side by a chair and on the other by a bedside locker. A wardrobe, dark and solid, stood at the foot of the bed looking not unlike the monolith in *2001: A Space Odyssey* (a movie that Finbarr counted among his very favourites, along with *Chitty Chitty Bang Bang*, *The Poseidon Adventure* and *Bullitt*). Its doors, like the main door, met opposition from the bed before they were fully open. This meant that he had to perch on his knees at the end of the mattress when he wanted to get at his clothes. There wasn't enough room to stand between bed and wardrobe.

Despite the *It's-A-Knockout* nature of the task, Finbar managed to pluck a clean pair of trousers — cleaner, anyway — from the wardrobe and wriggle into them with relative ease. Speed was of the essence here, he knew all too well. More than once, he'd hesitated over a clothes decision and found his knees locked when he tried to move.

3

Umberto did the trip from his house to Peter and Mary's in under twenty minutes that night, which was good going. But then his walking speed had always been directly proportional to his level of annoyance. It rarely took more than half an hour. Curiously, he had recently noticed that he didn't actually need to reach his destination for his mood to improve dramatically. It wasn't that it was a particularly pleasant walk – far from it. He always avoided going through town by cutting across some fields, but they weren't of the rolling, pretty variety. They were just big flat green squares with some cows and some cowshit in them. No, it seemed that the journey itself was therapy enough. The simple knowledge that he was leaving his parents behind and could look forward to mindless but entertaining chatter, some of it about sitcoms and computer games, was sufficient.

So it proved again. As he climbed over the final fence into the back of the estate where Peter and Mary lived, Umberto had already cheered up considerably. He was not the same Umberto who had slammed the back door of The Cottage in such violent disgust that a small Paul Klee print had fallen off a nearby wall (causing his mother to shriek so passionately that he heard her from halfway down the lane). Nevertheless, he felt the usual shiver of relief that he was only visiting and didn't actually live in the estate himself. Brookemore Lawns, as it was called, went up in the early nineties and was typical of its kind. The houses were airy and bright, if a little on the compact side. Each had a small garden at the back and a garage, which nobody seemed to use. This was the sort of home people were practically killing each other for, all over the country. It looked like Legoland to Umberto. Or like something you'd find in a rich communist state, if such a thing could be imagined. Every house the same, with the same year-old motors and the same plastic kids' toys littered around outside. As he climbed over the fence into Peter and Mary's back garden, he couldn't shake the feeling that everyone inside was watching state television, where The Leader was calmly assuring them that all was well.

When Mary answered the knock on the back door, both she and Umberto jumped a little in shock.

'You've been crying,' Umberto said after a pause. 'Your make-up is all over the place.'

'So have you,' she replied. 'And I shouldn't be able to tell.'

Umberto declined Mary's offer of tea or coffee – he claimed to have read disturbing reports about the effects of caffeine on male fertility. She pointed out that fertility shouldn't really be a major concern for a fourteen-year-old.

'I'm thinking long-term, *Aunt Mary*.'

'Well good for you, *Nephew Umberto*.'

They smiled as they took their seats at the kitchen table. He was given to calling her Aunt Mary as a gentle chastisement, usually reserved for those rare occasions when she spoke to him as a 'grown-up'. He knew it made her feel frumpy and old-fashioned. She preferred plain Mary.

'I've got decaf, you know.'

'Mary, *please*. Decaf! You either drink coffee or you don't.'

'Well, I like it. Although I suddenly can't remember why. Anyway. Go on. Shoot. What's the problem this time?'

'Ah, never mind me. I'm fine now. What's up with you?'

'Umberto, let me at least pretend to be the responsible adult here. You first. Start with the easy bit. Why, for the love of Christ, are you wearing make-up?'

He shrugged, but said nothing. Mary chewed her lip in thought for a moment.

'If you're going to get glammed up,' she said, 'at least come over here and let me do it properly for you. You haven't even accentuated your bee-stung lips, dear.'

He stared at the table.

'No point in asking your mother to help, is there? Sure what does that one know about applying make-up?'

He tutted.

'Nothing, that's what,' she went on. 'But I'm sure she could tell you all about its use as a tool to keep women in their place.'

Umberto cracked, a faint smile appearing very slowly on his pale face.

'Parent problems, so. You might as well tell me, Umberto. I can always ring Valerie and get it out of her.'

'Huh. You could try.'

'But . . . ?'

'But she wouldn't be able to shed any light. As far as she's concerned, I was acting like a mopey teenager all through dinner and then stormed out for no good reason. Oh, and I slammed the door, also for no good reason.'

'This doesn't explain the make-up.'

'The reason I was acting like a mopey teenager in the first place is that they failed to notice the fact that I was wearing make-up.'

'And you were wearing make-up . . . ?'

'To see if they'd notice.'

'Ah.'

'Yeah. *Ah*. And before you say anything, I am fully aware that this is a classic cry for attention, so don't even start that shit with me.'

'Language, Umberto.'

'Words are mere symbols and cannot harm us in themselves,' he told her in flat response. 'What? What are you looking at me like that for?'

'Nothing. It's just that I sometimes forget that talking to you is not like talking to kids in the shop. It's like, I dunno . . . finding a scalpel in your spoon drawer.'

'I'll take that as a compliment.'

'You should. And as for the make-up, well, at least you're not telling me you're gay or something.'

Umberto recoiled. 'Since when does wearing make-up make you gay? And what's wrong with being gay, anyway? Don't go all small-town on me, Mary.'

Mary slapped the table, causing him to leap in his chair. 'Don't you ever dare to call me "small-town",' she said.

Umberto brushed some fringe away from his eyes, shocked, and took a second to respond. It was the first time, ever, that Mary had even slightly raised her voice to him. Jesus . . . she even looked different, suddenly. Older, somehow.

'Well . . . I'm very sorry.'

She waved him away and then rubbed her temples. 'Forget it . . . I'm sorry I snapped at you. These days, I don't know what's . . . never mind, just ignore me. And there's nothing wrong with being gay. I was only thinking of the problems it might cause for you. Look at the slagging Camp David gets. And everyone knows he's not even actually gay. He's married, for Christ's sake.'

'OK, OK.'

'OK. So what, you sat there like Barbara Cartland through the whole dinner and they didn't bat an eyelid?'

'Dad looked at me weird a couple of times. I think he could tell that something was different but the penny didn't drop. They were too busy arguing anyway.'

He saw that Mary was surprised and knew why. His parents never fell out. Ever. It was common knowledge.

'They're fighting?'

'Cat and dog.'

'Oh? About what?'

'You don't want to know.'

She stared at the table. 'Not money, surely? I can't imag—'

'No, not money.'

'What then? Are they fighting over the remote control? Who washes the car? What?'

'Wave/particle duality,' Umberto said miserably.

Mary blinked. 'Excuse me?'

17

'You know. The nature of light. Sometimes it acts like a particle and sometimes it acts like a wave.'

Mary blinked again.

'Double slit experiment? Interference patterns?' Umberto ventured.

She shook her head.

'Not a popular science buff then,' he concluded. 'Well, good. Our house is full of those damn books and it doesn't promote peace and harmony, let me tell you.'

'No. I suppose not.'

'Mom said that light is made of particles that sometimes act like a wave, and Dad said it's a wave that sometimes acts like it's particles.'

'Oh *that* wave/particle duality . . .'

'He said she didn't know the first thing about physics and started laughing about some conversation they'd had about dark matter. She said something really stupid that day, apparently. Then she got mad at him for bringing the dark matter thing up, and then he said . . . well, you get the idea.'

Mary nodded that she did.

'I just wish they'd . . . be a bit less . . . you know . . . not so . . .'

She smiled sympathetically and patted the back of his hand. 'Yeah. I know.'

'Anyway. I'm all right now,' he said. 'So. What's up with you? And where's Peter?'

Mary glanced away very briefly. 'He's gone out somewhere, the pub probably. And never you mind what's wrong with me.'

Umberto nodded. He'd spotted the glance, and was well versed in the black art of glance interpretation. 'Would I be very wide of the mark,' he said, 'to assume that your recent tears and the suspicious absence of himself are in some way connected?'

Mary tapped the side of her nose. 'Grown-ups' business,' she told him.

Umberto noted a second sideways glance and let the subject drop.

4

Peter hadn't gone to the pub. He had gone to the pubs. McLaverty's first, because — and here he displayed something of the practical engineer in him — it was the first one he came across as he stomped furiously into town.

McLaverty's was one of the oldest pubs in Drumshanagh, dating from the turn of the nineteenth century. It was not a regular destination for Peter, who firmly believed that some of the original customers still drank there. Tiny old men in ancient black suits who took three days to drink a pint of Guinness and still argued in the present tense about Home Rule. This visit was only his second ever, the first having been on Camp David's twenty-sixth birthday. They did the whole town that night, but only lasted ten minutes in McLaverty's. Nearly everyone in town knew David Sheridan, and the crowd of well-wishers (and piss-takers) grew at every pub they visited. Until McLaverty's, that is, where the regulars regarded the whooping and cheering party with lupine stares. Even the barman looked scornful, and he was in his early twenties. They had one drink and filed out in silence, only to start whooping and cheering again as soon as they hit fresh air.

This second visit lasted about ninety seconds. All Peter wanted was peace and quiet to have a drink and think it through. McLaverty's was perfect, he assumed. He was sure that no one would bother him there. But as soon as he parked himself at the bar, he got talking – listening, rather – to an old man who was smoking foul-smelling roll-ups. The brief conversation centred on Peter's considerable height and the practical applications of same.

'Jazez, you're an awful length,' the old man gasped as Peter's drink arrived. 'You must be seven foot if you're a day.'

Peter might have found his companion perfectly agreeable on another night – a night when his wife hadn't more or less kicked him out.

'Six four,' he mumbled before taking a swig.

'It must be a powerful thing,' the old man went on. 'For seeing at the football and the like of that there.'

More or less? Who was he kidding? She'd pointed at the door and told him to get out of her sight.

'It's all right,' Peter said.

'I'm only wee meself, and it's no good. No good at all.'

Peter swallowed his drink and slipped off his stool. 'Give me a shout if you ever need anything off a shelf,' he said, and left.

Funnily enough, he was marginally more clear-headed with a drink under his belt. He marched up the street from McLaverty's, still fuming, and thought more seriously about which pub he should favour. Not one of his regulars, certainly not McShane's. So where? O'Brien's was too noisy. McNally's was too cramped. Daly's stank. The Still was full of provos. Hmmm. What about the Dead Leg? It wasn't a bad spot, really, but unpopular among Peter's crowd. Better yet, some middle-aged passer-through from Armagh had choked to death on what was assumed to be his own vomit in a toilet cubicle the previous summer and wasn't found for twenty-four hours. So it was clearly the sort of place where punters kept to themselves.

'Jameson, please,' Peter told the barman, glancing around nervously. Good. No overly familiar faces.

'And how are things in the high-tech world?' the barman said when he came back from the optic.

'Fine,' Peter said slowly.

'You don't remember me.'

Peter pocketed his change. 'I . . . eh . . .'

'You did the computers for me da – I was helping him out that day. In the garage. You and that other . . . funny fella.'

'Oh, yeah, right. The Renault place.'

'Aye.'

'Everything all right with the machines?'

'Wouldn't have a clue. They must be, or you'd have heard from the oul' man.'

Peter knew that this wasn't necessarily true. He once bumped into a customer on the street, a woman who ran a lighting shop. She nervously revealed that the PC he'd installed the previous week had packed it in half an hour after he left. She'd been afraid to call him, because she was sure she'd done something to make it break. Actually, she had done something: she'd kicked the plug slightly out of its socket. Still, the point, as Peter saw

23

it, was that people were funny about computers. The woman was so pleased that Peter a) 'fixed' it and b) didn't laugh that she gave him a nice lamp to take home. Mary said she loved it and him. Huh.

'Any problems, tell your da to gimme a shout.'

'Right, so.'

'Right.'

Peter turned and surveyed the room. The Dead Leg was a strange pub. It seemed to have been deliberately designed to appeal to no one in particular. There was no jukebox for the youth market. No TV for the sports fans. No mock antiques for whichever strange and unnamed section of society was supposed to find such things appealing. It wasn't moodily dark. It wasn't fashionably bright. It sported no romantic nooks. There were no weekly quizzes. No karaoke night. No pool table. Its seating was comfortable but anonymous: burgundy sofas, mainly, of the type usually found in hotel lobbies. The 'atmosphere', in Peter's opinion, was elevator-like. And yet it always drew a reasonable crowd. People who just wanted to have a drink and a chat, with no frills.

That was him, tonight. Except for the chat part. He took a seat in the corner and tried to arrange his thoughts.

Peter's father told him the fact of life not long after he turned fifteen. That was how the old man referred to it – in the singular. This was no red-faced, hand-rubbing explanation of the bio-mechanics involved in baby-making. (Peter had long since been thoroughly familiar with the technical details, on paper at least.) This was a father's genuine attempt to address his son as an emerging adult who needed certain information if he was to survive in the field.

The discussion was occasioned by Peter's arrival home from the Rugby Club junior disco a mere forty-five minutes after he'd left the house. He came through the back door like a bull, noisily gulping down tears in a manner that the worldly Mr Ford recognised instantly.

One week previously at the same event, Annette Boylan had surprised and initially terrified Peter by suddenly kissing him (with some violence) as they swayed uncertainly to 'Holding Back the Years'. He had been quietly stunned when she assented to a slow dance in the first place and was so flabbergasted by this new development that his hands abandoned their hard-won purchase on her hips and shot straight out to his sides. For a brief moment, he looked like someone about to take off in flight. Which was how he felt, as it happened.

They didn't exchange phone numbers or make plans of any sort, but she was, of course, going to be his wife. He smiled himself to sleep every night during the week, looking forward to technicolour dreams in which they walked hand in hand along the Seine, stopping periodically to clamp their mouths together with none of the awkwardness that had attended the event in real life.

He returned to the disco that Saturday night feeling none of his usual apprehension. He'd gone over the line and was untouchable. He'd been kissed, at last, and had kissed back. Life had nothing left to throw at him. He found Annette almost immediately. She was dancing with another boy. Their faces were mashed together. It wasn't even a slow song. The boy had one hand planted in the small of her back while the

25

other swept and patted the back of her head. His head rolled slightly on his shoulders and periodically withdrew, as though teasing. *Technique*, Peter said aloud as his stomach turned slowly over. When the kiss broke, Annette looked around, for approval perhaps. She caught Peter's eye. And she waved, smiling.

Back at the house, his father made him a cup of tea while he sat shivering at the kitchen table. His mother was away visiting her sister in Donegal. It was just the men. That was something.

'I'm going to tell you the fact of life,' Peter's father said when the tea had been drunk and relative calm restored. It was the first time Peter ever heard his dad deliberately swear.

'Women,' Mr Ford told his son, 'are mad in the fucking head. Every last one of them. Try not to mind. Because when all's said and done, they make this poxy life worth living.'

Peter was contemplating his dad's advice over whiskey number five in the Dead Leg when he felt someone sit next to him. He was perched head in hands, with eyes shut tight, and didn't turn around. He'd utterly failed to make any sense of the evening's events, but at least he was getting drunk.

'Women trouble,' said a voice to his left. It wasn't a question. It was a statement.

Peter made a sound that was neither confirmation nor denial.

'God knows, you have to watch out for the women,' the voice said wistfully.

Peter sighed. There was nothing for it. Conversation was inevitable. He reluctantly turned to face his companion. Your man, what was he called. Went into Mary's shop a lot. 'Oh, hello, eh . . .'

'Finbarr. Paul, isn't it?'

'Peter,' Peter said. 'What makes you so sure it's women trouble? Maybe my horse is still running. Maybe the car's on the fritz and I've no money. Maybe—'

Finbarr cackled. 'In my experience, most problems have a woman behind them somewhere. And sure look at the face you're pulling.'

'What face is that?'

Finbarr constricted his sharp features into a parody of misery, all twisted lips and heavy eyes.

Peter smiled a drunken smile, despite himself. 'Fast Eddie,' he mumbled.

'You're a what?'

'*You* are. A Fast Eddie. A student of human moves.'

This seemed to delight Finbarr. He threw his shiny head back and howled, slapping his thigh. 'Student of human moves!' he said. 'That's me, all right. Top of the class!'

For want of a better reply, Peter opened his throat and poured the remains of his drink down it.

'That wife of yours causing trouble, is she?' Finbarr asked seriously when his laughter had evaporated.

Peter shrugged, but said nothing. He didn't want to say anything that might be repeated back to Mary.

'Something irrational, I'm sure,' Finbarr went on. 'No offence to the missus. You probably don't even know what you did.'

Peter nodded, startled by this display of insight. 'That's about the size of it.'

'Was there shouting?'

'There was.'

27

'Dirty looks?'

Peter see-sawed his hand in mid-air, warming up. 'Little bit.'

Finbarr shook his head gravely. 'Nothing for it so but to get plastered and laugh it all out,' he said. Then he pointed a bony finger at Peter's whiskey. 'You'll have another one of them fellas,' he said and disappeared in the direction of the bar.

Peter had been all sorts of drunk in his time. He'd been tipsy. He'd been well-oiled. He'd been plastered. He'd made a few stabs at pickled and had dipped his toe in tanked. But he knew his limit. He was usually able to stop well short of the rubbery condition he thought of as simply *fucked*. That night in the Dead Leg, however, he watched in foggy wonder as his limit approached, passed, and fell away behind him.

After their first few drinks together, he discounted the possibility that Finbarr might squeal to Mary. It wasn't as if they were good friends, after all. He was just another customer, albeit a regular one. What's more, he seemed genuinely interested in Peter's difficulties and, surprisingly, had some interesting things to say on the subject of women.

'Birds,' Finbarr opined sadly at one point, 'are birds of a different feather. Not the same as you or me.'

Peter could only mutter his agreement. The point was beyond dispute, even if the word 'birds' sounded strange coming from a man who would never see sixty again. Now that he thought about it, no one said 'birds', not in Drumshanagh. He must have picked it up from TV.

'They don't know what they want,' Finbarr said a while later. 'They only know it's not what they've got now.'

More nodding from Peter who by now could feel his hard-luck story starting to crawl up his throat.

'It's like the old saying goes,' Finbarr eventually sighed. '"Why can't a woman be more like a man?"'

Peter drained his tenth whiskey at that point. Here's a man who knows what's what, he thought. An old hand. The voice of wisdom. A sagely spirit, sent to steer me right. Why be coy when help could be at hand? So he took the plunge and told his sorry tale.

Finbarr listened with pie-eyed attentiveness, nodding and grimacing as the details demanded. He shook his head dolefully when the story had ended.

'So she just started roaring?'

'Yes.'

'No warning?'

'No.'

Finbarr tapped his chin, considering. 'One minute she's apologising for the bad humour, as well she might, and the next . . .'

'"Get out of my sight." Her exact words were "Get out of my sight." She wouldn't talk, wouldn't explain, nothing. Just "Get out."'

'Christ. Oh, there's more to this one than meets the eye. I'll tell you that for nothing.'

Peter grew alarmed. 'You think so?'

Finbarr nodded firmly. 'No doubt about it. It's irrational behaviour, even by the standards of women. Mark my words, there's a bee in the bonnet.'

'Bee,' Peter echoed dumbly. His head was beginning to pound.

Finbarr folded his legs. 'Now what could it be, the bee? I don't want to pry into your personal—'

'Pry away,' Peter said. He was well past being circumspect.

'Well, let's see now. What do you do for a crust?'

'Computers.'

'Good man. Sure it's all computers now. And she has the record shop.'

'Correct.'

'So the problem's hardly . . . well, I'm being very nosy now, but it's hardly money, is it?'

Peter answered immediately. 'Definitely not. We're OK on that score.'

'Nice car? House?'

'Fiesta. Brookemore Lawns.'

Finbarr raised his glass. 'Good for you.'

Peter did likewise. They clinked.

'And there's no question of . . . ah, what am I on about, it's none of my business.'

Peter groaned. 'Go *on*, say it, man.'

'Well. You haven't been . . . straying, have you? Sideways glances, even?'

'No! Absolutely not. Are you joking me? I'm lucky to have her, and I know it.'

Finbarr smiled, displaying uneven dentistry. 'I'm glad to hear it. Nothing worse than a man who doesn't know when he's well off.'

'That's not me. No way. I count my blessings. I certainly do.'

Finbarr raised his glass in salute a second time. They clinked again.

'She's a fine girl. Even in the shop there, you'd know to look at her. Lovely manners. She'd always have a hello for you, and a smile, not like some of them in the town. Most of them, actually. If not all . . .'

Peter sighed that this was certainly so. 'The thing is, we never fall out, not properly. I mean, we have our rows . . . But she's been odd, lately. Not herself.'

'I'm stuck, so,' Finbarr concluded. 'It's a mystery. Chalk another mystery up for the birds.'

They fell silent and Peter became suddenly aware of the appalling condition he was in. He put weight on his legs experimentally and found them watery. Looking around the room, he was alarmed to find that his vision wasn't what it could be either.

'I think I better head for the hills,' he said, uncertainly.

Finbarr swirled the remainder of his drink around and downed it. 'Closing time anyway,' he noted.

They rose slowly to their feet and started to shuffle towards the door. Being vertical again was something of a shock to the system and Peter found simple locomotion quite challenging. It seemed to take an age for them to reach the street, where the sudden blast of fresh air was like one more unwelcome whiskey. At least one.

'I'm not well,' Peter managed to say, putting his right arm into the left sleeve of his jacket.

'You'll be all right,' Finbarr replied, rocking back slightly on his heels. 'Get a coffee or two in you when you get home.'

Peter frowned hard. 'If she hasn't changed the locks.'

Finbarr tilted his head in sympathy and gave Peter a friendly slap on the shoulder. But he timed it badly; Peter was still

31

grappling with his jacket and his weight was off-centre. He wound up, very quickly, on his ass.

'Sorry! Sorry!' Finbarr said, helping him up and dusting him off.

'It's fine, I'm all right,' Peter assured him. 'I think I should just go. It's not my night.'

Finbarr took a step back and saluted. 'Right you are. Take it easy on the way, now.'

They nodded at each other and went their separate ways. Peter had only gone a few steps before he heard Finbarr calling his name. He turned and lurched back down the street.

'Now I really am going over the line,' Finbarr slurred.

Peter shook his head. 'Go on.'

'Well . . . women today, as far as I can make out . . . ah, never mind.'

Peter groaned and stamped his foot. 'Go *on*, for fuck's sake.'

Finbarr coughed a phlegmy cough before continuing. 'Well . . . women today read those magazines, don't they?'

'Magazines?'

'The glossy ones. Filling their wee heads with all kinds of shite.'

Peter blinked in confusion.

'*Sex* shite,' Finbarr whispered. 'Do you follow me?'

'To be honest . . . no.'

Finbarr sighed and looked at his toes. 'They expect . . . things. You know . . . in the bedroom.'

Peter's eyes grew wide. 'Thanks for your concern,' he laughed. 'But we're all right in the bedroom. Jesus!'

Finbarr looked deeply embarrassed. 'Sorry. Sorry. No offence intended.'

'None taken,' Peter said, and meant it. 'Good luck, Finbarr. I'm away.'

They parted again. Peter laughed most of the way home. But not all the way. He was stonily silent and deep in drunken thought by the time he reached Brookemore Lawns.

5

Father Miles Duff had dressed for his first Sunday mass and was having a final cup of tea and a peek at the sports section when young Matthews knocked on the vestry door. He had already been up for two hours and so far, touch wood, he hadn't had a single fag. This meant that, in total, he had now sustained life without nicotine for a total of two hours and ten minutes, the last coffin nail having been mournfully consumed just before bed the previous night. A stickler for the rules, Father Duff didn't count time spent sleeping as time spent not smoking. Not this early in the campaign, at any rate.

'Father? Are you there, Father?' the boy said outside the door.

'What is it?' he snapped, rattling cup in saucer. 'I'm trying to prepare for the blessed sacrament in here, you know.'

'Sorry, Father. But there's a man. To see you.'

'What? Now? Sure mass is starting in fifteen minutes.'

'Yes, Father. Sorry, Father. He says it's important. He says it has to be now.'

'All right, all right. Give me a minute, Barry, like a good man.'

He speed-read the rest of the story about Sheffield Wednesday's latest home drubbing, silently cursing the time he had spent in that city and the mania it had bred in him. The words his grey eyes flickered over had a depressing familiarity. Boardroom squabbles. Nightclub arrests. Shambolic defence. Relegation candidates. Frowning heavily, he folded the paper away and rose to open the door.

'Sorry, Father,' Matthews said in the small corridor. 'He's out here. He says it's important.'

'So you said,' Father Duff replied, following down the corridor. This better be life and death, he thought as he surveyed with a shudder the cluster of livid spots on the back of the altar boy's neck.

They rounded a corner and came face to face with Eugene Brennan, a builder well known to Father Duff. He was a big, ashen-faced man, quiet and popular, a consistent mass-goer but not someone who was given to bothering priests about nothing at all. Father Duff felt his heart quicken slightly as he racked his brain, trying to remember if any of the Brennan clan were ill or due in court.

'Good man, Eugene!' he said as cheerily as he could, extending a hand. Brennan seized it and squeezed hard.

'Sorry to trouble you, Father,' he said.

'No trouble at all, Eugene. Nothing wrong, I hope?'

Young Matthews slipped away, and the shepherd stepped closer to his sheep.

'I don't know if you'd call it trouble, but I thought someone should tell you,' Brennan said.

Father Duff nodded for him to continue.

'Out the front, there now, I was walking in, with the wife, you know Imelda, and this fella comes up to us. A teenager, like, a young fella. And he says excuse me, polite and all, and stops us. He's doing a survey, he says, and will we take part?'

'A survey?'

'A survey, aye. So we said yes, gladly, and he takes out a notebook and asks us our names and we told him. Then he said there was only one question in the survey.' Brennan paused, apparently reluctant to go on.

'And what was it?' Father Duff asked, sounding more impatient than he intended.

There was another pause. 'I'm a wee bit embarrassed about it, to be honest, Father.'

Ah. This is about sex, Father Duff thought. He's going to tell me that some pagan rascal is out there asking people about their sex lives. On a dare, no doubt.

'Go on, Eugene,' he prompted.

'Well. The way it went was, he took out this notebook and he asks us . . . if we can tell him the ten commandments.'

Father Duff scratched the back of his head. 'Did he indeed?'

Brennan looked at his feet and then at his hands and then at the fire extinguisher hanging on the wall behind the priest.

'We got seven of them, Father. He caught us by surprise! Any other day—'

'All right, Eugene, don't annoy yourself about it.'

'False witness, I can never remember that one. Or the one about coveting . . .'

'All right, Eugene.'

'It's not that I don't—'

'Right, Eugene, it's all right, man. Is he still out there?'

'I think so, Father.'

'On you go into mass, so, and I'll see what's going on.'

'You can't miss him, Father. Young fella. Black hair. Big thick fringe.'

Father Duff nodded grimly. 'Don't worry, Eugene. I think I have a fair idea who it is.'

Once a year, the friendlier-looking priests and nuns in the area were despatched to the local schools on a recruiting drive. The idea was to take over some classes and talk about the religious life, trying your best to make it sound like a cross between being in U2 and actually being God. It was a task few relished. At best they could expect blank faces and yawns. At worst, it would be all smart-ass questions about the virgin birth and outright cheek about recent unfortunate scandals. Father Duff was a veteran of six of these missions, and liked them less and less each year.

Still, his trip to St Brendan's during the week had gone quite well. The assembled boys were perfectly attentive and he got a few laughs with his laboured celibacy gags. Even the dreaded Q & A seemed to start out OK. The first Q was about sodomy, granted, but the boy who asked it seemed to be motivated by genuine curiosity about the word's derivation, and not some childish desire to induce wholesale sniggering. He looked shocked and embarrassed, actually, when his question had just that effect. Father Duff gave a quick A and the boy nodded, apparently satisfied.

Half an hour later, the session was winding down nicely when a steady hand rose slowly in the ranks.

'Yes, son?' Father Duff said.

The questioner had delicate features, but a sturdy frame. Maybe a bit older than his classmates. He didn't look aggressive, but he was not smiling.

'How can you carry on with your work,' he asked in a clear voice, 'knowing full well that most of the so-called faithful live their lives in more or less total disregard for the essential teachings of the Catholic Church? It's not the sort of work I'd enjoy.'

There was no sniggering, but one or two students moaned.

'What makes you say that?' Father Duff said, trying to smile.

'It's obvious, isn't it?'

'Is it?'

'Well, yeah. "Christians" should follow the teachings of Christ, correct?'

'Of course.' Father Duff tried to decipher the boy's accent. It was local, but he pronounced some words with a definite twang. American? Canadian?

'But they don't. They quite clearly and obviously don't. Most of them couldn't tell you exactly what he's supposed to have said. Or the ten commandments even! I mean . . . if you really believe that God boiled his guide to life down to ten simple rules you should stick to them. I bet most people don't even *know* them. Not by heart.'

Father Duff took a few steps down the aisle. 'Do *you*?'

There was no hesitation. 'Yes.'

The class were interested now, switching their stares from the priest to the student, who had locked gazes.

Father Duff nodded and smiled. 'I'm sure you do. What's your name?'

'Umberto McKeown.'

There was low-key giggling.

'Umberto? Italian family?'

The boy seemed to grind his teeth. 'No,' he said, blinking once, very slowly.

'*Weirdo family*,' someone whispered. More giggling, louder this time, and sustained.

Father Duff ignored it, but saw his interlocutor twitch, as though he had just been pinched. 'I don't really think lists of rules are what's important in religion, do you, Umberto?'

There was no reply. The boy sat back in his chair and stared at his desk. Eventually, when the giggles had all subsided, he worked up a shrug.

Then a teacher knocked and walked in. Time was up for another year.

Father Duff walked briskly around to the front car park of St Michael's, checking his watch – ten minutes to ten. He really didn't have time for this. Umberto was standing inside the front gate with May Matthews, the altar boy's mother. As he quickstepped towards them, Father Duff picked out Umberto's distinctive voice.

'. . . so what's the point of all this church-going? If you can't even remember the simplest—'

'Umberto!'

Father Duff reached the pair gasping for oxygen and a cigarette. 'Sorry about this, Mrs Matthews,' he wheezed.

The poor woman looked as if she'd recently been slapped out of a hysterical fit. She was nodding quickly, her lips puffing in and out as she struggled to think of something to say. Father

Duff took Umberto's elbow and led him away. Mrs Matthews managed to croak, 'I'm going to mass,' as they receded. They stood under the only tree in the car park and looked each other in the eye. They were of approximately equal height, although Father Duff had several stones on Umberto.

'What do you think you're up to, lad? And don't just shrug!'

Umberto shrugged.

'Do you think this is funny? Clever?'

This time Umberto seemed prepared to form an answer. He opened his mouth, at any rate. It hung agape for a moment and then he spoke. 'I'm just . . . curious. I just wondered. Haven't you ever wondered?'

He didn't want to, but Father Duff smiled. There was something about the boy that made the maintenance of anger difficult. 'Not until I spoke to you the other day,' he admitted.

Umberto nodded but showed no pleasure at the answer. 'Do you want to know what I found out?' he asked.

Father Duff was sure that he didn't, but said, 'Go on then.'

'Based on my sample, I would say that practically all of your congregation know the ten commandments. And a surprising number know them in order. One old man gave me several specific examples of how they guide his everyday life. He frightened me a bit, actually . . .'

Father Duff did a reasonable job of concealing his surprise. 'Well, good. I knew it. Not that it's important, it isn't. It's not about learning off rules, Umberto. I suppose you're disappointed?'

'Disappointed?'

'Well, this is hardly the result you wanted, is it?'

Umberto looked genuinely affronted. 'I didn't "want" any result. I told you: I was just curious.'

Father Duff snorted.

'All right,' Umberto conceded. 'I may have had a ... preconception. But I still acted in the interests of science.'

'Are you curious about anything else?' Father Duff asked. 'Because maybe I can help you out, save you the bother of doing any more research.'

Umberto swept his fringe out of his eyes and thrust his hands into the pockets of his blue windcheater. He chewed his lip and thought about it for so long that Father Duff felt obliged to look at his watch again. He was on the point of telling Umberto that it had been a rhetorical question.

'Miracles,' Umberto said finally. 'Have you ever seen a miracle?'

'No,' Father Duff said, mildly exasperated. 'I have never personally seen a miracle. Now, I really have to go. Mass is supposed to be starting. I should—'

He stopped in mid-sentence. Umberto was suddenly smiling and holding his hands out to his sides at hip height. Father Duff looked from one palm to the other, blinking furiously, white noise whirling in his head.

Umberto's palms were running red, each sporting a little bloody bull's-eye in its centre. He smiled sweetly at the stupefied priest before turning and striding quickly away.

6

Peter lay very still in bed, trying to establish whether or not he was awake. He concluded that he must be, since he was aware of periodic noise in the room and of feeling slightly dizzy. He was also aware, even in the haze of his half-sleep, that he was in a great deal of pain. The agony was mainly concentrated in his head, which felt like a lump of solid metal that was being solemnly beaten with a tyre iron. However, the pain fairy had been both generous and scrupulously fair in her distribution of suffering – no area of his body had to go entirely without. When he eventually dared to crack open an eyelid, the flood of hot light that pierced his cranium caused him to snap it immediately shut again. He groaned and wondered if he was actually paralysed, or just felt so.

Some time later, he wiggled his toes and found them responsive. His fingers, likewise, seemed to be under his conscious control. Encouraged, he rolled over on to his back, keeping his head as still as possible. He lay that way for a few moments, like a weightlifter who has worked the bar on to his chest and needs a second's respite before going any further. Then, very carefully, he opened his eyes, millimetre by millimetre. His wife swam into semi-focus at the end of the bed.

'Morning,' he gasped.

Mary was in her underwear, trying to find the neck of an old Rolling Stones T-shirt. She located the aperture, and pulled it over her head.

'Hello,' she said.

Peter sucked and swallowed, trying to irrigate his Gobi gob. 'What's the time?' he said in an old man's voice.

'Nearly one. I left you sleeping and went to mass on my own.'

Mass was something they usually did together. Mary felt guilty if she missed it. Peter did not.

'Thanks. I don't think I would have been up to it.'

He was wondering how long he should keep up the chit-chat before asking if they were OK. Maybe he shouldn't ask and just assume that they were. She was at least talking to him. Albeit in clipped tones.

'So I gathered,' Mary said as she climbed into her tracksuit bottoms. 'The whole room stinks of booze.'

Peter closed his eyes and did his English Drawing-Room voice. 'It's my own rotten fault. I've been a bladdy fool.'

'Yup,' Mary said.

He rubbed his forehead and moaned. 'God, I had a really bizarre dream. You know on TV when some company or something publishes a report and they show a shot of someone's hands flipping through it? As if people wouldn't believe that the report existed unless they saw it being flipped through?

I dreamed that I got the job of being the guy who does the flipping for RTE. I wasn't a reporter or anything, I just ran around all day with a camera crew finding people who had published reports and then being filmed, you know . . . flipping through them. I was famous. People were stopping me on the streets to look at my hands. Then my boss called me in and said that they were considering getting someone else in, with younger-looking hands. I was going mad. I kept telling them that my hands were perfectly young and going on about how popular I was with the audience. I showed him all the gloves that the fans sent in. And I kept coming out with all these great hand jokes, saying I was "a safe pair of hands", and how you had to "hand it to me" for getting their ratings up. But the boss wouldn't listen. Then he said that they were not only going to fire me, but they were going to cut my hands off so I couldn't set myself up on some other channel as a rival to the new guy. Then I woke up.'

He opened his eyes. She had gone.

Half an hour later, Peter crept downstairs. He had endured a scalding shower and gulped down four Anadins. The apparent fissure running along the top of his skull hadn't closed over, but at least it had stopped widening. The pain had levelled off to the extent where it could now be described using human language.

He found Mary on the sofa in her Sunday afternoon uniform, the Stones T-shirt and shapeless tracksuit bottoms underlined by a pair of huge Winnie the Pooh slippers. She was holding her dirty blonde hair out of her eyes and gently nibbling her lower lip as she perused the headlines.

He cautiously took a seat beside her, lowering himself with great care.

'You still mad at me?' he asked, looking at her sideways.

She shook her head. 'No.'

Peter was unconvinced. 'I think maybe you are.'

'Maybe I am, then.'

'So why don't you admit it?'

She crossed her ankles and flapped her newspaper (a little theatrically, Peter thought), but said nothing.

'I'm trying to work out what I've done wrong, and I just don't get it,' he said, rubbing a tender temple.

Still no response.

'One minute you were apologising for being snotty with me, and the next minute you were shouting at me to get out.'

Mary maintained her silence, but had started to visibly fume.

'And now look at you! You're raging! What did I *do*? Tell me!'

He hadn't intended to raise his voice and regretted it immediately. Somewhere in the back of his mind, he began to seriously entertain the possibility that he might be obliged to vomit before he was very much older.

'You rewound the video,' Mary said slowly.

Peter thought he was hallucinating. 'Sorry?' he rasped. 'Did you say, "You rewound the video"?'

'*Yes.*'

He needed a moment to work it over in his mind, and to steel himself for more shrieking. 'I rewound the video? I rewound the *video*? That's why you went berserk?!'

She finally dropped any pretence that she was reading the

paper and turned to face him. 'I was trying to tell you something! I was pouring my heart out and you pretended to listen and then rewound the video so you wouldn't miss any of the film. The stupid film that you wouldn't even let me get in the first place. You didn't even give me a response. And you've done it before. You're *always* doing it.'

'Now wait a minute! That's bullshit. I wanted to get the James Bond, but no, I stepped aside—'

'It's not about getting the video, Peter.'

'What is it about then? Rewinding the video?'

'Yes! No! It's . . . never mind.'

'Go on.'

'I just told you. If you still don't get it . . .'

'*Mary*.'

But she would say no more. She sat like a child, pouting. After an ugly pause, Peter did his Winning Smile and placed both hands on her left knee. She pushed them away immediately.

'Don't touch me,' she said in a lush whisper that might otherwise have borne sweet nothings.

He felt a trickle of cold sweat meandering down his spine. 'Now you don't want me touching you? That's a step down from you don't want me rewinding a video.'

'I'm going to have a bath,' Mary said mechanically, as if she hadn't heard. Then she rose from the sofa and walked away from him, her Pooh slippers swishing on the thick carpet.

He stayed on the sofa for another twenty minutes, partly because he didn't know what else to do and partly because he still didn't trust his legs. Eventually, he made it to his feet and crept outside. For all he knew Mary had plans for the car that afternoon, but he didn't think it wise to check with her. Better to let her soak. So he climbed in, greasy and trembling, and drove to Camp David's. He didn't call ahead, satisfied that the trip would be worthwhile even if David wasn't home. At least it got him out of the house.

Driving, however, turned out to be every bit as problematic as walking. His feet felt uncertain on the pedals and his eyes were half closed in deference to the headache that still raged enthusiastically above them. To compensate for his reduced skills, he drove at a steady twenty miles an hour, whimpering periodically when a fresh wave of nausea crashed over him. David's house was about three miles out of town. It stood starkly alone, offset from the main road by a generous lawn. This was a two-car house with a two-car garage, shining testimony to the rude health of the Sheridan finances. David did the same job as Peter and made (Peter presumed) exactly the same salary. But his wife Fiona came from serious money. Construction. The way she told it, her family had built all of Galway and most of Limerick.

One of David's many idiosyncrasies was his habit of greeting any and all callers with a delight that was quite frankly off-putting. At work, he took his phone calls with a shrill 'David Sheridan here! What can I do for *you*?' in brazen disregard for the very real possibility that the person on the other end was apoplectic about some computer failure for which they held him wholly responsible. At home, he would sweep the door open at great speed, beaming like a man who was expecting the return of a skilful lover from whom he had been separated for several years. On this occasion, however, the sight of his debilitated colleague put an immediate damper on his glee.

'Holy mother!' he trilled as his smile collapsed. 'What in the name of God happened to you?'

'I am a hangover,' Peter said. He was about to correct his slip of the tongue but didn't, deciding that he had described his condition perfectly.

'You look like a corpse,' David marvelled. He wrinkled his nose and gagged. 'And you smell like a wino's burp.'

'I had a shower,' Peter said, hurt.

'No doubt. But you need some of my most powerful mints, my friend. Come in, come in.'

'New front door,' Peter said as he stepped inside. 'What happened to the old one?'

David threw his eyes north and flapped his hands. 'Nothing happened to it. My darling wife just decided that it wasn't quite the thing. You know what they're like.'

Peter shook his head. 'I thought I did. But it turns out I don't.'

Peter Ford first met David Sheridan in a toilet. It was 1985, the first day of secondary school for both of them, and there was a great deal of tension in the air. Rumour had it that first-years who didn't travel in a gang at lunch-time could expect to be rounded up, frog-marched into the toilets and 'ducked'. Depending on which correspondent you listened to, this could mean simply being held by your ankles and dipped up to your forehead into the toilet bowl, or it could mean something much worse. The most frightening scenario, outlined by a buck-toothed lad from Emyvale before the first bell had even rung, involved a recently used but (crucially) unflushed toilet into which the victim would be not only dipped but held. For anything up to ten minutes, according to buck-tooth. Some students were scornful of this horror story, pointing out that such treatment would inevitably result in death by drowning, but Peter was less confident. So he networked furiously during that first morning, seeking out acquaintances from his old primary school, and winning new intimates with his growing collection of funny voices (his recently perfected Margaret Thatcher Doing Knock-Knock Jokes was deemed a classic). By lunch-time he was part of something resembling a gang.

The safety in numbers ploy broke down, however, when it came to the necessarily solo pursuit of *voluntarily* visiting the toilet. There were only a few minutes of the lunch-break remaining when Peter finally accepted his bladder's word on the subject and admitted that he would need relief, and soon, if he wasn't to spend the afternoon in considerable discomfort. Reluctantly, to a volley of 'Good luck's and 'You're dead's, he left the pack behind and crept off towards the toilet block by the football pitch. As he walked, he reminded himself that he was big, or at least tall (five feet six inches already), and probably had nothing to fear. In any case, break-time at secondary school, so far at least, had proved itself to be very much like break-time at primary school, albeit with more illicit smoking.

He poked his head around the corner of the toilet block on arrival, finding it predictably unpleasant but quite empty. Although the release he sought was of the liquid variety, he nevertheless bounded in the direction of the stalls, with their lockable doors. There were three such chambers, which he tried in order from left to right. The first, unhappily, was home to a puddle of piss so deep and formidable that he didn't dare wade in, not in his new school shoes. The bowl of the second was piled high with sodden tissues, fag ends and other materials. The stink was almost visible. He didn't think he could stand there, not even for a minute. It was a bad sign, he mused, that the toilets were in this state halfway through the first *day*. What would they be like by Christmas? The door of stall number three was shut, but the faded lettering in its rusting lock declared it to be VACANT. Peter shoved it open, or rather tried to. Then three things happened at once. The bell for class rang out, the swinging door struck something solid, and a high, thin voice cried out, 'Lay one finger on me and I'll fucking sue you!'

Peter retreated in the direction of the urinals. 'What's the matter with you?' he shouted. 'I only want a piss!'

He fulfilled that ambition then, quickly and noisily. As he was zipping up, the stall door inched open and a short, doughy boy emerged, glancing around. He had blond hair, slightly wavy, and looked very nervous. 'Oh. You. You're in my class, I saw you earlier. I thought you were some bastard coming to duck me,' he said.

'Nope,' Peter said, moving towards the filthy sinks. He vaguely remembered hearing this boy give his name and home town during the morning introductions. Dermot something? Declan? Family just moved here from ... Cavan, was it? 'I think that whole ducking thing might be bullshit, anyway. To scare us.'

The other boy stepped towards him, hope blossoming. 'You think?'

'Yeah. Maybe.'

'Well, it certainly scared me. I've been in there the whole lunch-break.'

He had a funny way of talking, Peter thought. Up and down. Sing-songy. He sounded as if he was from Las Vegas, not Cavan.

'You never even locked the door.'

The boy shrugged. 'Don't like being locked in,' he said.

'And if you're going to threaten the duckers with something, I'd try some sort of violence, not the law.'

'Rightyo.'

Peter had never heard anyone his own age saying 'Rightyo' before.

'We have to go,' he said by way of response. 'The bell's gone. We'll be shot.'

'Would ye relax,' the other boy said. 'The teachers won't be in any hurry. They're as pissed off as we are to be back at school. Here, have a ciggy.'

Peter blinked at him, uncertain. Was this guy a frightened mummy's-boy or fag-sneaking hard man? Either way, he clearly spelled trouble. Peter declined the proffered smoke, and said he was off.

The boy followed immediately, pocketing his fags. 'Hang on!' he squealed. 'Wait for me!'

Great, Peter thought. I'm going to have this oddball tailing around after me for the rest of my life. Before long, however, David Sheridan had an enviable reputation. He was sent to the head's office twice in the first week, once for a series of thoroughly predictable smoking busts and once for repeatedly pretending to sneeze at the curvy science teacher while actually shouting, 'Ah-TITS-you.' He seemed to do these things for his own amusement and not for show, but everyone was impressed anyway. As the weeks wore on, he developed such standing as a 'character' that even his tendency to faint during cross-country runs couldn't lower his stock.

By Christmas Peter was glad to be able to call him his friend, and had to work very hard on his funny voices just to avoid being forgotten entirely.

'I know what you need,' David said after they had a cup of coffee and Peter had reported his sorry headlines. 'You need a nice game of pitch and putt. Fiona's out golfing, so there'd be a certain symmetry to it, don't you think?'

'Not a bad idea,' Peter consented, sucking on a startlingly hot mint. 'Fresh air, bit of exercise.'

They were both big fans of pitch and putt and played often. 'It's like golf,' David liked to say, 'only without all the Pringle wankers.' This was certainly true. Most players at the Highways Hotel course were under sixteen. (Peter wasn't sure if David considered his own wife one of the Pringle wankers, and never pressed the issue.)

They were there within half an hour and were surprised to find it largely deserted. It wasn't much more than a field, really, with flags fluttering here and there, but it was usually busier than this. 'PlayStation,' David said on arrival. He was fully convinced that every teenager in Ireland had at least one PlayStation in the house and that was why you never saw them out pursuing what he called 'wholesome outdoor activities'. Peter sometimes reminded him that this was somewhat hypocritical coming from a man who had spent much of his own youth crying and faking illness in an attempt to avoid wholesome outdoor activities.

It was a clear day and, for a change, sunny. Still, Peter was alarmed to find that the much-lauded fresh air had in actuality a mildly nauseating effect. He felt as if each breath contained too much oxygen and needed to sit down before they reached the flat bump of the first tee. Feeling increasingly wonky, he overhit his first shot by the entire length of the hole. David whistled sarcastically, then screwed up his own effort.

'I left a bit of the story out earlier,' Peter said, as they ambled up to the tiny bunker where David's ball had buried itself like some bizarre desert insect.

David sucked on a cigarette and frowned at his lie. 'Oh yeah?'

'Yeah. I set out . . . what's wrong with your eyes?'

'Nothing.'

'Why are you doing that then?'

David was holding his eyes open as wide as humanly possible. He looked like an astonished fish. 'I read it in one of Fiona's magazines,' he said. 'If you do this for an hour or so a day, it can help prevent wrinkles. Apparently.'

'Well, stop it. It's putting me off.'

'No.'

'Jesus. Anyway, I set out to get plastered on my own, like I said, but I didn't in the end. I got plastered with . . . eh . . . you know Finbarr what's-his-name? Oldish guy, you see him knocking about the town on his own?'

'Get out! Finbarr Grealey? How come?'

'He just sat beside me and started talking.'

'Isn't he a bit . . . you know? Peculiar?'

'You shouldn't judge people like that, David. He seemed all right to me. He was saying, you know, about Mary—'

David did a double-take. 'You weren't talking to him about the thing with Mary?'

'Well, I—'

'Jesus. What have I told you about talking to strange men?'

Peter ignored this. 'Anyway, he said something. He said maybe the reason Mary's being like this is that she's unhappy . . . in the bedroom.'

David was addressing his ball – that is, he was staring sadly at it with his bugged-out eyes – when Peter finished his sentence. He dropped his club immediately and gripped his sides as he shook with laughter. Peter found this habit of David's slightly irritating – that he literally held his sides when he found something more than ordinarily humorous.

'It's not funny,' he moped. His stomach audibly gurgled its accord.

'All right, all right,' David said. 'But don't tell me you're taking him seriously.'

Peter said nothing.

'Come *on*, for Christ's sake. He's an old man! What does he know about modern women? Or any women for that matter? You want to be careful who you take advice from.'

'Maybe.'

'And I don't care what you say, he's definitely strange. Everyone says so.'

'Do they? Who do you know who knows him? I mean really knows him. He strikes me as one of those people who everyone recognises but no one actually talks to. And anyway. Even if he is a bit . . . whatever, that doesn't mean he can't be right. Mary hasn't been herself this last while. What if she's . . . dissatisfied with me?'

'Oh, leave yourself alone,' David said, waving Peter away. This was an insult he reserved for people who were talking a load of old wank.

'You never know, David. We've been together, more or less, for a long time. What if she gets curious and starts looking around for comparisons?'

'My GOD, you're right! She'll be out putting up cards in phone boxes by the end of the week! They'll be queueing up round the house. She'll have to give out tickets, and call them in by number. "Now serving number thirty-four! Now serving num—"'

'All right, shut up.'

'Not gonna happen, Peter.'

'But—'

'If you're all that worried, why don't you just ask her?'

Peter bristled. 'No bloody way. What if it is about sex, and she *tells me so*? I'd rather die.'

'Forget about it then.'

Peter nodded that he would and went off after his ball, but he had already decided that he probably couldn't. There had to be some reason for her attitude, and she'd reacted very coldly to the very idea of physical contact that morning. What if Finbarr was some sort of idiot savant on the subject of women? What if she was bored with him in that way? Wondering about what she might be missing? He found his ball quickly and struck it almost thoughtlessly, sorry he'd ever agreed to this game and keen for it to be over quickly. To his surprise, the ball plopped neatly on to the 'green' (where the grass was merely an inch long, as opposed to the 'fairway', where it was about five inches). He wobbled off after it, patting his shuddering tummy. The sun felt very bright suddenly, he thought, and the twittering birds and the voices of the few other players sounded unusually loud.

Over at the greenside bunker, David lashed awkwardly at his ball and missed it entirely, striking the sand six inches behind it. 'Bastard thing!' he growled and tried again. This time he connected. The ball shot out of the bunker, over the green, and into a small clump of bushes. He stormed after it, passing Peter on the green. 'Me and that ball's gonna have words,' he said with a serious frown. It took him four more shots – including another trip to the same bunker – before both players were in a position to putt.

'If you ask me,' David said as Peter took aim, 'you should try to inject some romance, not more hot beef.'

Peter took a moment to decipher this. 'I am romantic,' he said eventually, before sending his ball whizzing past the hole. 'I'm always telling her how great she is.'

David shook his head. 'That's not romance, that's sucking up.'

'What do you suggest then?'

'The usual. Flowers. Chocolates. Candles. Maybe a bit of jewellery.'

'Nah. She hates all that clichéd soppy stuff, says it's a ruse invented by men to make women look weak. I think she got that line from Valerie, but that's not the point. It's our anniversary on Friday and we're not even getting each other presents or doing anything in particular. That's her idea, now, not mine.'

'Aha! That could be a test. She's just saying that. You'll show up with one arm as long as the other and she'll produce a diamond-encrusted Rolex. You're snookered then.'

'No chance. She's not like that, David.'

'You know what I think? I think she just says she hates "soppy stuff", as you call it, because she knows there's no chance you'll come up with the goods. Clichés only get to be clichés because there's something to 'em. Take it from your Uncle David. Nothing surer.'

Peter mulled this over as his partner holed out. Hmmm. Maybe David had the answer, not Finbarr. After all, he had always been spectacularly popular with the opposite sex, right from the off. Most spectators put his early triumphs down to some bizarre desire on the girls' part to 'cure' him of his obvious homosexuality. As the years passed, however, even the most slow-witted and unimaginative name-callers came to realise that David was not only straight as an arrow, but something of a rogue. In Peter's view, the Camp David nomenclature survived not out of spite but jealousy. This jealousy was set in stone for ever when David's rabidly successful dating career ended with his marriage to Fiona, who was a) gorgeous, b) exotic (there was Spanish blood in there somewhere) and c) loaded. And yet . . . it was hard to take him seriously as an expert, leaning there on his hired putter, with his soft belly hanging over his chinos and his unruly blond mop, as ever, six weeks overdue for a trim. The fish look didn't help either.

'Apart from the fact that she hates that stuff herself, Mary would probably die of shock if I showed up with flowers and chocolates,' Peter said. 'She knows I'm not into that shit either. She'd think I was having an affair.'

'You're making my point for me,' David replied. 'What you just said only goes to prove how sorely lacking in romance your pathetic sham of a marriage actually is. If *I* showed up with flowers and chocolates, Fiona would merely congratulate herself, yet again, on her excellent choice of spouse before rushing out to buy some more fancy bras.'

'You might be right,' Peter said unhappily. 'Sort of. Maybe I could surprise her on Friday, push the boat out a bit. Not with the flowers and chocs crap, though. Something meaningful. Something spectacular. I'll have to have a think about it.'

It was then, in that solemn moment, that his body launched its surprise attack, like an unstable nation sending troops over the border before diplomatic channels have even been exhausted. As he turned to his ball, chewing his lip in thought, the blood rushed from his head and, simultaneously, the contents of his stomach made a break for it. Shocked, but still in charge, he managed to drop his putter, straighten up, clench his throat shut and put his hand over his mouth in one swift movement.

'What is it?' David shrieked, stepping closer. 'Are you all right?'

Peter responded by running around in a tight circle, pointing to his revolting tummy.

'Puke?' David said. 'Are you going to puke?'

Peter made no formal response, but sped off in the direction of the bushes where David's ball had recently found a home. Regrettably, the grass was slightly damp underfoot and he was travelling with foolish haste. He didn't even make it off the green before his left foot, on contact with the ground,

59

slid forward an unsolicited three feet, causing him to do the splits. If he had been inclined to look on the bright side of this development (he wasn't), he would have noted that the sudden agony in his groin made him momentarily forget his headache and upset stomach. His legs opened to approximately 140 degrees before his feet stopped slipping in opposite directions. Then he fell, almost gratefully, on to his ass for the second time in twenty-four hours. He managed one quick whimper before the first splash of vomit gushed out on to his jumper. The second spasm had more range and made it into his lap. Flailing like an upturned turtle, he managed to twist over to one side and in the end delivered the bulk of his intestinal gift to the unkempt green.

7

'Of course we noticed!' Valerie said, shaking her match out. 'You could hardly miss it, could you? He looked like Siouxsie Sioux.'

Mary blinked in surprise. 'Then why didn't you say something to him?'

They were sitting on fat cushions by Valerie's hearth with large glasses of red wine. Mary had walked the two miles there, after finding Peter and the car gone when she emerged from the bath. Although she was fond of The Cottage, as Valerie and Jeff insisted on calling the renovated farmhouse where they lived, Mary was convinced that somewhere within it was a room she had never seen. A small, soundproof room where they went to yell and smash things. There had to be such a place – how else could you explain the house's other-worldly tidiness? They must be doing their mess-making somewhere. It was only human. Mary considered herself to be a neat person and even gave the same credit to Peter, but Valerie and Jeff were something else. It wasn't that they were minimalists.

They had hundreds of books and maybe a thousand CDs. They subscribed to the *New Yorker*, *Time*, *Nature*, *Sight and Sound*, *Modern Poetry Review*, *Modern Philosopher*, *Q*, *The Face*, *Architecture Today*, *Interview* and *Wallpaper*. They liked their flora too and had an army of yuccas and cacti. And, of course, they collected art. There were *objets* of it all over the shop. Yet Mary had never seen so much as a paperback left behind on a chair, let alone a film of dust on a bust.

The room in which they now sat was a case in point. Every cushion plumped and showroom straight, every magazine crease-free and lying square to the edges of the coffee table. Even the area around the open fire was spotless. If a spark or a bit of ash did dare to trespass, Valerie instantly seized her miniature brush and pan and returned it whence it came. The brush and pan were part of a fireside set Jeff had bought her for their tenth anniversary. They were designed by a Japanese architect whose work she admired and were one of only fifty ever made.

'Well, we didn't say anything . . .'

'Because you were too busy arguing?'

'Did he say that?'

'Yes, he did. He said you were too busy arguing about black holes or something to notice.'

Valerie took a long drag on her cigarette and tapped ash into the fire. 'Not strictly true, but we were having a lively discussion, I'll grant you that. I only realised that Jeff had noticed the make-up after Umberto . . . left. And Jeff thought *I* hadn't noticed. I suppose neither of us wanted to look like the disapproving adult, you know? We had a good laugh about it, actually.'

Mary pursed her lips and shook her head in disdain. 'Well, I'm not laughing, Valerie, and neither was your son. You'll have to have a talk with him. Where is he anyway, off with his dad?'

'Jeff's doing some sketching somewhere. Umberto, I don't know. He went straight to his room when he came back last night, and he was gone first thing.'

'My God, Valerie, how can you be so casual?' Mary asked. 'He's only fourteen years of age. You should take your responsibilities a bit more seriously.'

Valerie sipped her wine and avoided eye contact. Mary knew that her sister could endure any amount of criticism, could listen to it for days on end and not bat an eyelid. So she cancelled the lecture.

James and Elizabeth McKeown had their first baby girl in 1964. Over the years, Mary heard the story from both parents several dozen times. Her mother's favourite detail was the bit where her waters broke while she was hanging out the washing. There was a crossed wire somewhere and she swore, thinking it had started to rain. Her father liked to report that he spent the twenty-hour labour on his knees in the kitchen, lips moving soundlessly as he rubbed his rosary beads in cold fear. At the time, neither of them was of the school that said all babies are beautiful; James, in particular, thought most of them looked like drunken pensioners. But with all due modesty, they had to conclude that Valerie was an astonishingly gorgeous infant, long of lash and chubby of cheek. Visitors to the hospital lost their breath when they caught sight of her. Elizabeth was besotted, as any mother would have been. But *James* . . . James lost it. For the first three months, he left his daughter's side only to eat, visit the bathroom and, when absolutely necessary, sleep. Elizabeth told Mary that she had often discovered him bent over the cot in tears. She never asked him what was wrong; she knew that the answer, the genuine answer, was 'Nothing'. He returned to normal, or a version of normal, only when his wife pointed out that his milk round was suffering and their new daughter wouldn't thank him if they lost it.

Ten years passed before Mary was born. The gap was explained by simple economics. The McKeowns were never poor, but they knew where every penny came from, and they knew where every penny went. A second child was simply not an option. But in 1973 Elizabeth's Aunt Jean died of pneumonia, leaving her tiny house in Meath to her favourite niece. The resulting minor windfall put an end to James's frequent trips over the border to Godless Northern Ireland where condoms were so glamorously available, and before long Valerie had a sister. A second welcome consequence was that James no longer trembled and wept when considering the fate of his immortal soul. Elizabeth mentioned these details if she'd had a glass of wine; James never denied them.

When Mary arrived, the McKeowns could scarcely believe their luck, or so they said. Another beautiful little girl. James loved her absolutely, as did Elizabeth. (They both used that word, 'absolutely', when they talked about it, as if they'd got their stories straight in advance.) With Mary, however, there was no sleepless neglect of the milk round, no tears over the cot. Valerie was ten by then and had begun to display the traits that made her Valerie.

James told Mary that by the time she came along, as far as daughters went, he had lost his innocence.

*   *   *

The McKeown family photo album told its tale well. Mary spent many an hour poring over it in her youth, touching the photographs, and wondering, always wondering. The opening pages were full of grainy black and whites, poignant in their own way: James and Elizabeth picnicking in bright meadows or sunburning on rocky beaches. Then came the first baby photos. Valerie chewing on wooden bricks, her Disneyfied face lit up in simple delight. Valerie looking puzzled in her pushchair as the family cat strides past, ignoring her outstretched arm. Colour was introduced suddenly in the form of waxy Polaroids, around the time when Valerie first began to frown for the camera. The next few pages showed her alternating between sunny grins and anxious scowls. By the time Mary first made an appearance, her sister had entirely abandoned the former. She didn't look miserable or even uneasy in these later shots; her expression, Mary thought, was best described as 'serious'. Her mother once confided that the change was obvious only in retrospect. Looking back, they realised that you could make a flip-book showing her eyes growing slightly heavy, her lips turning inexorably down. But at the time, her mutation slipped past them in the general rush of everyday life.

If you asked James to put his finger on the exact moment when he knew for sure that Valerie was different – and Mary frequently did – he didn't hesitate. It was a murky winter's evening, not long after Valerie's eighth birthday. He was sitting in his favourite armchair by the fire, doing nothing in particular. Valerie wandered in and sat in the chair opposite. She was wearing a necklace she had made for herself. It consisted of a half-dozen dolls' heads strung together on an old bootlace.

Elizabeth had been understandably disturbed when she first saw it, but Valerie shrugged and changed the subject when challenged about its significance. Now it was just something she wore once in a while, and no one questioned it.

James nodded across the hearth at his daughter and she nodded back. He got the impression she wanted to ask him something and waited for her to do so. After a minute or so, she piped up.

'Daddy?' she said.

'Yes, darlin'?'

'What's time?'

James consulted his watch. 'It's nearly half-seven.'

Valerie shook her head. 'No. What *is* time?'

Looking back, Mary remembered her sister's teenage years as a period of unremitting tension. Valerie grew into the beautiful girl that everyone had predicted and before long the McKeown phone line was almost permanently tied up with an endless succession of warbling males demanding to know her whereabouts, her state of mind, her preference in cuddly toys. Most of these suitors were classmates at the mildly progressive – that is to say, mixed – school where Valerie long-sufferingly dragged herself every day. More than one voice, however, was fully adult. Mary took some of the calls herself and even then, she could tell that the people on the other end weren't calling to chat; they *wanted* something. She remembered her father spending a good deal of his time at confession in those years. He later told her that he'd been begging the priest for advance absolution, in case he woke up one day and found that he had blood on his hands.

But he needn't have worried. Valerie had long since decided that the people of Drumshanagh had nothing to say that she wanted to hear. And the absent-minded disinterest she developed for locals in general was nothing compared to her scorn for local *boys*. 'Ignorami,' she once told Mary, who was too young to make any response other than to laugh at the sound of the word. 'They have nothing to teach, and everything to learn.' Valerie's apparent appetite for knowledge was something of a mystery to her parents. If she was so intent on bettering herself, they used to say, then why were her school report cards littered with 'Can do better's and 'Not applying herself's? Her only consistently good grade was in art, and James claimed to be suspicious even of that. He had met her art teacher, a Mr McAuley, at a parent-teacher meeting and didn't like the way the man smiled as he praised Valerie's 'appreciation of form'.

Granted, she was often to be found at home with her nose in a book, but they weren't school texts, or anything that resembled educational material of any kind. Instead, she seemed to prefer fat, dog-eared library copies of novels that James and Mary had never heard of, authored by long-dead nobodies, many of whom sounded quite frankly French.

By the time she sat her Leaving Certificate in 1982, Valerie had failed to express any plans about, or interest in, the future. James and Elizabeth had begun to discount the possibility that she would ever be what they called 'a high-flier' and had taken to delighting in every minor achievement of Mary's. She was doing well in every subject, and, even better, she simply played with her dolls rather than decapitating them for jewellery.

The Leaving Certificate results were only a week away when

67

Valerie summoned her parents to the kitchen and informed them that she had a plan after all. Mary stood in the doorway and listened. She saw James clasping Elizabeth's hand underneath the table as Valerie stood there, tall and confident, telling them what she had decided. Her summer job in the textiles factory had been surprisingly lucrative, and she'd managed to save quite a bit. More than enough for a plane ticket to London, which was where she was going. The next day.

'To pursue the arts,' she said.

Over the next few years she wrote often, but made few phone calls, and visited not at all. The letters were uncharacteristically chatty and upbeat, providing homely details about her various temporary jobs (gallery gopher, stage-hand) and day trips hither and yon (Brighton, Oxford). There was no apology for the abrupt departure, just a repeated assertion that one day's notice had been 'best for all'.

James and Elizabeth – who were initially incapacitated with worry – comforted themselves with the notion that she was still alive and even seemed to be happy. Happier, at least. Mary was sorry that Valerie had gone, but lapped up the surplus attention. At the time, none of them knew the truth. It was only much later, in the last few years in fact, that Valerie had confided in Mary about the speed and the vodka and the acid, and the *men*, that tragi-comic parade of dusty sculptors and skinny poets (Valerie's virginity lasted precisely three weeks in London). They didn't know at the time – James and Elizabeth still didn't know – that she had received a black eye from one noted cellist and a tear-stained declaration of love from another. They were also unaware that she had written a 180,000-word novel and that she had burned it page by page over the course of a lonely weekend. It was early in 1985, Valerie later confessed, that she began to have serious doubts. This was the arts? These were the artists? These soup-stained bores, twittering in corners? But then what had she expected? And what had she wanted to be? She found that she couldn't quite say. It might have been different if she had begun to display talent of her own – in any field, she wasn't fussy. But she hadn't. Her paintings were still in her head, her novel was ash. She was still 'pursuing the arts' but she had a sinking feeling that the arts were going to get away. If Jeff hadn't turned up, in fact, she might have taken up one of the modelling jobs offered to her in dim bars by middle-aged men wearing bandannas.

His full name was Jeffrey Marshall Vance and he was one of the idle quite-well-off. His widowed father, also called Marshall, had died in 1981 leaving four Long Island restaurants and a chain of small hotels to his only child. Jeff told their managers to keep up the good work and let them know where they could deposit his monthly cheques. Then he took off, devoting himself to a life not so much of hedonism, but of whimsy: travelling, writing bad poetry, painting bad paintings, failing to learn the guitar.

He was a tall, broad-shouldered man with sad brown eyes and longish black hair. Women flocked around him, even those who were too dumb to smell the money. By the time he met Valerie (he was thirty-three, she was twenty-two), he claimed to have had nearly two hundred lovers, none of whom he loved. They met in a cramped but trendy bookshop in Fulham, where Jeff overheard Valerie ask the owner to recommend a novel. (This was a new strategy she had adopted with the intention of broadening her reading.) He introduced himself and wondered could he be so bold as to make a recommendation of his own. They ended up going for coffee, then dinner, then drinks, then back to Valerie's tiny flat, where Jeff sexually exhausted her. Afterwards, he recited one of his poems, a lengthy work entitled *To the Normal-Sized Child of Dwarf Parents* (Valerie still remembered part of it which she sometimes recited to Mary with tears of pride: 'No shame! No shame!/Stand tall/For you alone can see/What's going on'). Then he sketched her naked likeness on the inside cover of the A–M phone book. He had only a red Bic Biro to work with and declared himself unhappy with the result. Valerie loved it, even if it did prompt her first ever bikini wax. Just before dawn, Jeff read aloud from the novel she had bought on his recommendation. It was *The Name of the Rose* by Umberto Eco.

Mary and her parents first heard the name Jeff Vance eight months later in the same sentence as the words 'my new husband'.

After a proper honeymoon in Jeff's home town of New York, the couple presented themselves for inspection in Drumshanagh. Mary knew immediately that James didn't like his new son-in-law. Something gave it away – something in his eyes perhaps or his begrudging handshake, or maybe in the way he openly wept, mumbling about 'a gobshite'. Elizabeth put on a braver face. One evening, Mary heard her reminding James about Jeff's money and good bone structure. And Valerie was not only keeping her own name, she had vowed that her children, when they came, would be McKeowns. That was something. The strange thing was this: Jeff fell in love with the place immediately. He waxed lyrical about the space, the woods, the streams, the people. He could see himself living there, he said, despite . . . everything (Mary understood this to be a reference to James and his hateful looks).

It took him over a year to convince Valerie, who first consented to living in a rural area, then in an Irish rural area, and finally – with much bad grace – in Drumshanagh. She gave in, she later said, simply because she was pregnant. London had stopped being the kaleidoscopic centre of the arts and had turned into a series of concrete tunnels, fizzing with potential mayhem. She didn't want her child to live there. She could feel that in her guts. And now that there was Jeff, she didn't want a kaleidoscopic centre for the arts either. He was all that, rolled untidily into one person.

So they packed up and shipped off, making baby plans. One thing they had no doubts about was the name: Rose for a girl, Umberto for a boy.

'Are you all right?' Valerie asked. 'You seem edgy. You look tired. And this is the first time you ever showed up during the hours of daylight with a bottle of wine under your arm.'

'I'm fine,' Mary said. 'Well, a wee bit wound up, maybe. I had a row with Peter.'

'Oh? This morning?'

'No, last night. But it's been building up.'

'Yeah?'

'For weeks, really.'

'So what's the problem?'

'Never mind.'

'Oh, come on. I might be able to help.'

71

Mary gave this some thought. It didn't seem likely, but there had to be a first time for everything.

'All right,' she said. 'The problem, I think, is Peter. Last night, right, he suggested we get a film out, anything I wanted. He was very specific about that – anything I wanted. But when we got there, he stood all forlorn, staring at a James Bond like a wee boy.'

'The scoundrel.'

'I was supposed to go along with it for an easy life, as usual. But I wanted to get *Fargo*.'

'Mmmm.'

'Which we got in the end, after a bit of hoo-ha.'

'I'm with you.'

'Then back at home I felt bad and I tried to talk to him, to explain that I'd been out of sorts lately and I was sorry if I was being short with him. Which I was, I admit.'

'OK.'

'So, he lets me blabber on, nodding away at me, looking all interested and pretending to care and then when I finish talking, he rewinds the video so he won't miss any of it. Not a word out of him.'

Valerie nodded enthusiastically. 'It's good, isn't it? I prefer *Miller's Crossing*, personally, and Jeffward, the idiot—'

'Are you listening to me?'

'Sorry. Go on.'

'Actually, I was finished.'

'Were you? So, what, you're upset because Peter rewound a video?'

Mary shook her head, then nodded, then shook again. She thought she had worked it out overnight, had made sense of it in her own mind. 'He does it all the time!' she said. 'And it's not the rewinding in itself, it's the fact that he lets me talk and then he nods, says *nothing*, and rewinds. It's annoying at the best of times, but when I'm saying something important . . . And anyway, that's not the only thing. But it's things *like that*. Small things. This is what has me out of sorts in the first place. I think. I've only just realised how much he gets on my wick sometimes. Did you ever accidentally get a bit of silver paper in your mouth? Stuck to a sweet or a chocolate or something? It's *revolting*. That's the feeling he's been giving me lately. Like I'm chewing a bit of silver paper.'

'Oh dear. Does he leave the toilet seat up?'

'Are you taking the piss out of me?'

'No, really, I mean is it . . . man things? Can't ask for directions when you're lost? Doesn't know how the washing machine works? Farts and then laughs? Sitcom shit.'

'No. No. It's nothing to do with that. It's nothing to do with men. It's . . . him. It's all him.'

'What are you saying? You don't like your husband any more?'

'Of course not. It's . . . I dunno. He drives me mad sometimes. Just by being himself.'

'I need another for instance.'

Mary didn't hesitate. 'I could give you dozens. His funny voices. His Paddy Englishman jokes, his Knock-Knock jokes – his jokes, full stop. His collection of looks and routines that he does. The way he's always mentioning that he doesn't like *Star Trek* because he thinks it makes him look like less of a nerd. The way he thinks calling that hideous pouffe a poofy is funny. The way he does an explosion noise when something blows up on TV. The way he's always patronising me about computers. The way he thinks his dreams are interesting. The way he sings when we're having sex. The way—'

Valerie gagged. 'The way he *what*?'

'Never mind. I don't want to go into it.'

'What does he sing? Tell me, tell me, tell me.'

'Love songs, all right? He sings me love songs. And once he did "Hungry Like The Wolf". But really, I don't want to go into it.'

Valerie smiled. 'I think that's cute,' she said.

'I used to think so too,' Mary said miserably. 'Is there any more wine?'

Valerie did the honours. 'It doesn't sound like too serious a problem, if you ask me.'

'I knew you'd say that,' Mary said. 'I shouldn't have mentioned it.'

'What I mean is you can easily do something about it.'

'Like?'

'What do you mean, "like"? Talk to him, for God's sake. Tell him what's eating you. He'll probably laugh.'

'Tell him what? "You know something, Peter, I think I've worked out what's been bugging me, and it's you. You drive me clean mad a lot of the time."'

'Of course not. I mean when he does one of these specific things, point out that you find it irritating.'

'I've tried, haven't I? Every time he puts on that computer expert face he does and says a chip is sort of like the computer's "little brain", I tell him that it drives me crazy and please stop doing it. And he says he will, but he can't help himself. That's what has me so wound up – these small things are all part of him. They're stitched, they're *woven* into him. So if I start hating them, maybe I'll end up hating him. And that can't be good, can it? Friday's our anniversary. A year only. What'll I be like after twenty?'

'You'll be grand,' Valerie said. 'It's a phase, that's all. Bound to happen when you've been together for ever, like you two. You have to look at the length of the whole relationship, not just the marriage.'

'That doesn't help, Valerie. How does that help?'

Valerie thought for a moment. 'I'm not sure. Anyway, you know what you need?'

'I know what you *think* I need, and you're wrong.'

'It'd change everything. You'd have a whole new perspective. You'd forget all about all this other . . . froth.'

'Valerie, please . . .'

'Have you even discussed it with him?'

'Of course we've talked about it. And we're in perfect harmony on the subject. I want kids and Peter wants kids, but neither of us – neither of us, mind – wants them right now.'

'I still say—'

'Listen, if you're so keen on children, why is Umberto an only child? Answer me that.'

Valerie threw her eyes to heaven. 'You wouldn't ask that question if you'd ever given birth. Ha! "Given birth." You don't give birth, you have it torn out of you. Jesus. I'm not going through *that* again.'

'Well, which is it? Children are the greatest thing since sliced bread, or childbirth is a living hell?'

'It's both. You'd know if you had one.'

They took stereo sips of wine and said nothing for a

while. A spark leaped from the fire and Valerie pounced on it.

'What about you and Jeff?' Mary said to fill the silence. 'Did you ever have a phase like this?'

Valerie bunched her knees up to her chest and rested her chin. 'I wish I could say yes,' she said. 'But I can't. Jeff hasn't got any habits or quirks that annoy me. Sorry.'

'Really?' Mary said. There was more surprise in her voice than she would have liked, and Valerie noticed.

'Why? What does he do that annoys you?'

'Nothing. Nothing.'

'No, go on, there's obviously something.'

'I think Jeff's great, Valerie, you know I do.'

'But . . . ?'

'Well, OK, don't take this the wrong way, we're just talking, aren't we?'

'Of course. Just talking.'

'OK, then. To be honest, if I was in your shoes, I don't think I could put up with the whole "Question" thing.'

'What "Question" thing?'

'You know. The way he says "Question" before he asks you a question. Like "Question: have you ever been to Madrid?" Or "Question: what type of cheese is this?"'

Valerie smiled behind her wine glass. 'What else?' she said.

Mary smiled back. She was beginning to feel a bit tipsy. 'Let's see. OK, I've got one. If Jeff was here now, drinking this wine, he'd propose a toast, wouldn't he?'

Valerie nodded, and Mary elaborated. 'He always proposes a toast, even when there's nothing going on! That'd drive me mad, now, in your shoes. Why can't we just drink it, for God's sake, why does there have to be this whole ceremony? If he can't think of anything sensible to toast, he says "To us" which, come on, means absolutely nothing. It's just words.'

'He's such an asshole!' Valerie laughed. 'I don't know how I put up with him.'

Mary laughed along, trying to think of some more of Jeff's habits. There was that noise he made with his tongue, but he didn't do it often enough for it to qualify.

'Now that you point it out,' Valerie said. 'I see what you're on about. But I'm lucky, I suppose, 'cos Jeff only has one or two annoying tics. It must be hell being married to someone with *dozens* of them.'

Mary's tittering slowly subsided. 'Yeah,' she said.

'No wonder you're all in a tizz about it. I would be too. *In your shoes.*'

It finally dawned on Mary that she had put her foot in it. 'OK, I'm sorry,' she said. 'I shouldn't be sitting here bitching about Jeff. I should be bitching about Peter.'

'Exactly. More wine?'

8

When he turned his back on Father Duff, Umberto more or less ran away. He figured that the guy probably wouldn't follow him if it was going to require serious energy expenditure. He didn't look like the athletic type. And besides, he had a mass to do.

Umberto made his way to St Anne's, his old primary school. He often went there and strolled around its tarmacked playground, kicking stones and peering through the windows. It was in an out-of-the-way spot, down a side road on the edge of town, and he found it peaceful. He had certainly been happier there than he was in his secondary school. One of the things he liked about primary was having just one teacher, someone who you could get to understand if not actually like. Take Mr Maguire, who Umberto had for two years in a row. You knew that he would sometimes accept ridiculous excuses for tardiness or undone homework but was down like a ton of hot shit on anyone who talked during a class. At secondary school, there was a different teacher for every subject, and it was hard to keep up with their likes and dislikes. A crime that went virtually unpunished in one class could get you lifted off the ground by the hair in another.

What Umberto really liked about primary school, however, was this: he hadn't felt different there. Everyone always said 'Children can be so cruel', but Umberto disagreed: adolescents were the ones you had to watch out for. Children, he felt, lacked the experience and know-how necessary for the formation of a genuinely cruel jibe. Adolescents, on the other hand, had lived long enough to know how to really hurt a person.

In primary school he suffered nothing more serious than sometimes being called 'Bumberto'. In secondary school it seemed that his entire existence was up for grabs. His father was not only a Yank, but rich. His mother dressed like a burglar and swanned around like she owned the whole town. Neither of them had a real job and both of them were stuck-up gobshites who thought they were better than everybody else. Worse still, somewhere between leaving primary and starting secondary, he suddenly began to have opinions. In his youth (as he thought of ages 0–12), he'd been entirely untroubled by them. There were so many heartfelt convictions flying around in his house, most of which he didn't understand, that he couldn't imagine the day when he would want to contribute to the din. Sure, he liked brown sauce more than he liked ketchup and he thought Batman had cooler moves than Spiderman, but these were mere preferences. If a classmate said they liked Spiderman more, Umberto would shrug and move on. Each to his own.

Those days were gone. He had started to form a picture of the world and became intrigued and energised when it was violated. Now he raised his hand at least once during every class. Wasn't it true that . . . ? But hadn't he read somewhere that . . . ? Did the teacher really believe that . . . ? He questioned everything, from the chemical composition of air to the underlying causes of World War One. At first, his interjections were welcomed by all. Teachers were impressed by his intellectual rigour, his desire to get to the bottom of everything. Classmates simply welcomed the break, for the exchanges often turned into full-blown debates with the lesson at hand completely forgotten. But it wasn't long before this argumentative tendency was simply added to the list of things that made him an easy target. He was never bullied, exactly, but he was the butt of the joke more often than he would have liked.

It could be worse, he knew. He could be Spazmo Lavery, who had a lisp, poor skin and holes in his clothes. Not a day went by when Spazmo wasn't spat on, tripped up, or simply punched in the stomach for no good reason. His case wasn't helped, of course, by his personal unpleasantness. Umberto tried several times to strike up conversation with him, and was told every time either to fuck off, get fucked or go fuck himself. Although he eventually stopped trying, he still couldn't help but wonder what kind of adult Spazmo would become. Not a very happy one, he guessed.

You had to count your blessings.

Sitting on a step outside the main school door, Umberto fished around in his pockets and withdrew two empty blood capsules. He'd bought them the previous Hallowe'en, along with a fake severed finger and a box of stink bombs. He had no real plans for any of these items at the time – he just thought they were cool. He lost the finger and threw the stink bombs away, deciding that they were childish and beneath him. But he kept the capsules, more or less on a whim.

The stigmata idea came to him only after the priest's visit to his class. Umberto found everything about religion deeply interesting but was especially fascinated by miracles. Did people actually believe in them, or were they merely some sort of metaphor? He had intended to ask the priest about it, but his classmates' laughter put him off. That was when he decided to do some research in the field. He would find a suitably credulous mass-goer, an old woman ideally, and put her to the test. His subject would no doubt see right through his amateurish sleight of hand and laugh in his face. He would laugh along, then ask her how come she believed other people's stigmata stories (or apparition stories or overnight cure stories)? The ten commandments quiz was merely a curtain-raiser, albeit an entertaining one.

The tubby priest had bounced over and interfered, however, just as he was finally getting ready to go for it. Umberto didn't mind: a genuine paid-up servant of God made an even better lab rat than the old dear. And the capsules worked pretty well, he thought. The colour was a tad vibrant perhaps, but they burst as soon as he squeezed them. He had used a Biro beforehand to draw a small hole in the centre of each palm and, looking at them now, had to admit that the result was quite impressive. They wouldn't have survived close inspection, of course, but he only flashed them for a second. The look on the priest's face . . . Umberto laughed out loud. What was he doing now? Was he on the phone to the bishop, tearfully recounting the miracle? Or, more likely, was he sitting in his favourite armchair, questioning his entire faith? It was an interesting dilemma for the guy.

He laughed again and began to walk home.

When he walked through the door and found Mary and his mother sitting by the fire, it was immediately obvious to Umberto that he had just missed something good. Mary was in full flow and making some kind of gesture with her hands, one of which was clutching a glass of wine. She seemed to stop mid-word. Then she and his mother made eye contact. Both pairs of eyes widened ever so slightly.

'Didn't hear you come in there,' Valerie said. 'Where have you been?'

'Out and about,' he said, taking a seat.

Mary cocked an eye at him. 'Sounds very mysterious.'

'Nah. Not really. So, were you talking about me or what?'

'Sorry?' Valerie said.

'A minute ago. You were saying something I wasn't sup-posed to hear. Would you like me to leave again?'

'We're not always talking about you, you know, Umberto. We do have other conversations.'

Umberto looked to Mary. She looked away immediately.

'I'm leaving anyway,' he said. 'I'm gasping for a drink. You're fine on that score, by the looks of things.'

They both looked at their glasses to confirm that this was so. 'Yes, ta,' Mary said.

Umberto got up and headed for the kitchen. He closed the door behind him and immediately put his ear to it. Seconds passed. Nothing. He should have been able to hear them. They were either sitting there in total silence or else they

83

Damien Owens

were speaking in very low voices. The latter, for sure – he couldn't imagine his mother maintaining silence for more than a few seconds. Then he heard Mary saying something, but he couldn't make anything out except for the word 'Peter'. He stood there for another couple of minutes, but the acoustics didn't improve.

Mary in tears one day. Wine in the afternoon the next. Serious conversations about Peter stopped on a dime. Something was most definitely up.

9

On Monday morning, Mary kicked the shop door half a dozen times and used every swear word in her vocabulary before she realised that she was using the wrong key. This sort of thing always happened when she didn't get her ten hours. No doubt the day would be spent giving people the wrong change and picking up the stapler every time the phone rang. It was not an enticing prospect. Nevertheless, she was no longer at home. That was a good thing . . . or was it? Could it be a good thing to prefer work to home? Surely not.

Musique Boutique was the only real record shop in town. A couple of the supermarkets made half-assed attempts at music sales, but they had no knowledgeable staff and never ventured beyond the shallow waters of the top twenty. Mary was only twenty-four when she bought it and all of its pitiful stock after the original owner finally accepted that a successful business has to open for more than a couple of days a week and threw in the towel. He was a former show band leader called Billy Carey and might have made a go of it had it not been for his frothing hatred of all music written after 1960 on the one hand, and his rampant alcoholism on the other.

She was on her fourth full-time job at the time (personal assistant to a creepy accountant) and had no third-level qualifications or real business experience. But she had ideas, passion, and a correspondence-course certificate in Basic Book-keeping. The first bank manager she called on hummed a tune while she outlined her plans and called her 'my dear', as in 'I'm not willing to take the risk, my dear'. The second had watched the shop's decline with dismay, however, privately wondering why no enterprising local person wanted to take it on. When Mary showed up, all nervous enthusiasm and rapid chat, he listened hard. And he called her by her name.

She opened for business a month later.

'No,' Mary said. 'It hasn't arrived yet.'

'Any idea w—'

'No. None. Sorry. Try next week.'

Mrs Sheedy muttered under her breath and made her exit. She'd been in the shop every day for the past fortnight, looking for the new Daniel O'Donnell video. Its consistent failure to arrive was beginning to affect her health, Mary thought. She looked thinner and frailer each time she came through the door, her face flickering between hope and fear.

Before she opened the shop, Mary had assumed that Daniel O'Donnell was essentially a media creation. He provided an easy target for lazy comedians and third-rate impressionists. She didn't think for a moment that people actually bought his records. But they did. And his calendars and videos and his mugs. Every time she dropped one into a bag and faked a smile for the customer, she felt herself die a little. In the first few months of trading, she'd told all and sundry that her shop was going to be nothing like Billy's. She kept the ridiculous name, of course, but she meant it to be ironic — Musique Boutique mark two was going to be something entirely new and entirely different. She was sorely disappointed to find that for every punter who wanted to know when the new Teenage Fanclub album was due, there were a dozen middle-aged Danielites, hopping from foot to foot, waving their wrinkled cash at her. They kept her in business, granted, but she felt entitled to resent them just a tiny bit anyway.

Mrs Sheedy came and went at about ten thirty. She was the only customer of the entire morning. These frequent lulls in activity originally terrified Mary, but she soon got used to the idea that approximately half of her business was done on Saturdays. It had just turned noon when the shop door swung open and the second customer of the day strode in. He was a boy of about sixteen, dressed unseasonably in a black T-shirt and ragged grey board-shorts. The T-shirt bore the legend 'My Other T-shirt is a Jumper'. Mary wondered why he wasn't at school but said nothing.

'Hi,' she said as he ambled — stumbled, really — up to the counter. He put his right hand under the T-shirt and scratched his pot belly vigorously for a moment before responding.

'Yeah. I'm looking for *Kill the Dead*.'

'Excuse me?'

He sighed deeply. 'Cockstump?'

'Cock what?'

Another sigh. 'Cockstump.'

'That's what I thought you said. Is that . . . a band?'

He avoided her eye and snickered. 'Forget about it,' he said. 'I didn't think you'd have it.' He turned and stumbled back towards the door.

'Wait! I can order it!' she said.

'Never mind,' he said from the doorway. Then he turned and sneered as only a teenage boy can. 'That was an album too. Have you heard of that one?'

'Cheeky wee shite,' she said to the closed door.

Customer number three showed up immediately after lunch. Mary was staring into blank space at the time, wondering if she should be listening to anyone as melancholy as Emmylou Harris, given her current state of mind.

'Hello,' Finbarr Grealey said as the door shut behind him. 'Not a bad day.'

'Not bad, no,' Mary assented. Finbarr smiled and then turned away from her to face the A section of Rock and Pop. When he first started to frequent Musique Boutique, Mary used to make small talk with him, as she would with any customer. He was never snappy or unfriendly, but he seemed to physically squirm when she spoke to him. Just not a talker, she supposed. Instead, he simply browsed methodically, starting inside the door at Rock and Pop – A and ending in the centre display at Country and Western – Z. He never left empty-handed, not once. Mary thought he had wonderfully eclectic taste (even if she didn't always approve of his purchases) and told him so one day. He blushed bright red and almost ran out of the shop. It was the last personal comment she made to him. He was practically her best customer and she didn't want to lose him. From that day on, it was strictly Hello, How much do I owe you, Thank you and Goodbye with them. So it was something of a shock when Finbarr turned towards the counter, cracked a crooked smile and asked her how she was keeping.

'Keeping?' Mary said. 'How am I keeping?'

'Keeping. Getting on. How are you doing?'

'I know what you mean,' Mary said. 'I was just . . . I'm fine, Finbarr. How . . . how are you?'

'Grand,' he said, turning back to the racks. 'Never better.'

Mary smiled and tried to think of something else to say. Nothing suggested itself. She knew something about most of her customers and could ask about their families or their jobs. Finbarr was a closed book. She knew his name and she knew that he was retired and lived alone, but that was all. Hardly the building blocks of an interesting conversation. She was on the point of saying something about the weather when he ended the awkward silence himself.

'How's that husband of yours?' he asked, still rifling through the CDs.

Mary stiffened. In her mind's eye, she saw Peter hopping around on one foot in front of the washing machine, wincing and trying to extricate himself from his vomit-stained clothes. She'd found him in that condition when she returned from Valerie's and simultaneously felt like laughing and crying. Mostly crying.

'He's fine too,' she said. 'Do you know Peter?'

Finbarr shrugged. 'Only to see. I know his face, like. From around town.'

'Oh. Right.'

'I never married, meself,' he said. 'Never met the right woman.' He turned to face her, cracked a peculiar grin, then went back to the racks.

Mary really didn't know what to say. This was a conversational deluge by Finbarr's standards.

'Well, you're not missing a damn thing.' She smiled. 'Take it from me.'

She meant it as a joke, but Finbarr didn't seem to take it that way. He froze, then turned slowly on his heels and walked towards the counter. He wore an unreadable expression.

'Now why would you say something like that?' he asked her, folding his arms.

Mary thought she detected shades of anger in his tone and took an involuntary step back. 'I'm only jok—'

'You should count your blessings,' he said. 'You wouldn't want to be on your own, would you?'

Mary swallowed hard. 'Of course not.'

'Because it's no fun being on your own.'

'I'm sure it isn't. I was only—'

'You should count your blessings,' he said again.

There was a pause in which they stared at each other. 'I do count my blessings,' Mary said then.

He smiled so suddenly that Mary jumped. 'Of course you do.'

She smiled back, a weak approximation of the leer that had overrun his face.

Finbarr reached forward then, causing her to jump again, and picked up a magazine she'd been thumbing through earlier. 'Been doing a bit of reading?' he asked, flipping it over to see the cover.

'Yeah. I have,' she said testily. She was starting to find this new familiarity unsettling.

'*Mojo*,' Finbarr said, reading the cover. He pronounced it '*Modge-o*'. 'Any good, is it?'

'Yeah. Keeps me up to date.'

He placed it back on the counter. 'So many magazines on the go these days. Do you read any other ones? Non-music ones?'

There was something in his eyes that she didn't like. It suddenly occurred to her that he might be chatting her up. Her toes curled. 'I suppose I do,' she said nervously. 'Passes the time, doesn't it?'

'You have to be careful though, don't you? You were in a hurry, you might pick up the wrong one.' He scratched the tip of his nose and smiled. 'You know. One of them sexy magazines.'

Mary started to wish there was someone else in the shop. This was definitely turning seedy. She felt butterflies in her stomach and when she spoke, her voice was not steady. 'Like what? What do you mean? *Playboy*? I'm not likely to buy *Playboy* by mistake, now am I?'

Finbarr laughed, or at least pulled a face and made a noise deep in his throat. 'No, I'm sure you wouldn't. I mean the women's magazines. They've gone all sexy. Not like in my day. They used to be full of nothing but recipes and fancy clothes, from what I could see. You know the sort of rubbish women like. Now they're all sex sex sex . . .'

He looked embarrassed when he said this, and Mary relaxed a little. He was just trying to make conversation and was obviously out of practice. She allowed herself to smile. 'I

91

suppose you're right, they are all going that way,' she said. 'The times, they are a-changing.'

He failed to pick up on the musical reference, despite the fact that she'd sold him the album only a fortnight previously. But he seemed pleased at her response, satisfied somehow. He nodded, turned away and picked up a CD without even looking at it.

'I'll take this,' he said, handing her a copy of *True Blue*.

By now, Mary simply wanted him to leave. She bagged his purchase and took payment without another word.

10

'It's not funny,' Peter told Mairéad. 'I could have been seriously injured.'

She covered her mouth with both hands and shook her head. 'Terrible. Terrible. It's very sad.'

'Oi, stop laughing. For all I know, I *have* been seriously injured. I might never walk properly again. I could have—'

The phone interrupted him. Mairéad tried to put the brakes on her laughter and let it ring a few times before she felt able to answer. 'Data Force, good morning. Oh, hi, Fiona . . . no, nothing's wrong . . . no . . . no, I just heard something funny, that's all . . . yeah, he just got in . . . oh, right . . . hang on, I'll put you through.' She punched a button and shouted through to the main office. 'David! That's Fiona. She's lost her keys or something. Line two.' Then she turned to Peter again, still smiling. 'Walk over to the wall,' she said. 'I want to see it again.'

'I'm not your plaything, you know,' he said. 'I do have other roles around here.' But he obliged anyway. Mairéad's laugh was light and musical and Peter liked provoking it, even under circumstances such as these. He rotated slowly and hobbled away from her desk, shifting his weight slowly from one foot to the other as he went. When he reached the wall he executed a tortuous about-turn and made his way back, wincing all the while. She laughed as loudly as she had when he first came through the door but at least had the decency to feign genuine concern this time.

'It does look . . . uncomfortable. Maybe you should see a doctor. I know a good groin man, he could fix you right up.'

'What a funny lady.'

'I'm serious. If not for yourself, do it for Mary. It can't be much fun for her, having you out of action like this.'

Mairéad was in her early fifties, but she was given to making oblique references to the sex lives of everyone in the office on a daily basis. They usually responded in kind. When Peter failed to do so, she allowed her smile to fade.

'Ah, I'm sorry, Peter. It must be very sore. Our Terry got a groin strain playing football one time and he was like an Antichrist for a week. Go on in and I'll bring you a cuppa.'

'Thanks, Mairéad. I could do with a sit down.'

'And I'll pop into the shop at lunch-time and give Mary that doctor's number. In case she gets desperate.'

Peter didn't laugh or even smile. Mairéad shrugged and went to get the tea. 'You've lost your sense of humour,' she called out over her shoulder. 'Must be as painful as it looks.'

David and Pat the Boss were sitting at the large oval-shaped table in the main office when Peter limped in. They called it the 'main office' to distinguish it from the only other office, a cupboard-sized room that Pat occupied when he wasn't out hustling for business. Besides the table, it was home to a desk each for Peter and David as well as several piles of dejected-looking computers, keyboards, monitors, mice and printers. Some of these machines were beyond repair, and others just needed a bit of love and attention. Some worked perfectly. At least once a week, Pat vowed to find out which was which.

'Jesus,' Peter said, noting their glum faces. 'Who died?'

David looked up, winced. 'Pat's grandmother.'

Peter swallowed. 'You are joking, of course?'

David shook his head slowly.

'Shit,' Peter said. 'I'm sorry, Pat, I didn't know. You'd think Mairéad would have told me.'

Pat leaned forward to get a view of the tiny reception area where Mairéad worked. 'Mairéad!' he yelled through the open door.

She was still in the kitchen and her voice was faint. 'Yeah?'

'I forgot to tell you. My granny died last night.'

She was in the office within two seconds. Peter, who had his back to her, guessed that she must have hurdled over her desk.

'Ah no,' Mairéad said, leaning on the door frame. 'I'm very sorry. I didn't know she was ill.'

Pat sat back in his chair, looking, as usual, like a fat, balding fifteen-year-old in his dad's suit. 'She wasn't ill, as such. She just . . . died. During an ad break in *The South Bank Show*. So they said.'

'Poor thing,' Peter said.

Pat smiled at a memory. 'She loved *The South Bank Show*. There was something about Melvyn Bragg's hair she found comforting. She told me all about it, last time I went to the home to see her. She said she never knew what he was on about, but she couldn't take her eyes off his hair. She commandeered the TV every Sunday night, made them all watch it, all the oul' ones. I think she fancied him, actually.'

Everyone nodded.

'She had a good innings, though. Eighty-two.'

Everyone nodded again. There was a momentary silence. Then the phone rang and Mairéad went back out to answer it. 'Sorry for your trouble,' she said over her shoulder.

'Anyway,' Pat said. 'Life goes on. Thing is, the funeral's on Wednesday, so there's no way I can go to Dublin now. One of you two'll have to do it.'

Peter and David flicked their eyes at each other, then back to Pat. 'It' was a two-day course in Upgrading to Microsoft Windows 2000. They attended about a half-dozen such courses every year, or rather one of them did and then filled in the other two on whatever was new in the software when he got back. Pat the Boss usually did the honours, partly because Peter and David were invariably too busy with actual paying customers and partly because he was the only one of the three who could be trusted to pay attention and take notes. The courses themselves were frequently pointless and always extremely boring.

'Well I don't think I can do it,' David said, before Peter could speak. 'I've got a lot on this week. Wednesday especially. Looks very bad for me, Wednesday. Thursday's not much better.'

Peter scrambled to think of a good reason why he couldn't go either. It was too . . . he had to do a . . . there was no . . . his groin was . . .

'Down to you so,' Pat the Boss said as his mind spun. 'Remember to steal lots of pens.'

11

'That's a pawn, Seamus. Not a bishop.'

'Is it?'

'It is, yes. No doubt about it.'

Father Grehan lifted the piece up close to his face and peered at it in the firelight through his Coke-bottle glasses. 'It is and all,' he admitted. 'Sorry about that. Let me see now, give me a second . . .'

'No hurry,' Father Duff said, sitting back in his armchair. 'Take your time.'

Father Grehan rubbed his chin and surveyed the board. 'Wait'll I see now . . .' After a minute's reflection he pointed to his one remaining bishop, which had been lying inert at the side of the board for some time. 'This lad's a bishop, correct?'

Father Duff nodded. Christ, he could do with a fag. 'Yes. That one's a bishop. You're under no obligation to move a bishop this turn, you know, Seamus, you can move other pieces as well. Your queen, say.'

As usual, Father Grehan had despatched his queen from the

safety of the back rank at the earliest opportunity. When he did so, Father Duff advised him for perhaps the hundredth time that such a move was a strategic error that was sure to end in tears. But the older man waved him away, vowing with his usual relish that, given free rein, the piece would 'wreak havoc' on the open board. In fact, Father Duff could have taken the queen three times during the first ten moves but instead pretended not to notice its existence. He had long since realised that the sole challenge in playing chess with Father Grehan was in seeing how long you could plausibly allow his pieces to remain on the board.

'Me queen?' Father Grehan said dismissively. 'She's grand where she is.'

Father Duff sighed. His own previous move had placed the white queen once again in immediate danger of being taken ('gobbled', Father Grehan called it). He had no real intention of taking it, of course. He had merely hoped that his opponent would see the danger and react. He knew that such escapes thrilled Father Grehan, who liked to think of himself as a fly-by-the-seat-of-your-pants sort of player.

Cautiously, Father Grehan moved his bishop one square closer to the centre. Then he rubbed his hands together and grinned, as if he had just sprung a cunning trap. The fact that the bishop could now be taken by the same black knight that threatened his queen passed him by completely. Father Duff shook his head in disbelief and then shunted a pawn harmlessly forward, hoping to get another few minutes out of the game. He had discovered chess only six months previously and embraced it with a convert's zeal, teaching himself with a library book, first the surprisingly simple rules and then some elementary strategy. The only problem was finding an opponent. There was a chess club in the town but he wanted to play in comfort, in his favourite armchair at the priests' house, not on some plastic stool at the community centre. He could have bought one of those chess computers, he supposed, but where was the fun in that? It was supposed to be a social game. And so, once he was satisfied that he knew what was what, he began to badger Father Grehan who doubted that he would be any good at it but agreed to learn – out of simple kindness, it seemed. Nevertheless, he too was soon hooked, although his concerns about his abilities were well founded. It wasn't just his rapidly failing eyesight. He seemed to be congenitally incapable of following the flow of play. It was as if his memory had been wiped clean every few seconds. He frequently moved individual pieces only once, apparently deciding that having disturbed their rest, he should let them have the remainder of the game off. His 'attacks', when they arose, were exercises in wanton carnage with every piece thrown recklessly forward, only to be mown down at Father Duff's convenience. His idea of defensive play was to shuffle his king back and forth in whatever strange corner of the board he had himself trapped it until his opponent grew restless and ended the misery.

Despite all this, Father Duff enjoyed their games. He had always liked Father Grehan personally and found his respect for the man growing with every inevitable victory. He had never met anyone who so clearly believed in the old chestnut 'It's not the winning, it's the taking part'. He would have enjoyed a real game – he had never played anyone else – but that was life, he supposed. No point in complaining about it.

After a long pause, during which he peered at the board

101

from a distance of about four inches, Father Grehan settled on a piece from the second rank and tentatively slid it four squares along a diagonal.

Father Duff shook his head once more and smiled to himself.

'That's a pawn, Seamus. Not a bishop.'

The game ended soon afterwards, when Father Duff decided that it should. As ever, Father Grehan was philosophical in defeat.

'I sort of ran out of room to manoeuvre there,' he said. 'Sure I'll get you the next time.'

They watched the fire for a while then, both lost in their own thoughts. Father Grehan wore a slight smile and periodically broke into a full grin. He was replaying the game in his head, Father Duff suspected, making plans for the next one, vowing not to make the same mistakes again. Father Duff's own thoughts were elsewhere. On the lad, the stigmatic.

'I met a peculiar young fella in the school last week,' he said casually.

'Oh?'

'A big lump of a lad, fourteen or fifteen. Different from the rest of them in his class, you could tell right away. More serious, maybe, or more mature. Different anyway.'

Father Grehan nodded.

'We were talking, the whole class, about the priesthood and so on. The usual questions, you know yourself. Then your man sticks up his hand. How can I stand to be a priest, he says, knowing full well that people don't even know the ten commandments.'

'Get away. The cheeky pup.'

'Anyway, I gave him an answer, and he seemed interested in what I was saying, and that was that, I thought. But then yesterday, I was getting ready to do the ten o'clock and who's standing at the gate only himself. Asking the people going in whether they can tell him the ten commandments. Doing a survey, he says.'

'The wee get!'

'So I went out to talk to him, and to cut a long story short, he, eh . . . he tried to cod me that he was a stigmatic.'

Father Grehan folded his hands on his chest. 'You're joking. What did he say?'

'He didn't say anything. He had ink or ketchup or something all over his palms. He showed them to me and then he ran off.'

Father Grehan pushed his glasses up his nose and sniffed. 'That's a good one. What's he up to, do you think?'

'I wouldn't have a clue. Umberto McKeown, he's called. Who are his people, do you know?'

'McKeown. McKeown. There's a few McKeowns about the place. What kind of a name is Umberto?'

'It's Italian, but he isn't. I heard somebody in the class slagging him about his parents. Weirdos, he said.'

Father Grehan nodded. 'Could be James McKeown's grandson, then. He has an oddball daughter you hear stories about now and then.'

'I don't suppose you know where they live? I wouldn't mind having a word.'

'I don't, but it wouldn't be hard to find out. Are you worried about him, Miles? Is he a bit . . . disturbed, would you say?'

Father Duff pursed his lips. 'Not disturbed, no, not the way you mean anyhow. But there was something funny about him, the way he carried on, the way he looked at me. He was . . . *interested*. I'd like to talk to him.'

'Interested? In what?'

'A job, maybe. I think we could make a priest out of him.'

12

It could well be, Peter mused in bed on Monday night, that I am going stone mad. His concern arose from the fact that his normally reliable and rational thought processes had fractured and split to such an extent that there were now literal voices in his head. They were having an argument. Peter felt that he was listening, rather than taking part.

Just because somebody says something, that doesn't necessarily make it so, one of the voices said. That's blindingly obvious isn't it? You don't have to believe someone just because they formed a sentence. What if they'd said that Mary is acting like this because you're no good at gardening or because you have poor taste in socks? Wouldn't make it true, would it? You'd laugh it off. Like you should laugh their other ideas off.

This voice was calm and authoritative. Peter found it convincing. For a moment. Then the other voice spoke up, shrill and passionate.

Maybe, it said. But you felt something didn't you? You felt

something in your stomach, both times, Finbarr and David. You felt a little thump. A little thump of recognition. You knew they could be right, either of them. Or both of them.

Oh, for Christ's sake, the first voice replied. 'A little thump.' I never heard such crap. That was *pride*, you twat. No man wants to entertain the possibility that he's no good with women, either in bed or out of it. They could have suggested that to anyone and he'd have his doubts, if only for a moment. Grow up.

The second voice grew slightly hysterical. But what about when she saw your limp and you told her you had done your groin in? You cracked that great joke.

'I'm done for,' you said, in your Plucky Soldier voice (one of your best voices, by the way). 'Go on without me.' And what did she say? 'Typical.'

So what? voice number one said.

Voice number two sighed. You don't have to be Sigmund fucking Freud, do you? You told her you were having groin troubles, and she said, 'Typical.' Peter waited for the first voice to respond. It didn't. The second voice had wind in its sails now and blustered on. And then you tried to start a conversation about the anniversary. Not only did she not join in, the whole idea seemed to make her physically uncomfortable. Face the facts, Peter. Something's gone badly wrong.

'*Crap*,' he said aloud. Mary murmured in her sleep and rolled even further away from him.

13

Every year after his parents died Finbarr bought himself something nice for Christmas. There was no one else to do it and he had usually been good, so why not? The fun part was surprising himself, which he found quite easy: he would simply get fantastically drunk, stagger into town, pick a gift and then rush home to get it wrapped before he started to sober up. Christmas morning, he'd tiptoe down to the kitchen bleary-eyed and rip the parcel open, eager to find out what he'd bought. Most times he was delighted with his present: a good winter jumper, perhaps, or a pen and pencil set.

He was bitterly disappointed in 1998, however, when he woke to discover that he'd bought himself a portable stereo. It was a wildly inappropriate gift. For one thing, he couldn't really afford it, having recently retired from his job as a postman ('I'm a man of letters,' he used to tell people). More importantly, he had no real interest in music. His parents enjoyed listening to the radio as they silently built their nightly house of cards but Finbarr could never hear what all the fuss was about. Music was nothing more than noise, one song practically indistinguishable from the next. Why his subconscious should suddenly decide to give it a chance at this stage was a mystery to him. Nevertheless, he played along and spent the holiday period roaming around the dial at random. To his astonishment, he found it delightful. The music, that is – the DJs drove him to distraction, with their pathetic quizzes and unasked-for opinions. He wasn't crazy about the constant ads either. The solution was obvious. When the shops reopened, he went straight to Musique Boutique and spent more money that he really couldn't spare. His first purchases were *Fear of a Black Planet* by Public Enemy and *Songs for Swingin' Lovers!* by Frank Sinatra. He loved them both, and before long he was buying at least one CD a week, more or less at random (although he did have a penchant for brightly coloured covers). He cursed his extravagance every time, but forgot about pounds and pence as soon as he hit the play button. The parps and toots, the trills and warbles! Finbarr was transported, every time. One rainy morning in February, he approached the record shop counter with an especially heavy load: Pearl Jam's *Ten*, Loretta Lynn's *Greatest Hits*, and *The Best Dance Album in the World Ever, Volume II*. Young McKeown smiled at him and told him he was starting to be her best customer. Finbarr took it as a compliment – the fourth of his life by his count.

True Blue was the first album he ever bought that he didn't love. He thought it was all right, but not great. It sounded too . . . plastic. Shiny. Or maybe he was just feeling down, on account of poor Peter Ford. (Finbarr often felt down. He'd spent whole weeks in bed in the past. It wasn't too bad once you got the hang of it.) He felt so sorry for him. The look on your woman's face when he mentioned those magazines . . . there was no doubt about it – she'd been doing some reading. And now she had all sorts of ideas.

When the CD ended, he went to make himself a cup of tea. He liked his tea strong and made it in a mug with three tea-bags, each heartily squeezed. The mug said The Far Side on it and it had a picture of some cows. In honour of what, Finbarr had no idea. It had been his mug during those final few years in the post office. His cups of tea were a source of great hilarity there. 'You could nearly stand a spoon up in that,' Liam Sweeney said to him one day years ago. Liam was one of the few souls who had an occasional word for Finbarr, and was sorely missed after he upped and moved to Canada.

When the water in the mug had turned almost black, he fished out the mangled tea-bags and dropped them into the white plastic bag that served as his kitchen bin. Then he added a drop of milk. Just a drop. He puckered up and sucked noisily at the edge of the mug before releasing a TV commercial 'Ahhhhhhh' of satisfaction.

Probably wouldn't even stoop to making poor Peter a cup of tea, your woman. That'd be too old-fashioned, wouldn't it? Too much like being a normal wife. Probably off in the bedroom on her own instead, reading about what she was missing. Finbarr could see it all clearly. The next stage would be coming soon – the affair. Probably has her eye on someone already, he thought. Weighing him up, checking against what the magazine said.

It was heartbreaking. And typical of women, Finbarr guessed.

*   *   *

109

Who would she have the affair with, that was the question. She was good-looking, for sure, and could probably take her pick. A customer maybe, or some lonely sales rep. Peter was crazy about her, that was obvious. He'd be devastated when he found out the truth. Finbarr wished there was some way he could warn him, let him know what was in store if he didn't get out with his dignity while he still could. It was what you did for a friend.

He had no evidence, though. Just his gut instinct. It was good enough for Finbarr himself, but probably wouldn't hold much water with Peter. What he needed was something tangible, some physical thing that would spell it out loud and clear. He could follow her, he supposed. With a camera. It would be something to do, apart from anything else. But it sounded like a lot of work. Besides, she might not be at that stage yet. She might still be at the thinking about it stage.

Then a light went on in Finbarr's head. He could save everybody a lot of time, and Peter a lot of grief, by helping matters along himself. She was going to wander sooner or later anyway. Why not get the whole ugly mess over with? There were no children involved. It would be like stripping a plaster off very quickly. There was no chance that he could coax her into her first infidelity himself, of course – Finbarr was nothing if not a realist – but he could pose as an anonymous admirer. If he made some disguised approach, she might be tempted. Send her flowers or something and a note. Invite her to meet him at some romantic spot and get the photos that way.

Nah. A photo of her standing around looking at her watch in some dark lovers' lane probably wouldn't do. She could be waiting for anyone, a woman friend or whatever. And, knowing his luck, he would almost certainly get caught. If he could get her to write a letter or leave a message somehow . . . Yeah, that was good. A phone message. Get it straight from the horse's mouth.

The only problem was, Finbarr didn't have a phone, much less an answering machine. He had never seen the need, for the same reasons that he had never seen the need to decorate the house. This was an emergency though. Exceptions had to be made. Besides, hadn't he been having dreams lately about those happy-go-lucky young people in the ads for mobile phones, laughing and chatting and arranging nights out? Wasn't this just the excuse he needed? So what if no one else would ever ring him on it. Just owning the thing would be good for morale.

And hang the expense. Wouldn't Peter do the same for him, if the tables were turned?

14

James and Elizabeth came to visit on Tuesday night. Peter heard about it when the doorbell rang. It was one of Mary's first sentences to him that evening.

'Oh yeah,' she said. 'I forgot. Mum and Dad are coming over.'

He was on the sofa in his socks, channel-hopping and scratching himself. 'What?' he said, sitting up. 'What for?'

Mary shrugged. 'A visit.'

He didn't mind having them around. Quite the reverse in fact, especially since his own parents had retired to Donegal. He usually got some notice though. Mary was out into the hall and had let them in before Peter had even made it into his shoes. He was still wrestling with them as the trio came bustling through the living-room door. Mary carried on into the kitchen, babbling about tea and biscuits. James and Elizabeth, as ever, stood just inside the door, waiting to be invited to sit.

'I hope you're not putting shoes on for our sake,' James said.

Peter smiled up at them. 'I wouldn't bother normally, but there's holes in my socks today.'

James smiled, or rather upgraded his frown. Then he gripped Peter's hand and gave it his habitual three brisk shakes.

'So how are you keeping?' Peter asked. 'Sit down, sit down.'

'We are very well, thank you for asking us,' Elizabeth said as she perched daintily on the end of an armchair. For some reason that Peter couldn't quite fathom, his mother-in-law sometimes spoke to him like someone who had learned English from a tape. 'Are you busy now in your job?' she asked.

'It's gone a bit mad recently, yeah. And I have a course to do in Dublin, tomorrow and the day after.'

'A course?' James said. 'What kind of a course? I thought you were supposed to be an expert.' In contrast to Elizabeth, James had burrowed his frame down into his armchair so thoroughly that his neck had disappeared. The posture lent his words a certain menace, but Peter knew he wasn't being malicious. He was used to this treatment from James and understood it to be a sort of compliment. It was better, for example, than the way he treated Jeff.

'Just brushing up, James,' he said. 'Things change very quickly in computers. You have to—'

'Tell me this,' James interrupted. 'What happened to the millennium bug? You scared the shite out of me about it last Christmas. D'ye remember him, Elizabeth? Going on and on and on?'

'Watch your language,' his wife told him. 'You're not at home now.'

'I remember him going on and on and on,' Mary said,

appearing with a tray. 'Planes were going to fall out of the sky, there'd be no electricity, there'd be no food, we'd all have to—'

Peter butted in. 'Thank God the skilled professionals in the information technology industry were able to act in time and save us all. *Phew.*'

He said it with a smile, but he wasn't able to keep the gravel out of his voice. Elizabeth moved even closer to the edge of her seat and was now in real danger of coming off it. James burrowed deeper into his and stared hard at his lap.

'What a hero,' Mary said, returning to the kitchen.

Peter saw James and Elizabeth exchange nervous glances.

'So how's the toe, James?' Peter asked quickly, pouring tea. 'Healing all right, is it?'

James had recently dropped a sledgehammer on the big toe of his left foot. It wasn't a serious injury – there were no broken bones – but nevertheless he had phoned Mary four times since with breathless updates on his progress.

'I don't know what's keeping that toenail hanging on,' he said solemnly. 'Must be habit. What's it like, Elizabeth? Tell him.'

His wife shrugged. 'It's very sore looking.'

'Tell him about the colour of it.'

Elizabeth sighed. 'It's purple.'

'Purple me arse, it's black.'

'Dark purple, yes.'

'It's black! Lookit . . .'

Mary came back with the jug of milk she had forgotten as James tore angrily at his laces. 'Are we all taking our shoes off now?' she said.

115

'Your father's just showing us his toe,' Peter said, trying to make the sentence sound reasonable.

'For the love of God . . .' Elizabeth said quietly, covering her eyes.

'Black,' James said simply. He had his shoe off now and was carefully working on his coarse brown sock. Wide-eyed with concentration, he tugged it down the length of his foot, flinching slightly.

'Is it still sore then, Dad?' Mary said, taking a seat.

'Brutal,' James confessed. 'I hardly got a wink of sleep last night.'

Elizabeth raised her eyebrows over her teacup. 'What was all the snoring for then?'

James didn't answer. He finished peeling off his sock and extended his leg to give everyone a better view. The digit in question was surrounded by ancient grey cotton wool held on by Christmas wrapping tape. The tape had snowmen on it.

'Ah, Dad,' Mary said. 'What good's that? Could you not have gone to the doctor? Get it done properly. Or at least buy decent bandages.'

'Or proper sellotape,' Peter said.

'Waste of money,' James said. Mary looked helplessly to her mother, who shrugged. The tape and cotton wool fitted over the big toe like a bearskin hat. James pulled it off gingerly, blowing short bursts of air and wincing as he did so.

'Look at that now,' he said. Everyone except Elizabeth leaned over and stared. His hairless foot was as grey as the cotton wool and sat twitching on the rug like a landed fish. Peter found himself sniffing and hoped no one heard. It didn't reek, exactly, but it smelled like a foot all right. None of James's toes was in great nick. They were all unusually long, like mini-fingers, and sported a number of weals and scars. His toenails had evidently been allowed to grow unfettered for some time. They curled round gently at the top, each trapping a sliver of dirt. But these minor imperfections were of no consequence compared to the wreck of his big toe. It was grossly swollen and seemed to be visibly throbbing.

'Jesus Christ!' Mary said.

'Oh, indeed and it was a lot worse looking than that,' James assured her, evidently pleased at her reaction. 'Some of the blackness has gone.'

As far as Peter could see, all of the blackness had gone. Still, the remaining colours were dramatic enough in their own right.

Elizabeth leaned over, stole a peek and then nodded to herself. 'Dark purple,' she muttered.

James turned to look at her. 'What are you on about?' he hissed. 'It's black! Under the nail! Black! Lookit!'

Elizabeth said nothing and looked away.

'You're going blind, woman!'

Mary patted him on the knee. 'Come on, Dad, calm down now and have your tea.'

'Calm, me shite! That foot could fall off and she wouldn't care!'

Elizabeth looked at Peter, cocked her head and bit her bottom lip. It was a gesture of apology on her husband's behalf. Peter smiled at her to indicate that no apology was necessary.

Mary said, 'Now you know that's not true, Dad. Just put your sock back on and we'll—'

James interrupted her with a growl and snatched at his cotton wool. 'I'd have to lose a leg before *she'd* pay any attention. I'd have to come hopping in on one foot, carrying me severed frigging leg before—'

'What is the subject of your computer course, Peter?' Elizabeth said amiably.

James turned to Mary and simultaneously pointed at Elizabeth like a tattle-tale child. 'Do you see that now? Do you see the way she just flat out ignores me when it suits her? The like of that there now . . . that drives me mad. That drives me clean mad.'

Peter wondered if he should answer Elizabeth's question. He was still deciding when she shook her head and said, 'Did you ever, in all your born days meet such a hypocrite? He spends half his life ignoring me.' She said it to Peter, as if James wasn't actually there.

There was a tense hiatus. Peter found that he was gripping his knees, white-knuckled. Although he was well used to hearing them sparring like this, the atmosphere was usually more good-natured. This was beginning to sound like a real row. But the potential for ugliness vanished immediately.

'Wheesht! Did you hear something, Mary?' James said, winking. 'I thought I heard a noise there. Did someone say something?'

Elizabeth slapped him gently on the shoulder. 'A comedian,' she said. 'I married a comedian.'

James pretended to look around for the source of the noise,

looking straight through Elizabeth. 'There it is again! Did you hear it that time, Peter?'

Everyone laughed, except Mary.

They stayed for over an hour, which was quite a lengthy visit by their standards.

'We better tip on,' James said, when he had drained his third cup of tea. 'Let you get on with it.'

'Would you listen to him,' Elizabeth said. 'What he means is he wants to get home before *Friends* comes on.'

'Rubbish!' James said, getting up. 'You'd sit here all night, if I left it up to you. Getting in their way.'

'I don't know why you won't just admit you like that show. Or rather you like the women in it, I should say.'

James folded his arms and then unfolded them. Then he folded them again. 'It's very well written,' he said unsteadily. 'It's very clever.'

'Monica or Rachel?' Peter said.

James looked at his feet. 'Phoebe,' he muttered.

.Later, when they had cleared the tea things away, Peter and Mary sat in silence on the sofa.

'What are you smiling at?' Mary said after a while.

Peter's grin expanded. 'Your mother and father.'

'And what's so funny about my mother and father?'

He was surprised by her accusatory tone. 'I'm not laughing *at* them, Mary. I just think they're amusing.'

'Do you? What's so amusing about them? Amusing how?'

'Have you been watching *Goodfellas* again?'

'Eh?'

'Never mind. You're only embarrassed because they're your

parents; everyone else thinks they're a scream. I certainly do. And they're a great ad for being married.'

She sat up. 'Are you serious? If that's a good ad, I'd hate to see a bad one.'

'Well, they still have a laugh together, still pick on each other, take the piss.' He paused. 'I think it's . . . encouraging.'

She made no reply. Peter understood that he had somehow put his foot in it again, but he was getting used to that feeling. So he let the silence drag on. When it dragged on to the point where it was becoming uncomfortable, he groped around for the remote control.

'Might as well see what's on the box.'

The tube warmed up and Lieutenant Commander Worf appeared.

'Shite,' Peter said, switching channels. 'More bloody *Star Trek*. It must be on five times a day. Dunno what people see in that programme. I really don't.'

Mary silently rose and went upstairs to bed.

Early, again.

15

For as long as he could remember, Umberto's parents had repeatedly warned him about an unsavoury group of people called the Philistines. They were the lowest of the low, these characters, and if he even so much as talked to one, he could expect nothing from his life but misery and boredom. Philistines, they explained, were not only profoundly ignorant and unpleasant in themselves, that was how they wanted everyone else too.

As a young child, he listened hard, nodding with all the gravity he could muster and offering his assurances that he would run a mile if he ever met one. Valerie and Jeff didn't know it, but their warnings were in vain. Umberto hadn't quite grasped the message, unfortunately, and consequently grew up with an irrational fear of the Flintstones. He was eleven years old before he realised his mistake but even now the sight of Fred and Wilma caused him to shudder and recoil.

To the surprise of all who knew them, Valerie and Jeff had no major objections to the medium of television. There were several arts reviews shows that they never missed, of course.

If it had a drunken artist, a controversial feminist, and at least one angry poet, they were all over it. But they also delighted in watching any show featuring members of the general public, or 'Les Stupides', as they called them. *Family Fortunes* was a particular favourite. Valerie actively encouraged her son to watch it, claiming it provided the perfect showcase for all that was wrong with the world. 'It's not only shallow and pointless in itself,' she told him, 'it makes you wonder how some people can find their way out of bed in the morning. Watch and learn. *This* is what you don't want to be.' Umberto tried hard to enjoy it on the same level as his parents. But he couldn't. He just thought it was dumb. So why watch it?

He was flicking idly through the channels at around seven thirty, thinking these and other thoughts, when The Cottage doorbell chimed. He dropped the remote control and padded across the floor in his socks, wondering who it could be. His parents were out and his own visitors were few and far between. They were too remote for ticket-sellers and survey-takers. He opened the door slowly and suspiciously.

'Hello, Umberto,' Father Duff said, smiling broadly. 'How are the wounds of Christ?'

Umberto's first reaction was to lean outside and look around for spies. His reputation was poor enough as it was. It would be just his luck if Helmet McGuiney or some other yahoo from school was passing by on his way to the woods looking for magic mushrooms. Social calls from the local religious would provide them with yet more ammunition that they didn't really need.

'How did you find me?' he said, stepping back inside, but not inviting his visitor to do likewise.

Father Duff chuckled. 'This is a very small town,' he said. 'It wasn't difficult.'

'You didn't contact the school, did you? Because—'

'No, Umberto, I didn't. It was guesswork, really. Are your mother and father in?'

Underneath his fringe, Umberto's eyes widened. 'What do you want them for? They're out anyway, having dinner. What do you want them for?'

'You're repeating yourself, lad. And I don't want them, particularly. I called to see you.'

'Why? To give out to me?'

Father Duff chuckled a second time. 'Are we going to have this conversation on the doorstep or are you going to ask me in?'

Umberto looked down the lane into the dusk again. Then he looked back into the house. His parents weren't due back for hours, but he couldn't risk it. What if the restaurant was double-booked or something and they came back early?

'I suppose we could go for a walk,' he said, uncertainly.

'Good man,' Father Duff replied, patting his gut. 'I could do with the exercise.'

Umberto was a fast walker and Father Duff had difficulty keeping up.

'Do you always go at this speed?' he puffed, pumping his arms slightly for momentum.

Umberto shrugged. 'If you're going somewhere, why wouldn't you want to get there as soon as possible?'

'But we're not *going* anywhere. We're going for a walk. It's an end in itself.'

'Suppose.'

'Don't you ever go for a walk? Just for the sake of it?'

Umberto thought of his frequent desperate treks over the fields to Mary and Peter's. 'I walk, yeah. But not for the sake of it. Look, why are you here? What do you want?'

'Why does my being here make you so uncomfortable?'

'Why are you answering a question with a question?'

'Why shouldn't I?'

'Didn't anyone ever tell you it's bad manners?'

'Do you think priests all have perfect manners?'

'What makes you think I ever give priests any thought?'

'Why did you try to fake stigmata?'

Umberto stopped. 'So that is why you're here, I knew it.'

Father Duff waddled level and stopped too. 'It was an interesting thing to do, Umberto. It was a new one on me, that's for sure.'

He smiled then, and Umberto understood that whatever else he was, he wasn't angry.

'You obviously weren't fooled, then.'

'Fooled? No. Intrigued, yes. What was it, ink?'

Umberto looked up and down the lane again, not sure what he was looking for. 'Blood capsules. Hallowe'en things. Maybe ink would have worked better.'

'No, no, you did well. I was impressed.'

'But you didn't think it was possible.'

They started to walk again, following the tapering lane round the edge of the woods. The pace was slower now.

'I'll put it this way. It didn't seem *plausible*.'

Umberto sniggered.

Father Duff said, 'Did I say something funny?'

'I would have thought that a priest, above all people, would find the idea perfectly plausible.'

'Why do you say that?'

'Are we starting the question game again?'

'Do you want to?'

'Do you?'

Father Duff shook his head and laughed.

Umberto managed a smile. 'Don't answer this one with a question. If I told you I had seen a vision of the Virgin Mary, would you believe me?'

'*Did* you see a vision of the Virgin Mary, Umberto?'

'That's another question!'

'All right, OK. It would depend.'

'On?'

'On the evidence.'

'So now you're looking for evidence. Where's the evidence for Fatima? Or Lourdes? Or that other one, Medgysomething.'

'Medjugorje. And they're different.'

'How are they different?'

Father Duff started walking again and Umberto followed.

'They've been well documented, Umberto. There've been cures and—'

'Oh, gimme a break. The number of so-called cures at Lourdes compared to the number of visitors is statistically insignificant. Those people would have got better sitting at home.'

'It's largely a matter of faith though, isn't it?'

Umberto snorted. 'I don't believe in faith.' Then he looked away, wondering if that made sense.

'Is that right? I'm sorry to hear that.'

'Well, it has its place, I suppose. Which is *after* . . . you know . . . facts. A person can believe whatever he or she likes, as far as I'm concerned, so long as it doesn't contradict what he or she *knows*. Hume has a lot to say on this. Maybe you should take a look.'

'Who's Hume? John Hume?'

Umberto snorted. 'David Hume. The philosopher.'

'You seem very knowledgeable on the subject. For someone your age, that's . . . unusual. Been doing some reading?'

'Yeah, I have, actually. *Hume for Dummies*, if you must know. So what? What are you smiling at?'

'So you're interested in all this. You're . . . curious.'

'Maybe I . . . oh. Ohhhh. I just got it. *Jesus*. You're recruiting!' He laughed long and loud, then turned on his heels and began to troop home.

Father Duff trotted after him silently, trailing by several feet. It was getting properly dark now. Seconds passed before Umberto spoke.

'What if my mom and dad had been at home? Would you have whipped out a brochure or something? Because, lemme tell you, you'd be on a loser there.'

Father Duff stepped up his pace and drew level. 'No. Not at all. I wouldn't have embarrassed you, Umberto. And I know your parents aren't religious. I was hoping they weren't in, to be honest. If they'd been there, I was going to make something up.'

'Like what?'

'Nothing very clever. I was going to say I was lost, ask for directions.'

Umberto sniffed. 'How long have you been priesting in Drumshanagh?'

'"Priesting"? I've been "priesting" here for seven years, give or take.'

'Wouldn't have been much of a lie, would it? Lived here for seven years, and doesn't know his way around yet?'

Father Duff shrugged and sighed. 'Maybe I'm not as good at deception as you are.'

'I'll take that as a compliment. And if you look at me and see a priest in the making, you're not much use at judging character, either. Besides, isn't this against the rules? Hassling people like this? What would the bishop say? If he found out that one of his pawns was chasing after—'

Father Duff halted abruptly and slapped his palms together. 'Wait! Hang on. Do you play chess?'

'What?'

'Bishops, pawns. Are you a chess player?'

Umberto folded his arms defensively. They were within sight of The Cottage now, and for a moment he considered making a run for it. The urge passed. 'Maybe. Why?'

'Me too! Me too! Are you any good at it?'

Umberto's mind raced, trying to anticipate the unwieldy chess metaphor that was surely just around the corner. 'Jesus always plays white' maybe, or 'God wants you to castle on the King's side of your heart'.

'I'm OK at it,' he said eventually.

Father Duff had lit up. He was practically dancing on the spot. 'Umberto, I'm going to ask you for a favour. Never mind everything else, I'm not going to hassle you, as you put it, about the priesthood or anything else. But please –

will you give me a game some time? Anywhere. At any time. Please.'

'I don't think so.'

'Please, Umberto. Please. I'm only a beginner, I just want the competition.'

For a moment, he was tempted. He was a little rusty, but he was sure he could take the priest. That would be fun. But no, it was obviously a trap. They'd get halfway through a game and then your man would start babbling about the religious life, the joys of helping others, the certainty of salvation.

'I'll think about it,' he said with no intention whatsoever of doing so. Then he bolted for The Cottage and slipped inside.

He locked the door, too.

16

Wednesday was Mary's day off, when Musique Boutique was left in the capable if somewhat under-informed hands of Fidelma Hughes. Fidelma was an old schoolfriend of Mary's and got the job on that basis. She certainly didn't get it for her musical taste, which ran the gamut all the way from Bryan Adams to Bryan Adams.

Despite, or perhaps because of her limited interest in music, Fidelma was much better than Mary at dealing with the likes of Mrs Sheedy. Every Saturday, when the shop was busy enough to require both hands on deck, they did their best to divide the customers between them according to type. It was an unspoken agreement, but it worked well. Mary handled the grubby teenagers sullenly enquiring after stuff that they didn't have but could order, while Fidelma fielded the tweedier patrons. She was lucky to have the help, she knew. There weren't many people willing to work just two days a week and cover for the occasional crisis. And the Wednesday morning lie-in was a weekly luxury she couldn't live without.

Peter left for Dublin at dawn, taking the car. He knelt by the side of the bed for some time first, presenting Mary with a lengthy description of the relative merits of this course of action. The earliest bus didn't go until seven thirty, he explained, and although his training didn't start until ten thirty, it would be a tight squeeze. She had always assumed that he would take the car, and was offended that he felt it necessary to justify himself. Then she realised that he was just tiptoeing around her, afraid that he was going to incur her further wrath. The guilt gripped her around the middle and squeezed hard. As Peter rose from her side and pottered around the room packing, she realised that she was close to tears. He would be gone for two days now, and mightn't even call. She probably wouldn't, in his shoes. Why set yourself up for more misery?

He was humming as he moved around, a tune she couldn't identify. He was doing it to make noise, she knew, to break the silence. She found herself wanting to say something. But what could she say? That she had started to find him irritating in a thousand different ways? That the feeling had sneaked up on her so slowly, over so many weeks or months that she'd only just worked it out for herself? That she couldn't picture their lives together in ten or even five years' time, because she was sure she would have murdered him long before then?

The previous night hadn't helped. Watching her parents' pantomime of slur and counter-slur had merely reinforced her concerns. Was that her fate? To wind up as the straight woman in an unfunny double act, the pair of them sick to death of each other's foibles, but too tired and old to do anything about it? The fact that Peter found them charming only made it worse.

130

So she said nothing. She just lay there, unable to make out what he was humming and later mumbling. When she finally peeked out from under the duvet and found the room empty, she realised that it had been goodbye.

With nothing to get up for, she stayed in bed until after eleven, dozing but not quite sleeping. When she finally worked her way out of bed, she had a quick shower, but didn't dress properly, opting instead for her Sunday afternoon uniform. This sloppy attitude was a break from the norm. Mary knew that a day off could dissolve before your very eyes if you didn't make some kind of effort to do something. She was usually up and out by now, shopping or arsing around in the garden. If she was feeling especially social she might even call on Valerie to hear all about her latest opinion. Valerie did a nice line in opinions. You could knock on her door at any time, day or night, and she'd be ready to go, all fired up about the latest Wim Wenders film or somesuch. Today, however, Mary felt like lying on the sofa and staring at the ceiling. So she did.

There was a small black stain up there, next to the light fitting. It was shaped like a teardrop, an inch or two in length. She spent a good twenty minutes looking at it, wondering first how she had failed to notice it before, and then how the hell it could possibly have got there. It was irritatingly familiar. She had seen something very like it before, she was sure. When the answer came to her, she snapped her fingers and felt immediately silly for being so literal.

It was a kick mark. There were others in the house, at ankle level. Peter's doing, of course. He had a thing for heavy black boots and she sometimes got the impression that he couldn't quite control them. It was as if their weight caused him to swing his feet too hard, scuffing any walls and doors unfortunate enough to be in his way at the time. That still didn't explain this current stain, not without serious offence to the laws of physics anyway. To Mary's trembling horror, Peter once professed admiration for Lionel Richie's 'Dancing on the Ceiling', but as far as she knew, he was still subject to gravity himself.

There was really only one possible explanation. He must have thrown a boot up there at some point. But why? At what? A fly? Yeah. That made sense. He hated flies. Was passionate about hating them, in fact. Somewhere along the way, he had assembled a few facts and figures on the subject, which he regularly spun out into a mini-lecture entitled 'Flies and Their Disgusting Habits'. It was part of a series that also included 'Speech Recognition is the Holy Grail of Modern Computing' and 'The Irish are a Nation of Begrudgers'. Mary knew them by heart.

The fly scenario was easy to imagine. Peter tearing about the room with a rolled-up newspaper, taking violent and inaccurate swipes, swearing and fuming. The fly heading out of range to the ceiling. Peter losing his temper and looking around for something heavy to throw at it.

Christ. He could have used a book or something. Something that didn't leave a mark. She stared on for the best part of an hour.

By lunch-time she had moved on, without really knowing why, to thinking about safaris. Valerie and Jeff were going on one in the summer and were beside themselves with excitement

(Umberto would be staying with Peter and herself; he said it was bad manners to go on holidays anywhere where the locals are all poorer than the tourists). Mary had no moral objections to the idea, but couldn't see the attraction either. It would be hot and dusty and uncomfortable. And they had perfectly good animals in the zoo.

Her trance was broken when the phone rang. It was Fidelma.

'What's wrong?' Mary said, worried. Fidelma never bothered her on her day off unless something had gone seriously awry.

'Nothing,' Fidelma said. 'There's nothing wrong, exactly. But something's happened.'

It was Fidelma's conversational style to leave such statements dangling, inviting the other party to drag it out of her. Mary took the bait.

'Go on,' she said. 'I'm all ears.'

'There's something here for you,' Fidelma cooed. 'A delivery, a few minutes ago.'

There was a pause. This time Mary refused to play the game.

Fidelma caved in after a few seconds. 'Flowers,' she said. 'You got some flowers delivered. Interflora.'

Mary gripped the handset a little tighter. 'Really?'

She had to hand it to Peter, in a way. Even after all the rancour of the last few days, he still hadn't given up on her. Flowers, though. Yuck.

'What does the card say?' she asked.

Fidelma lowered her voice. 'It says, "From an admirer". Actually, it says "From a admirer". Typo. And there's a phone number. Which I don't recognise. Has Peter got a new mobile?'

*   *   *

Mary dressed and made it into the shop on foot within twenty minutes. There was only one customer there, a scruffy young man she didn't recognise.

'Red roses,' Fidelma said, producing the flowers from underneath the counter. 'Not very original, but that's hardly the point.'

Mary stared at her gift in silence and then plucked the card from the front of the package. She read it at once and put it into her bag.

'None of my business and all,' Fidelma said, 'but have you any idea who sent them?'

'Not a clue.'

'But not Peter?'

'Nope.'

'Maybe it's someone local. You could ask around in the flower shops. They might be able to tell you. Self-Raising Flowers, I'd start there.'

This possibility had already occurred to Mary. 'You're assuming I want to know,' she said.

Fidelma leaned towards her. 'Well, you do, don't you? I mean, simple curiosity?'

Mary shrugged. Then shrugged again.

'Maybe,' she said.

17

Peter's course was run by an outfit called Computer Training Ltd, based in Fitzwilliam Square. On the drive down, he tried and failed to imagine the meeting where the founders decided to call their computer training company Computer Training Ltd. Mind you, he supposed, it wasn't much worse than his own Data Force, which sounded like a 1970s TV show about a group of crime-solving robots.

Although he found essentially everything about training courses fairly dreadful, there was one particular aspect of them that Peter dreaded just that little bit more: the pre-training mixer. No one actually called it a mixer, of course, but that was what it was. Standing around with a complementary coffee, peering at name badges and declaring yourself delighted to meet a representative of Compu-this or Micro-that. What else would you call it? It was the sense of forced giddiness that got to him. The laughs were always too loud and the smiles were always too bright. It was as if the students were trying to convince each other and possibly themselves that their attendance at such a mind-numbing affair in no way diminished their status as Interesting and Vibrant Human Beings.

The Computer Training Ltd mixer took place in a small reception area on the first floor. It was a windowless space that immediately made Peter feel bored and sleepy. On arrival, he was presented with a registration form and a badge upon which he printed his first name in chunky capitals. No sooner had he done so than a smiling man in a wrinkled suit approached with hand extended.

'Good morning to you ... Peter,' he beamed. 'Gerard Mullen. I'm teaching this course, for my sins.'

'Hello,' Peter said. Jesus. The guy had put an exclamation mark after his name on the badge. That was a bad sign. It suggested enthusiasm. No doubt he was one of those teachers who expected everyone to not only remain conscious but to actually listen.

'Have you come very far?' Gerard said, still beaming. For a moment, Peter thought he was talking about the great journey of life. He was on the point of saying something about his hopes and dreams when he realised it was a simpler enquiry.

'Monaghan,' he said. 'Drumshanagh. It's about six—'

'Ah, sure don't I know it well. The wife's from Donegal and if I passed through Drumshanagh once, I must have passed through it a thousand times. With the big square there, with the church? I know it like the back of my hand.'

Peter struggled to think of a response. He came up with 'Yes.' They stared at each other for a moment.

'Here's another arrival,' Gerard said then, looking over Peter's shoulder. 'Better meet and greet. Get yourself a tea or a coffee, like a good man, don't be shy.'

136

Peter smiled as serenely as he could and went over to the table where an angry-looking youth was dispensing hot drinks. He nodded several hellos at his fellow students on the way, but didn't pause long enough to allow conversation.

'Tea, please,' he told the youth, who didn't look old enough to shave. Work experience, maybe. That might account for the hateful look he sported as he grimly sloshed some grey liquid into a Computer Training Ltd mug and pushed it across the table towards Peter.

'Milk?' he sighed, as he added milk.

'Yes,' Peter said. 'Just as well, too.'

'What?'

'Never mind. Thank you.'

The youth frowned and muttered something under his breath. Peter was suddenly furious. What would it have cost him to smile? To be nice? To pretend, if necessary? What was *wrong* with people? But his anger passed instantly. He had no idea what was going on in this boy's life, and he had no right to judge. For all he knew, his dog might have just died. Or his mother, or his girlfriend. Maybe he was ill. Or hopelessly lonely. That was often the case with other people's misery. There was no guessing the reason. If they decided not to explain, then that was the end of it – you didn't find out. Simple.

He moved away from the table to an especially dim corner of the room and sipped his coffee, wondering if Mary was up yet. Ten fifteen. She was probably up and gone. Not one for sitting around doing nothing, Mary. It was one of the things he admired about her. Personally, he could sit around for Ireland.

As she sometimes pointed out. With a smile, though – she pointed it out with a smile.

He felt his features clouding over and realised that he had squeezed himself as far into the corner as was physically possible. That wouldn't do. He may not have relished the mixing prospect, but it was better than marking yourself out as a lonely curmudgeon before the course had even begun. He looked around for a likely conversational target and settled on a trio of men right in the centre of the room. He started towards them, but found his path blocked by a fleet-footed woman who suddenly appeared, ambush-style, from behind a pillar.

'Peter Ford!' the woman squealed, bouncing on her toes. 'My God, are you still growing?'

In common with many of his college classmates, Peter suffered from a debilitating condition known as Regina Clarke Syndrome. Well, that was what he called it. The others might have called it Regina Clarke Disease or Clarkitis or the Regina Complex or something along those lines.

The condition had only one symptom: a crippling fear that the sufferer could, at any moment, bump into Regina Clarke. It usually manifested itself in public places. Peter's attacks tended to occur while he was out shopping, for example. Not so much in Drumshanagh, where he felt relatively safe, but in other towns or cities, where every dark nook was a potential hiding place from which the Clarke might suddenly spring. It was an irrational fear, of course, like the fear of flying. Every nervous flyer knows that he or she is statistically safer in a plane than in a car or train. But knowing and feeling are two different things. In the two years since he graduated, Peter hadn't so much as glimpsed Regina from afar, yet still he trembled every time he caught sight of a fast-moving young woman with an uncontrollable mass of pitch black curls. It was only a matter of time, he knew, before their paths crossed and he wound up pinned to a wall, hearing all about his many faults and how to fix them.

Now that the moment had come, it was almost a relief. Almost.

'Regina!' he managed to croak. 'Long time no see!'

'Long time no see' was a phrase Peter despised. He resented being shocked into using it, but forced a smile anyway. Regina smiled back in her usual way, with teeth parted and eyelashes flapping.

'It *has* been a while,' she said. 'Here for the course?'

'Yup. You?'

'Well, duh! What do you think? I'm certainly not here for the fun.'

Peter nodded. 'You haven't changed a bit,' he said, meaning that it was entirely in keeping with her old self for Regina to mock him for asking the same polite but silly question she'd just asked.

'You're not unrecognisable yourself,' she said. 'Bit more forehead showing, maybe.'

Peter pretended to laugh, by saying 'Ha ha' while throwing his head back and smiling.

'So where did you end up working?' he asked. 'I seem to remember you having job offers before we graduated.' He also remembered the drunken evening in the students' union bar when he and several friends joined hands and prayed that she would take the one in San Francisco.

139

'Cork,' Regina said, with a flourish in her voice. Her tone implied that Cork was somewhere in the south of France. 'I'm in charge of Management Information Systems at a pharmaceuticals company. A very well-respected pharmaceuticals company.'

Peter couldn't resist. He said, 'You know, you can say "MIS" to me, Regina. I know what it stands for.'

She didn't miss a beat. 'In my case, it stands for a Golf GTi and a nice big apartment by the river. So what are you doing with yourself these days? Something other than doing it with yourself, I hope.'

Peter did the 'Ha ha' thing again and wondered why there was never a blunt instrument to hand when you wanted one.

'I work for a small company back up home. We do installations and maintenance for local businesses. Nothing fancy.'

Regina cocked her head to one side and bit her lip. 'Not to worry,' she said. 'I'm sure things will pick up for you.'

It was just as well, Peter later thought, that Gerard chose that moment to call the students into class. Blunt instrument or no, he still had his bare hands.

The classroom was typical of its kind, cramped and hot, with long benches where the students gathered two to a PC. The PCs, on which they would later test their new-found knowledge, were grimy and old. Their keyboards were blackened with use and their screens appeared to have been recently used as sneeze guards. Each space had a folder packed with course notes, together with paper and pens. There was a whiteboard and another PC at the top, for the teacher's use. That machine was hooked up to a projector and screen so that everyone, even those at the very back, could see how colossally boring the subject was.

Peter sat with Regina, principally because he couldn't see how to avoid it.

'Good morning, everyone,' Gerard said. 'You're all very welcome to this course in Upgrading to Microsoft Windows 2000.'

That was the last sentence Peter listened to with both ears. He was reasonably confident that he could upgrade a customer to Windows 2000 after ten minutes with the manual and didn't see the need to waste valuable brain space on the minutiae. He was careful, however, to nod intently when Gerard looked in his direction. He even feigned note-taking by periodically writing his name and address in the margins of his course notes.

'Having an identity crisis, are we?' Regina whispered when she caught him doing so.

'Just testing the pen,' he replied. 'It seems to work fine.'

'You write like a child,' she said. 'Has anyone ever told you that?'

Peter struggled to maintain a whisper. 'Yeah, Regina. You have. Repeatedly.'

Peter saw his first computer in 1983, at his friend Daniel's house. It was a Sinclair ZX Spectrum, a small black rectangle with blue rubbery keys. Besides the usual letters and numbers, the keys were marked with strange symbols and alien half-words like TAN and CLS. Daniel said it was 'all right, but not great'. He didn't really want to play with it and thought they should go outside and throw stones at something. Peter could only shake his head, staring silently at the Future.

Eventually, Daniel went out alone and left him in the bedroom on his own. Peter suspected that he was being rude, but couldn't drag himself away.

A Spectrum cost £129, an absurd sum, he thought, and one that was probably beyond his parents' reach. His father was a mechanic – a 'humble mechanic,' as he said himself – and although Peter had no idea what his income was, he suspected that the Spectrum might easily account for a week's worth of it, maybe more. He had several sleepless nights, wondering what kind of son would be selfish enough to put his parents through that kind of financial stress just because he wanted to play some games and practise typing his name. But his hand-wringing always ceased by morning, when he ate breakfast behind a conspicuous copy of *Sinclair User* magazine while waxing philosophical about the passage of time. Why, it seemed like only yesterday that he'd had a birthday and, look at this, the date was almost upon them again.

Realising that there was almost no chance that his parents would risk insolvency to provide their only child with a toy, he took every opportunity to highlight the educational and social benefits that would inevitably accrue from their ownership of what he called 'a powerful techno-tool'. The key to success, he felt, was in stressing that this would be a *family* computer. It would not only propel Peter instantly to the top of his class, but would also manage the household finances and help his mother keep track of recipes. In a moment of desperation, he heard himself telling his father that you could play poker on it too. Probably. For all his efforts, he received no promises beyond 'We'll see.'

His birthday was a Saturday and began in traditional fashion with cards and hugs. Well, his mother hugged him; his father slapped him on the shoulder and said, 'Good man yourself.' They made no mention of a present of any kind, let alone a computer. Peter felt that this was a positive sign, and played along. He pottered around the house all morning, smiling and pretending that he had forgotten all about computers and was happy simply to be a member of such a wonderful family. After lunch, his father announced a special treat – they were off to Armagh to see a film. It was *War Games*, with Matthew Broderick. Peter's hopes, already high, rose even further. *War Games* was about a teenage computer whiz who accidentally hacks into a military installation and almost starts World War Three. It was the greatest movie Peter had ever seen, and sitting there in the dark, he felt almost embarrassed by the sudden overwhelming affection he felt for his parents. Did they think this was subtle? That he hadn't guessed? It was so *cute*. His mother had dallied inside the house before they left. 'What the hell's she doing?' his father said in the car, drumming his fingers impatiently on the steering wheel. Peter knew what she was doing all right. She was putting his new computer on the kitchen table for him to find when they returned.

On the drive back to Drumshanagh, Peter thanked them profusely for the movie. He saw satisfied grins growing on their faces and couldn't help but add, 'This is the best birthday ever!' like a television child.

It never occurred to him, not even for a moment, that they had let him down. There was a Sinclair ZX Spectrum sitting on that kitchen table. He would have bet his life on it.

By the time they reached home, his legs had turned to jelly. He frantically tried to remember if there was anything good on

143

TV at this time of day. He would need to commandeer it for the computer . . . unless they'd bought a portable telly too! No. He was being greedy. The computer was more than enough.

'I'm gasping for a cuppa,' his mum said, putting her key in the front door. 'Anyone else?'

'I've never said no to a cup of tea in me life, and I'm not starting now,' his dad said.

Peter didn't answer. He was so excited that he couldn't speak. Mrs Ford strode off into the kitchen and her husband followed. Peter took a breath and stepped slowly after them. It was getting dark by then and the kitchen was gloomy. No one spoke. Peter stared at his feet until someone snapped on the overhead light.

Then, to his utter embarrassment, he began to cry. Not for his new computer. For the predictability of his parents' love.

The birthday present was the first step on a road that led directly to Dundalk Regional Technical College and a diploma in computer science, then to his job with Data Force and now here, to this creaking plastic seat next to Regina bloody Clarke.

Ordinarily, it gladdened Peter's heart to look back down that road, to wonder with a shudder where he might be now if his parents had let him down. Just before lunch-time, though, at the moment when Regina leaned over and suggested that they should have dinner together, that most memorable of birthdays looked a lot like the first step on the road to hell.

18

Self-Raising Flowers wasn't the only place to buy flowers in Drumshanagh in the same way that Musique Boutique wasn't the only place to buy records. But it took nearly all of the business that was going and was the logical place to start enquiries.

The two shops were on almost directly opposite sides of the square. Mary left Fidelma in a state of extreme excitement – she loved any kind of scandal, that one – and marched halfway there before stopping in her tracks. She was being silly. It would be a mistake, possibly a serious mistake, to do any snooping. On the other hand . . . But then . . . Supposing . . .

Coffee. She needed coffee, and some thinking time.

The lunch-time rush was in full swing and Mary was lucky to find a table to herself at the back of the Coffee to a Tea café. She had a cappuccino and a doughnut, and a full view of the other patrons. Old women, mostly, and some schoolkids. There was one middle-aged man sitting alone by the window, staring sadly at the *Irish Times*. He seemed to feel her looking at him and glanced up. They smiled at each other. Then he went back to his paper.

Could be him, she thought. Could be anyone. Could even be Peter, taking the piss, wondering if she had the nerve to call a strange number. Waiting on the other end with one of his bloody voices. That would be just like him. Trying to create some spicy intrigue, never once realising that what he was actually doing was setting a cheap trap, deceiving his own wife.

No. She was being unfair. Again. He would never be so underhanded. If Peter was anything, it was up-front. He'd been like that from the get-go. His first words to her, ever, were, 'You're lovely. What about a snog?' You had to make allowances for the fact that he was sixteen at the time, and had three and a half pints of cider sloshing around inside him, but still. Machiavelli, he was not.

You're lovely. What about a snog?

Nah. But I'll dance with you.

That was how they started, in the Rugby Club junior disco, September 1989. They never did kiss that first night, although he did plant his mouth on her neck during the slow set, before making a farting noise with his lips. Normal people did that on their infants' tummies, if at all. Peter Ford used it as a sexual tactic. When she finally let him kiss her, two discos later, she was pleasantly surprised. Her only previous kissing experiences were the unhappy result of Spin the Bottle games, and were memorable only for the astonishing foulness of her partners' breath and their inability to stop laughing. One of them attempted to cop a feel, too, right in front of everyone.

Peter not only respected the gravity of the moment, but had evidently consumed several hundred Tic-Tacs while her back was turned. He wasn't so much minty fresh as scorching hot. She appreciated the gesture, though, and agreed to meet him again. Then again. And again. He began referring to himself as her 'Ford escort'.

Soon they were practically famous among the local teens. It was unheard of for people their age to go out for more than a few months. By the time Peter and Mary passed the two years mark, no one even commented on it any more. What was there to say? It was 'a wedding job', anyone could see that. Peter and Mary – even their names seemed to go together, like a happy but sexually conservative couple from a Catholic marriage manual.

Then he went off to the technical college in Dundalk. Interest in their couple status picked up again. It was only a matter of time, well-meaning friends told her, before he came home one weekend and made an announcement: There was this girl in his class, see . . .

But it didn't happen. If anything, they became closer. He wrote and phoned as often as he could. And he took a bus home every single Friday. As soon as *Cheers* was over, the doorbell would ring and there he'd be, smiling down at her. He always held her hand as they walked down the path but never kissed her until they'd gone around the corner and were out of sight. He was old-fashioned like that, even though he knew her parents both liked him. If they weren't home, of course, he'd be scrambling around under her shirt and down the front of her jeans within minutes. She sipped her cappuccino and smiled, almost despite herself, at the memory.

147

His first year in Dundalk coincided with her Leaving Certificate. When they finally came, her results were good – better than Peter's – but she found that she didn't want to go to third level. There was simply nothing she wanted to study. She didn't even realise it until the offers arrived. Philosophy? Archaeology? French and German? Why had she even chosen those courses? She couldn't remember. Her teachers were disgusted. All that time and effort . . . Her parents took a more relaxed attitude. She wasn't off to pursue the arts in London, that was the main thing. And she could easily find work in Drumshanagh, her mum told her, bide her time until something 'caught her eye'. Some of her classmates had stayed put too, so she wasn't lonely. Better yet, Peter spent his college holidays at home, while his new friends took off to London or Munich or New York. His dad could usually find some work for him in the garage and there were always bar jobs going. She sometimes felt guilty about it, as if she were holding him back. But he was happy. It wasn't the kind of happiness you could fake. She felt it too.

They had sex for the first time during the Christmas holidays of his second college year. St Stephen's Day, to be precise. At around four in the afternoon. Her parents were out visiting. There was nothing on TV.

'I'm bored,' he said. 'Are you?'

They'd talked about it plenty of times, of course, usually while drunk. She'd always backed out. She was afraid. Not that it would hurt, or that she'd get pregnant. She was afraid of the whole concept. What would it mean? Would it mean anything? Looking back, she found this highly embarrassing. They'd been together for over three *years*, for God's sake.

They were both adults. Kids today certainly didn't dither the way they had. She heard them in the shop, discussing positions and giggling about the wet spot. Some days she was appalled. Some days she envied their cool.

It wasn't great the first time. Peter nervous-talked his way through the whole thing, the hurried undressing, the last-minute doubts, the banana-fingered fiddling with the condom (he had one with him 'by chance'). He kept asking her if she was OK, did she want to stop. No. Did he? No bloody way. He didn't launch into song on that occasion – the singing came much later, after they were married – but he did find time to tell her a joke.

'Knock, knock,' he said, between hitching breaths.

'Who's there?' she panted. But he didn't answer. He was too busy gurgling and choking. It was over already.

She never did find out who was there.

By 1994 they'd already been together for five years. He was twenty-one, she was a year younger. They began, simulta-neously it seemed, to find themselves strange. If only one or other of them could admit to some foolish indiscretion. An intense sexual liaison with some passing dancer or poet would have been ideal, but a drunken snog with a pimply local would have sufficed. There was nothing. They began to wonder about each other. It wasn't normal, was it, this level of constancy in people their age? What were they, swans? They tried to laugh about it. It wasn't easy.

Peter's graduation only added to the pressure. They weren't on hold any more. They were proper grown-ups, both of them. In five years, they had never once discussed marriage. Not seriously, at any rate. People their age didn't get married, it was ridiculous. But then so was their entire relationship, it seemed. The weeks after he left college were unlike any of their time together. They had their first awkward silences.

Mary was the first to mention the possibility of a break. They were in his house, in the front room. An old episode of *Monty Python* was flickering on the TV. She said it casually, and he responded casually. There were no harsh words, no tearful storm-outs. They discussed it like business people who were calmly considering letting some of the staff go. It was a brief conversation, depressingly so, given its subject. Peter's unemployment gave them their excuse. They had always known that he would have to look beyond Drumshanagh for IT work. It had always seemed like an approaching bump in the road. Now it looked like a brick wall. He would move to Dublin and they would 'see how it worked out'.

The separation lasted for a little over eighteen months, during which time Peter worked at the Allied Irish Bank computer centre and lived with two colleagues in a rented house in Drumcondra. He had three girlfriends. The best of them lasted a fortnight. Mary had four boyfriends. The best of them lasted seventy-two hours.

They maintained more or less the same level of contact by phone and letter and met for a drink every time Peter came home. Mary even visited him in Dublin a few times. After a year, they began to joke that nothing had changed except for the fact that they no longer had sex. They circled around each other in conversation for several more months before Peter finally suggested that one other thing had changed: they were both miserable. The separation ended noisily and sweatily over the course of a weekend in Drumcondra during which they left the bedroom only to visit the bathroom and order more pizza.

Neither of them regretted the break. It had proved something important: that they belonged together. So what if they had met at a junior disco? Wasn't that the stuff of romantic fantasy, the whole childhood sweethearts thing? It was nothing to be ashamed of. They began to discuss the possibility of Mary moving to Dublin. She wasn't a fan of city life, but there didn't seem to be any alternative.

Then they heard something interesting. There was a guy in Drumshanagh called Pat O'Donnell. Pat had never studied computers in any official capacity – his day job was fitting alarms – but he was a genuine geek and knew a lot. And everyone in Drumshanagh knew that he knew a lot. When local businesses wanted advice or technical assistance, they talked to him, rather than some stranger in Dundalk or Armagh. Pat had recently realised that he was making more money from the computer nixers than the alarms, and had abandoned the latter in favour of the former. Rumour had it that business was good and that Pat was looking for help. Peter called Camp David, who was living in Galway and was also working in computers. They hadn't fallen out, but had drifted steadily apart since their schooldays. David knew Pat O'Donnell through his elder brother and could vouch that he had a good head on his shoulders. He made a phone call, and suddenly Peter was back in Drumshanagh. Better yet, so was David. Pat's business wasn't just good, it was booming. It turned out that there were hundreds of computers in the area, and almost none of them was working. He was at it twelve hours a day and still had

151

to turn work down. With staff, he could expand, get a proper office, make real plans. Data Force was a success right from the start.

With so much good fortune in the air, it seemed like bad manners for Mary and Peter to delay the inevitable. They talked about it for fifteen minutes and then declared themselves engaged.

They were absurdly happy. Both of them.

Mary blinked and realised that her cappuccino had gone cold. The *Irish Times* man was gone. She grabbed her jacket and left for home, trying to forget about the florist, thinking instead about curiosity and cats.

19

Regina Clarke seemed to have suffered one of those bizarre brain injuries that you sometimes read about in the Sunday supplements. Peter was talking and she was clearly listening, and even nodding, but it didn't seem to be making any sense to her. Any second now, he expected her to mistake him for a hat.

'Honestly, Regina,' he said. 'I don't think I'm up for it.'

'I quite fancy a Chinese,' Regina said. 'Hmmm. Have you ever had Chinese food, Peter? I bet you'd like it. You mustn't be afraid to try new things.'

'I'm quite tired, you know, after the drive down and then class and all . . .'

'Or maybe Indian. I know a nice Indian in Ballsbridge. Popular though. We'd be lucky to get in.'

'Another time, maybe, when I'm not so—'

'About eight, eight thirty say. Give us time to have a shower and unwind a bit. And I'm sure you want to catch *Home and Away* or something equally awful on the telly.'

They were standing on the street outside Computer Training Ltd. Class was over for the day. It hadn't been merely boring. It had been something else entirely, some new strain of super-tedium for which Peter knew no name. If something merely boring had suddenly happened, he would have waved his arms in the air and cheered like a kid on a rollercoaster. And they were still only halfway through. All he wanted now was a hot bath and some room service. Maybe give Mary a ring and see what the humour was like. A nice quiet night.

'Regina—'

'I bet you didn't even have a proper lunch. I could smell the beer on you when you came back. Talking rubbish with this friend of yours in the pub, no doubt, instead of eating something sensible. It's no wonder you're so lanky.'

Her initial suggestion of dinner had rattled him so badly that he literally ran away from her at lunch-time, shouting something over his shoulder about meeting a pal. In fact, he spent the hour alone in a pub, nursing a pint and a ham toastie, glancing around like a hunted animal, certain she had followed him. Later, when the mid-afternoon tea break finally came around, he panicked and cornered Gerard rather than give her the opportunity to expand on the dinner idea. That was a mistake. Gerard asked him what he thought of the course so far and Peter was sure that his nebulous answer ('It's . . . good') had left his teacher in no doubt about his level of interest, which was close to zero. Compared to his level of interest in dining with Regina, however, it was pulsating frenzy.

'I'm just not up to it tonight, Regina. Honestly. I'm really not.'

He seemed to get through this time. Regina stood momentarily on her toes and then relaxed again. For the third or fourth time, he caught her staring at his left hand.

'What's the matter, Peter?' she said. 'Afraid someone will see you out on the town with an attractive young woman who is not your wife?'

'Attractive?' he said. 'Is someone coming with us?'

He was pleased with his retort and expected her to laugh. He really did. And while she was laughing, he hoped to slip away. Instead, she froze, horrified. There was silence. The traffic seemed to stop. Peter took immediate conciliatory action. He smiled as vividly as he could, then raised his eyebrows one at a time, first the left, followed by the right, before lowering them both while simultaneously increasing the wattage of his smile still further. This was his Cheeky Chappie look, one that had served him well in many an awkward moment with Mary. Like that time she put one of those wash-in, wash-out super-blonde dyes in her hair and he said it made her look like a prostitute. If it hadn't been for the mollifying effects of the old Cheeky Chappie, she probably would have been annoyed at him.

When Regina didn't reciprocate, he considered saying that it had been a joke. But he quickly decided against it. To come right out and literally say that he was joking would be to acknowledge formally the existence of the other possibility – that he was not. What was her problem? Didn't she know that he would never say such a thing if she actually was unattractive? Not that he fancied her or anything. She was easy enough to look at, but . . . Jesus. All day long, he'd been wondering what it would be like to take a swipe at Regina, to knock one of her barbed comments back over the net at her. Fun,

155

he imagined, but not worth it. That analysis was spot-on, it turned out.

An ancient memory flickered in his mind, like a not-quite subliminal advertisement. The image was of his cousin Tony, aged six, on a holiday visit from Donegal with his parents and older sister. Tony was into pinching at the time. He wasn't a bad child and he did no real harm. It was just a game, albeit an annoying one. He would sneak up behind his victim, give them a little pinch and then run off squealing, inviting a chase. Everyone obliged, including Peter. He was four years older than Tony and mature enough (he congratulated himself) to allow an act of such gross disrespect in his own home.

When the visitors were leaving at the end of the week, the two families gathered in the front drive for the farewell hugs and handshakes. Tony skipped up to Peter and got off one final salvo, a four-fingered bite on the forearm. He laughed as he did it, and Peter laughed back; as ever, it wasn't even sore. There was no malice in Peter's mind as he seized Tony's wrist and gave it the briefest and gentlest of Chinese burns. In the half-second when he decided to do it, it seemed that it would be a fitting coda to the holiday. Educational, too: Tony would learn, relatively painlessly, that you can only pinch for so long before someone takes a stand. A 'Thank you' would not have been inappropriate, Peter thought at the time.

The boy screamed like a dunked lobster and collapsed immediately to the ground. Peter was stunned. He'd hardly touched him. Now his aunt and uncle would surely beat him to death with one of his own legs. And if they didn't, his parents would. He was surprised and relieved when Tony was scooped up, told to pipe down, bundled into the back of the car and then driven away at speed. He didn't get so much as a dirty look himself, and understood that his cousin was deemed to have been asking for it. That didn't make him feel any better.

'Suit yourself,' Regina finally said. 'It was only a dinner invitation. I was trying to be *nice.*'

There. He was home free. All he had to do was say something bland and non-committal – 'I'll see you tomorrow' would have done – and that would have been the end of it. Her expression, though. It was the same look that Tony had sported as he pulled away in the back of the car. Hurt, but more than that – mystified too.

He made fists in his jacket pockets, wondering when medical science was going to come up with a conscience-ectomy.

'What's the address of the restaurant?' he sighed.

Peter wasn't a frequent diner-out, never had been. He blamed his parents. They weren't the type. As far as he knew, they had never eaten out in their lives, not counting weddings. (And funerals. Some people put on a great spread for a funeral.) His inexperience led him to assume that ethnic restaurants would always adhere to the relevant cultural stereotype. In the case of the Balti Palace, he expected to find stuffed tigers and jewelled daggers. Music, if there was any, would surely take the form of a twanged sitar – possibly played live by a cross-legged swami who would drop enlightening titbits between numbers. The waiting staff would undoubtedly be sporting turbans.

When he arrived and saw the reality, he cringed at his preconceptions. Maybe this was how racists began their careers. One minute you were looking for swamis in an Indian restaurant and the next you were trying to block the ports.

'You're impressed,' Regina said when they'd been shown to their table. 'I can see it on your face.'

'It's very nice, yeah. Are you a regular in here then?'

'When I'm in Dublin. I don't get to come up as often as I'd like, though. I swear, they can't do without me down there . . .'

Peter had concocted a strategy for the meal. He would stay as quiet as possible, offering nothing more substantial than conversational jump-starts, as required. Let her talk about herself and her brilliance as much as she wanted, and on no account be tempted to . . . comment. That way he could avoid conflict and more or less tune out.

'Big company, is it?' he asked.

'Huge. HUGE. I have a team of eight techs and we look after, lemme see, around two hundred PCs. They're all useless, naturally. The techs – not the PCs. I couldn't even trust one of them to take this course. I've got better things I could be doing, you know. Sometimes I envy the likes of you. A small-time operation, no pressure, strictly nine to five. There are days when I don't get out of the place until eight, nine at night. Honestly. Don't be jealous. Someone like you is as well off in . . . what's it called?'

Here we go, Peter thought. 'It's called Data Force.'

Regina didn't even try not to laugh. 'It's called *what*?'

He presumed it was a rhetorical question and said nothing.

'What, are you superheroes or something?' she sniggered. 'Do customers shine a big logo into the sky when their mouse stops working?'

'It wasn't my choice. The boss likes it. Nothing I can do.'

'I'm sorry, I know I shouldn't laugh. I forget how lucky

I am sometimes. So what's a typical day for you? Talk me through.'

'I'd rather not.'

'Oh? Why not?'

Because you don't want to know about my typical day, he was tempted to say. You just want an excuse to take the piss. Like you need an excuse . . .

'Business talk is boring, that's why.'

Regina smacked her lips and sat back. 'OK. Personal talk then . . . tell me about wifey. What's she called, for a start?'

'Mary.'

'Well, that's nice and . . . plain. Homely. Peter and Mary — sounds good and . . . safe.'

Peter ground his teeth. She was within reach. He could just reach over, grab her by the throat . . . For the second time that day, she was saved from certain death by the interruption of a third party, in this case a waiter. French, judging by his accent. A critical voice in Peter's head pointed out that, bizarrely, the waiter wasn't wearing a beret and didn't have a string of onions around his neck. Fancy that. Peter told the voice to shut up. The waiter deposited menus, took their drinks orders and left.

'Wait a minute,' Regina said when they were alone again. 'Don't tell me it's the same girl you were so tied to at college? She was a Mary too, wasn't she?'

Tied to?

'Yes,' he said. 'It's the same girl. Why? What's wrong with that?'

'There's nothing wrong with it per se, but . . .'

'But what?'

'Well. Correct me if I'm wrong —'

159

'Don't worry, I will.'

'— but wasn't she your, how will I put this? Wasn't she your original girlfriend? If you follow.'

Peter flapped his menu open and stared at it without reading. 'No. I don't follow. What does "original" mean? As opposed to a copy, is that it? Did you know people with fake girlfriends at college? Did they take them to be appraised and got a terrible shock?'

He was rambling, he knew. Anger made him do that. The waiter returned with their drinks. Beer for him, sparkling water for her.

'I mean original, as in first,' Regina said. 'This Mary character was your first ever girlfriend, wasn't she? So you've been together since for ever, since, Jesus, since school? That was her, wasn't it? The girl you started going out with at school? Everyone in our class knew about your set-up. We thought it was weird *then*.'

'For one thing, she isn't a character. She's a person. And for another thing, so what? What's your point?'

'Nothing. No point. It's unusual though, isn't it? To be so . . . faithful?'

'Jesus. I thought women liked faithfulness.'

'Fidelity, Peter. Say "fidelity". We like fidelity within a relationship, granted.'

'What?'

'Oh, never mind, Peter. It's unusual, that's all. Forget about it. Now, what will we eat?'

He reminded himself of the strategy again, and decided to let it drop. The menu was long and, to Peter, almost entirely incomprehensible. He recognised words like 'chicken' and 'beef' but few others. Had he been alone or with Mary, he would probably have gone for chicken curry on the grounds that he knew what was in it – chicken and curry. But he sensed that it was a boring choice and that Regina would seize upon the chance to lecture him about his blandness. So he scoured the menu for the most obscure-sounding dish he could see. He was still scouring when the waiter returned.

'Are you ready to order?' he asked in the eager manner of a man who lived to hear what people wanted to eat.

'I'll have aloo chop to start,' Regina said. The waiter beamed and rocked gently on his heels. He seemed delighted. 'And chicken curry.' More beaming and some scribbling. He took her menu.

Crap, Peter thought. Maybe chicken curry wasn't boring after all. Maybe it was cool. But he couldn't order it now anyway. She'd lecture him about not having a mind of his own. The waiter's beam was aimed squarely in his direction now.

'Eh . . . I think I will have . . . eh . . .'

Thirty seconds passed. Regina drummed her fingers on the table. 'He doesn't get out much, bless him,' she told the waiter, who nodded sympathetically.

'I can come back later,' he said. Peter looked up at him, checking for sarcasm. There was none.

'No, no,' Peter said. 'I will have . . . eh . . . this to start.' He pointed at some words he'd never seen before in his life. 'And . . . this lamb . . . dish.' To Peter's surprise, the waiter looked every bit as delighted with this choice as he'd been with Regina's. Part of the job, he supposed.

'Would you like anything from the wine menu?'

'Certainly,' Regina said. 'You choose, Peter. Something fruity.'

Peter swallowed. Did she mean something poncy? Probably not. He gazed at the wine list. It meant even less to him than the food list.

'I'm not really a big wine buff,' he said. 'Eh . . .'

Regina snapped the menu from him. 'Why don't we have the '96 Merlot?' she said after the quickest of scans. The waiter moaned with pleasure, scribbled again, and departed.

Peter grew more relaxed over the course of the meal. The food was sensational and the strategy held up well: Regina talked ceaselessly about herself and only occasionally paused to criticise him ('You're chewing all wrong'). The wine played an important role. Peter topped up their glasses every few sips, hoping to induce numbness in himself and increased loquacity in Regina. It worked a treat – he timed one of her monologues at twelve minutes and barely felt its effect. He ordered a second bottle before the first was empty, but was sparing with his own measures thereafter. The last thing he wanted was to get drunk and take another swipe . . .

Besides all that, he didn't want a repeat of the Finbarr scenario. If he lost the run of himself and blabbed to Regina about his problems, he'd never hear the end of it. She would probably write a book or maybe produce a television series about the variety and extent of his failings as a husband. But what was the story with that 'fidelity' remark of hers? Shite. He should have pressed her on it while the subject was hot. It would be dangerous to interrupt her now. She was in full flow, jabbering about some sofa she'd bought.

It was very expensive. It was very difficult to find. It was very comfortable. It was a thing of uncommon beauty. And so on. If he butted in, she could turn nasty. Nastier. 'We like fidelity within a relationship,' she'd said, with heavy emphasis on 'within'. Meaning what? That they don't like fidelity outside a relationship? No. That made no sense. What then? He'd have no peace till he found out.

'Regina?'

'. . . finest Italian . . . what? I'm *telling* you something here.'

'What did you mean, that fidelity remark?'

She adopted a puzzled look. An obviously faked puzzled look. It didn't seem very likely that Regina would ever forget her own words. 'When?'

'You know, tonight. Earlier tonight. I said that fidelity was a good thing and you said that it was only a good thing "within a relationship".'

Now she seemed to be faking slow realisation. 'Oh, right. Right. And?'

'Well . . . what did you mean by that? It doesn't make sense. How can you be faithful outside a relationship?'

She shook her head and looked at him like he was simple. 'You can't. That's not what I was getting at. I meant that fidelity is fine when you're the beneficiary. In this case . . . what was her name again?'

She knew. Why was she pretending not to know? 'Mary,' he said.

'Yeah. Mary. I'm sure Mary thinks that the creepy level of fidelity you two seem to have is just fab. She would, wouldn't she? She's the beneficiary. But—'

163

'I think the word "creepy" is—'

'I'm talking about the outsider woman's point of view. Mine, in this case. To the outsider, it's a real turn-off. It's sooooo boring.'

Peter's jaw fell open. He'd been right in the first place. The sofa story was better than this. 'What the hell makes you think I'm trying to turn you on?'

She snorted. 'Nothing. I'm sure you aren't. Of course not. I'm just saying, that's all.'

'Because I'm not trying to turn anyone on!'

'Huh. I hope you're trying to turn your wife on.'

Peter's heart did a backflip. His fingers splayed, involuntarily, and then regrouped to form tight fists. His voice, when he finally forced it out, was low and steady. 'I think, Regina, that the territory we are straying into is just a wee bit too personal. All right? Maybe I should tell you about my typical day after all.'

He was hunched forward over the table now, his face close to Regina's. He saw her lips curl ever so slightly upwards.

'Oh dear,' she cooed. 'I think I hit a nerve.'

The strategy was looking increasingly shaky. Peter knocked the semblance of a smile together from the ruins of his grimace.

'Don't take offence at this, Regina,' he said. 'But you and I are not close friends, OK? We weren't close friends in college even. And I am not comfortable with all this turn-on talk. It's my fault, you can blame me, I should have let that fidelity comment go. But please. Let's just get back to the normal How-have-you-beens?'

She shook her head, in sadness rather than defiance. 'Poor Peter. I can see how much you need someone to talk to.'

'Regina. I do not need someone to talk to. End message.'

'I'm no psychiatrist, Peter –'

'Jesus.'

'– but that's twice now you've spat the dummy when I mentioned your marriage.'

'I can't believe I'm hearing this.'

'Don't be afraid. Talking helps, you know?'

'Is this a joke?'

'And I'm a good listener, always have been.'

'Am I hearing things?'

'Listen to yourself. Everything in the negative. You're in denial. Open up, Peter. Let someone in. You'll feel better, I promise.'

She reached out and lowered a moist hand on to his. It was her left. No ring. She gave him a gentle squeeze and he looked up. In his mind, a certainty was born.

This awful bloody woman was coming on to him.

20

Kurt Cobain was lying supine on a stage somewhere, still flailing at his guitar, his dirty sneakered feet kicking feebly. A cymbal stand fell and crashed by his head. He failed to notice.

'Ah, there's poor Kurt,' Valerie said, soberly. 'Tragic. Tragic.'

In the armchair beside hers, Umberto twitched. He'd been channel-hopping and had accidentally paused on MTV. By the time he realised who was on, it was too late. She was off. *I'll never forget where I was when I heard . . .*

'I'll never forget where I was when I heard. Seems like yesterday. You were at your Aunt Mary's for the afternoon, do you remember? I was driving back to get you, not a care in the world. Then I switched on the radio . . . They announced it just like any other piece of news. Like it was a strike or a football result. They had no idea. None.'

Her voice trailed away. On the TV, Kurt was on his feet again and was enthusiastically smashing his guitar on the floor.

'He had such energy,' she swooned.

Umberto bit down on a sigh and dropped the remote control to the floor. He was stuck with this rubbish for the time being. Still, he counted his blessings – at least his dad was missing, gone to Carlingford for the day to take some photographs. The merest mention of Kurt Cobain (or Bob Dylan or Paul Simon) could prompt the old man to reach for his guitar, and it wasn't a pretty sight. Or sound, for that matter.

'Mary thought I'd been in an accident, I was in such a state. I could hardly speak. Trembling. I was in shock, I suppose. Remember? Umberto?'

He nodded dumbly, hoping that this would be the abridged version and not the full production.

'When I calmed down . . .'

Good. It was the abridged version. In the full production, she gave a lengthy list of the other guesses that Mary had made while her sister trembled and wept. Jeff had been in an accident. Their mother had been in an accident. Their father had been in an accident. Peter had caused an accident.

'. . . and I finally got the breath to explain, she couldn't have cared less. Shrugged her shoulders and said she was relieved. She thought it might have been something serious. Serious! She just didn't get it. Not just Kurt, the whole thing.'

Umberto didn't get it either. By his reckoning, his mother had been pushing thirty years of age at the time. She was simply not part of the appropriate demographic. He was glad that he'd been too young to be embarrassed at the time. *Grunge*, for the love of God. Horrible name, horrible music. He was an S Club 7 man himself. The brunette, especially.

'And now she claims to be an authority on music! She doesn't know the first thing. Ask her to name all the members of the Velvet Underground. Wouldn't have a clue. Oh, she's learned the names of a few bands and albums she should name-check, but that's as far as it goes.'

Umberto was impressed. She was really speeding along. She'd left out all the stuff about hugging Umberto and thinking of Frances Bean, the candle-lighting ceremony and its multi-faceted significance, and that line about some stars shining a little too brilliantly. Straight to the climax, and real point of the story: Mary's ignorance of music.

'Or the Clash. Ask her to tell you three significant facts about the Clash. She couldn't. But I was *there* ... shortly afterwards.'

When she talked about anything even vaguely connected to her years in London, she tended to pronounce a phrase or two in feeble Cockney. 'Tow ya' she said in this case, for 'tell you'. Umberto wondered about that sometimes. He also wondered why his mother was so interested in Mary's knowledge of music, or alleged lack thereof. Was she jealous of the shop's success? Did she wish she'd thought of it first, or what? It was strange. On the plus side, he had his excuse to speak up.

'Is she all right these days, do you think?' he said.

'Who?'

'Mary.'

'What do you mean?'

'In general. Feeling all right, I mean.'

'Why wouldn't she be?'

'I dunno. No reason. She just wasn't herself when I saw her

the other day. And she seemed quiet when she was here on Sunday, too.'

'Oh? Not herself how? She didn't say anything to *you*, did she? Jesus . . .'

There was a certain edge to her voice. It might have been suspicion; it might have been anger. She made frequent comments about her son and her sister being 'thick as thieves', and in an unguarded moment once described Mary as 'your other mother'. Umberto knew that whatever these comments were, they were not jokes.

'Say anything about what?'

'You tell me.'

'Is there something to say?'

'How would I know? You're the one on the inside track.'

Christ, it was like talking to the priest all over again. Circular, pointless, questions answered with questions. She obviously wasn't going to tell him what was going on.

'So long as she's all right.'

'She'll be fine. She's having a bit of a crisis, that's all. Nothing for you to get excited about.'

'What kind of crisis? It's something to do with Peter, isn't it?'

Her mouth formed a perfect O. Then it formed a hyphen. 'How do you know that?'

'Just from the way she was carrying on the other night when I went round. He wasn't there, and she was . . . upset. I asked her what was wrong, but she wouldn't tell me. It was obviously about him, though, the way she was acting. I'm not stupid, you know, I've got eyes and ears. What is it?'

'Never you mind.'

'But—'

'But nothing. It's adults' stuff. And you're not quite an adult yet. So leave it. It's not our affair. Now listen, it's just us for dinner, will I nip into town for a pizza? You know what your father's like when he gets a camera in his hand, he won't be back till it's pitch dark.'

Adults' stuff? Not our affair? Christ on a bike – an affair! Peter was having an affair! The *bastard* . . .

'Umberto? Did you hear me?'

'Yeah, OK. Pizza. Great.'

As soon as she had gone, he picked up the phone and dialled Mary's number. But he hung up before she could answer, unsure what he was trying to achieve with the call. There was nothing he could say that would help, and besides, he wasn't even supposed to know what was going on. Best leave it, for the time being anyway.

Jesus, though. An affair . . . it was worse than he thought. If anyone had asked him to guess what the problem was, he would have said it was something to do with kids. He often heard his mother saying that Mary and Peter would never be 'complete' until they had some. Or one, at any rate. Umberto had his doubts. They always struck him as being fairly fully formed. If anything, it was his own parents who had bits missing.

Who could she be, this other woman? Someone from work maybe? Nah. There were no eligible women in Data Force, just that middle-aged secretary type. What was she called? Mairéad. Umberto had met her one evening when he joined Peter and David for a game of network Quake at the office. She seemed nice and all, but she was too old. Who then? A customer?

171

That was more likely. He must be meeting new people all the time and some of them were bound to be women. It stood to reason that some of them must be attractive women. Yeah. Umberto could see it very easily. He gets a phone call one day, a honey-toned female voice complaining about a wonky printer or scanner or something. He pays a visit, does his thing. They get talking, the way people do. She's his age or thereabouts. Single, lonely. From out of town maybe. Doesn't know anyone here. Blonde, say. Tanned. Big blue eyes, short black skirt, crisp white blouse straining to contain her heavy . . . Hoo. Umberto was getting a woody. Again. He patted his trouser tent and tried to think about something else for a moment. The priest. If anything was death to unwanted woodies, it was priests. (And the peace process, for some reason. Umberto had decommissioned more than once by conjuring up an image of Martin McGuinness.) Conflicting images swirled in his mind: Father Duff, the blonde with the computer problems, Mary in tears. Hang on . . . This whole ugly business was priest territory, wasn't it? Marriage counselling, that sort of thing. They had training, didn't they? They must know a few tricks, some handy pointers they could pass along.

Hmmm.

21

Finbarr's new mobile rang for the first time on Wednesday evening. He was lying spread-eagled on his bed at the time, enjoying a nap. The noise that interrupted him made no sense at first. Biddle-de-dee, biddle-de-dee, biddle-de-dee, rapid beeps repeating over and over. He lay there with an ear cocked to the bedroom door, running through a list of possibilities, including doorbell (unlikely), TV (not switched on) and ghosts (no such thing). When the truth dawned, he bounded off the bed and semi-tumbled down the stairs, swearing violently as he went. In the shadowy kitchen, the mobile stood lit up, like some sort of navigational beacon, between the toaster and the kettle. He snatched at it and poised a quivering digit over the keypad, wondering what you did to answer the thing. The girl in the shop had offered to show him how it worked, but he'd declined. He was in a hurry, he said. In truth, he had wanted out of there as quickly as possible. She asked him a lot of personal questions: would he be using it during the day or at night, how many calls did he expect to make, and so on. It made him feel nervous, like an undercover agent being stopped at a checkpoint.

Biddle-de-dee, biddle-de-dee. Ah, fuck. None of the buttons said 'Answer' or anything like it. One of them had a picture of a little green phone, though. That might be the chap. He was on the point of pressing it when he remembered that he wanted a recorded message, not a conversation. He had to let it ring out. Goggle-eyed and breathing heavily, he waited for the biddle-de-dees to end. It took an age.

'That's the girl,' he whispered. 'Don't forget to wait for the beep . . .'

He stood there for a minute or two, imagining her voice. Uncertain, but excited. Thanking her mysterious admirer, wondering who he was. Suggesting a meeting, with any luck. That would be pure gold, the bull's-eye, the World Cup. He felt nervous, suddenly. It was actually happening. It was working. He had his proof. But what would he actually *say* to Peter? How would he put it? He wasn't much good with words. Then again, he wouldn't have to say a whole lot. A brief overview of the facts would suffice. The message would do the rest. Wait a minute . . .

'Shite,' he spat. 'How the hell do you listen to your messages?'

For such a small device, the mobile phone came with a lot of literary baggage. Finbarr counted eight different booklets of varying hues and sizes. Some of them seemed to be nothing more than ads for other rubbish you could buy, covers and earpieces and guff like that. One ran to sixty-four pages and read like a manual for building your own jet fighter. Another was devoted to using the phone abroad. Finbarr had never been abroad and hoped he never would. He tossed them all aside.

Simon's C25 User Guide, he read, peering at the next contender. That sounded hopeful. But no. It was thirty pages of incomprehensible gibberish about sending text messages (whatever that was) and changing your biddle-de-dee to God knows what, doodle-de-doo maybe. It was while he was scouring the index of this publication that Finbarr suddenly realised that Simon's wasn't Simon's, it was Siemen's. He took a giggling break for a minute or so. It didn't do to be serious all the time.

Something called the *Pocket Reference Guide* was next. It was encouragingly slim. Finbarr's hopes rose . . . Diverting Calls, Changing Your Password, Call Waiting – bingo. Receiving Your Messages. It turned out to be quite easy. Dial 121 and press the button with the green phone on it. Finbarr took a breath and did so.

There was some beeping, and then a sort of buzz. 'The number of new messages is . . . one,' a voice said. Finbarr's palms were slick with sweat.

'Here we go,' he said.

The next voice he heard was male and completely alien to him. A Dublin accent. 'Howiye Keith,' it said. 'It's Eamo. Listen, me fucken battery was dead earlier but I'm back up now, so gimme a buzz. Any time suits me really, but after nine would be better. Right so. Talk to ye.'

Finbarr was gutted. 'BOLLOCKS,' he declared. A fucking wrong number. Never mind. He had to be cool. Patience was

175

of the essence in this sort of game. She was still thinking it over, no doubt, maybe waiting for Peter to leave the house before she made the call.

Finbarr could wait. He was good at waiting.

22

'Eleanor Rigby' was one of the few singles the McKeowns had owned when Mary was a child, and the only one by the Beatles ('Some of their songs had a good beat,' she remembered her father reporting, 'but sure they were hopeless drug addicts. You couldn't be up to them, the same Beatles').

She found it one Sunday afternoon while rifling through their album collection, somewhat out of place among the Roger Whittakers and the Tammy Wynettes. Mary couldn't remember how old she'd been – eight or nine, she guessed, based on the fact that she didn't have any records of her own and that Valerie was away in London. The first time she heard it, she was impressed. It was a beautiful tune and he had a lovely voice, your man. Not as good as thingy from the Monkees, but not bad. She didn't really listen to the lyrics too closely on that first play. If truth be told, she got the impression that it was a love song. As soon as it ended, she lifted the needle and played it again, this time paying close attention to the words as well as the music. By the end of that second outing, she felt sick. Why, she didn't know.

She played it again. This time, it made her cry, even though it skipped twice, once at the line about the face in the jar and again at one of the lonely peoples. She ran to her bedroom and closed the door.

Lying on her bed, she tried to understand why the song had bothered her so much. She'd heard sad songs before about lost love and puppy love and unrequited love, and had understood them, or at least got the gist. But they'd had no real effect on her. They were sad songs, that was all, little stories you could forget as soon as they were over. What was different about this one?

It was a while before she worked it out. 'Eleanor Rigby' was about adults who were simply unhappy in general. Nothing to do with love. It had never occurred to Mary before that adults might be capable of unhappiness. Up until then she had figured that they had it made. They had money, they could stay up until all hours, they didn't have parents telling them that their face was dirty or their jeans didn't fit them. They were sorted. This, apparently, was bullshit. Adults could be just as miserable as children. Possibly more so, given the song's testimony that they were prone not only to crushing loneliness and pointless, wasted lives, but to sudden death as well. Misery could happen to her parents.

Perhaps it had already happened to them.

'What's wrong? Is something wrong?' James said hurriedly when she came through the kitchen door that Wednesday night. He was sitting in his favourite chair by the range with an *Evening Herald* splayed in front of him. The headline, Mary couldn't help but notice, screeched something about murderous immigrants.

178

'I'm delighted to see you too, Father dear,' Mary said. 'What makes you think there's something wrong?'

He folded his newspaper away and joined his hands on his chest. 'Did I dream it or were we not round in your house last night? Two visits in two days, that's all I'm saying.'

'Some welcome that is.'

'Ah, would you be quiet. You're always welcome. Now make yourself useful and stick the kettle on.'

'The host with the most. So, are you on your own?'

'She's at confession.'

'Oh? What's she been up to?'

He wagged a finger at her. 'Now. Less of that, missy. It wouldn't kill you to go an odd time.'

With the kettle on, Mary took the armchair opposite his, on the other side of the range. 'I do go. Often. Not that I have anything to confess . . .'

Or have I? she thought. No. Nope. Nuh-uh.

'Good girl. I'm sure you don't. But you might have a word in that sister of yours's ear, try to steer her in the same direction. Or to mass, at the very least. For the sake of her son, if nothing else.'

'Which son is that?'

He pursed his lips but said nothing for a moment. This was an old game with them. Mary had heard her father say Umberto's name perhaps a dozen times, ever. Each time, he went cross-eyed and almost choked. He usually called him 'Valerie's son' or 'the grandson' or, to his face, just 'son'. Mary was sure that Umberto noticed all of this and was equally sure that he didn't care.

'Kevin, I think you call him. Or maybe it's Declan. Or

179

Michael or David or Anthony. Something like that. One of those nice normal names.'

'Are you sure it isn't Umberto?'

'Positive. Sure that's not even a word.'

'Do you know what "denial" is, Dad?'

He rubbed his chin. 'Is it a riv—'

'And don't say "Is it a river in Egypt?"'

'Well then I'm stuck.'

They smiled at each other and she rose to make the tea.

'So. How's the toe?' she asked, when they were comfortable.

'Much the same,' he said sadly, and leaned forward to reach for his shoelace.

Mary shivered. 'It's OK, I don't want to see it.'

'I'm only—'

'No. Really. Once was more than enough for that particular treat.'

He sat back and took a swig of tea. 'You're your mother's daughter, that's for sure.'

Mary felt a frown form, unbidden. 'Meaning what?'

'Meaning she couldn't care less either.'

'Is that what you really think? That she doesn't care?'

He shrugged a single shoulder. 'Dunno.'

'You don't *know*?'

She knew by the way he looked at her that she had spoken harshly. It was the same look Peter had been giving her lately. She wondered when exactly this had started, this inability to control her tone.

'What's up, Mary?' he said.

She blinked. 'Nothing.'

'Hmmm. Don't think so. I've been your father for a long time. I know my Mary. You're not at yourself these days. There must be something annoying—'

'Nope.'

'Your mother noticed it too.'

She swallowed some tea and avoided his gaze. 'Nope.'

'You did this when you were a wee girl too. I mind it well.'

'Did what?'

'This. This "Nope" business. When something was bothering you but you didn't want to spit it out, you'd come looking for me or your mother and mope around us until we dragged it out of you. And "dragged" is the word for it. Took all day sometimes. You were big on "Nope" then too.'

He paused, apparently hoping he had said enough for her to crack. She stayed silent. He continued.

'Like the time Valerie went to London and you had that wee crisis. Remember?'

She shook her head.

'I think you do,' he said, lowering his chin to his chest. 'If I can remember it, I'm sure you can.'

Of course she remembered. She just didn't want to talk about it. The summer of 1982. Not long before the 'Eleanor Rigby' revelation. When Valerie announced that she was off, the McKeown household went into a state of shock, and not merely because it was all so sudden. Even as a child, Mary recognised that Valerie was an anomaly in the family and that her absence would be somehow meaningful. Without her they would be . . . ordinary. She couldn't hope to fill the Valerie-shaped space herself. She still played dressing-up, for Christ's sake. It was only a matter of time before her parents noticed the void and started to resent her. A matter of time? It happened immediately. They were distracted, distant, right from the day she left. Her mother wandered around the house in silence, watering the same plants again and again. Her father sat in front of the television, apparently watching soap operas. He hated soap operas. Mary ricocheted between them, chirping banalities. They responded with small smiles and few words. In desperation, she even tried to interest them in her homework. They were nonplussed. She didn't really blame them. How could her half-page essay *The Most Exciting Day of My Life* compete with, say, Valerie's papier-mâché sculpture of a man with three breasts and a penis that almost reached the floor (*Tomorrow*, it was called)?

As time passed, her efforts became ever more frantic. One evening she invented a dance. Left arm out, right leg out, right arm out, left leg out, all limbs in, jump. Left arm out . . . It wasn't a big hit. 'Oh,' her mother said. 'Ah,' her father said.

After a week or so, her mother sat her down at the kitchen table and wondered if anything was the matter. She remembered shaking her head and staring out of the window. And she might have said, 'Nope', she really couldn't recall. Then her dad joined in, leaning back against the sink with folded arms. Was she sure she was all right? She was 'acting funny'.

Mary remembered thinking that was a bit rich. If anyone was acting funny, it was them, with their blank stares and their weighted sighs. When she made little or no response, her dad launched into a rare speech. About Valerie's departure, about 'the choices people make in life', about 'the way things change but stay the same'. It went right over her head, but she nodded along anyway. Her mum did some nodding too, sitting with her fingers tightly intertwined. Then she asked Mary if she knew that her parents loved her. She was embarrassed – they didn't have this sort of conversation, as a rule – but said that she did. Her mother asked a follow-up question. Did she think that they loved her more or less or about the same because Valerie had gone away? She said about the same. It seemed to be the correct answer. They smiled at her and hugged her in turn. That was the end of it.

'Maybe it rings a small bell,' Mary said.

Her father took a tremendous gulp of tea. 'So . . . are you going to tell me what's up now?'

'There's nothing up, Dad. Honestly. I'm grand.'

He nodded. 'Everything all right with Peter?'

'Why wouldn't it be?'

'No reason. We just thought maybe the pair of you were a bit . . . you know . . . last night.'

'We?'

'Your mother and me.'

'That's a good one . . .'

'Meaning?'

'Meaning the two of you were at each other's throats.'

'We were not!'

'You were! You're always sniping at each other. Every time I see you, you're having a go. If it's not about your toe, it's about the right way to do scrambled eggs or who played who in old movies. You never let up, the pair of you.'

'You've never mentioned this before.'

'Well . . . maybe I've only just noticed.'

'But sure you know we're only messing!'

She thought about it for a moment. 'Sometimes I think—'

183

There was a sudden shuffle outside the kitchen door. Then her mother walked in, unwrapping her headscarf.

'Oh, hello, Mary,' she said. 'Two days in a row! Is there something wrong?'

She stayed for another half an hour, give or take. To her great relief, her father dropped the thread of their previous conversation. They small-talked instead, about whether or not Mary and Peter should have a second car amongst other things. James thought they should; Valerie and Jeff swore by it. Elizabeth thought it was unnecessary extravagance. Mary said she liked walking, because it provided good thinking time. That comment earned her strange looks from them both.

'Time was, confession of a Wednesday would be jam-packed,' her mother said at one point. 'You'd want to see it now. Half a dozen of us, maybe. And all oul' ones like me. You still go, don't you, Mary?'

'*Yes.*'

'Well, I'm glad to hear it. Most young ones don't give a damn.'

'That didn't last long, did it?' James said. 'You're only out of it half an hour and you're swearing already.'

'Swearing? What swearing? What are you on about now?'

'You said "damn", that's a swear.'

'No it's not.'

'It is.'

'It *isn't.*'

'Oh, I think so.'

'Mary, tell him.'

'I don't know,' Mary said. 'I wouldn't worry about it either way.'

'Anyway. I had Father Duff. He's—'

James coughed. 'There's another one.'

'What?'

'Telling us who you had for confession. You shouldn't do that. It's supposed to be a secret. You'll have to tell that in confession the next time.'

'You made that up. He's always at that, Mary, did you ever notice? He makes up his own religious rules when it suits him. He's not even a Catholic at this stage, he's something else he came up with himself. Anyway. I had that' – she gave her husband a look – 'FATHER DUFF. He was all chat. Wanted to know all about the family, how everyone was keeping. I didn't know he knew us from Adam. He's not that sort of priest, I always thought. Not like Father Fleming, God rest him. He knew every man Jack in the town by name.'

James said, 'He knew which end of a whiskey bottle to suck on as well.'

She ignored this. 'He was asking after you, Mary, and Valerie.'

'Was he?'

'He was. And Umberto.'

'Eh? How would he know Umberto?'

'Don't ask me. He wouldn't know him from mass, Valerie neither. I can tell you that much.'

James sat up, looking alarmed. 'I hope he's not one of those . . . you know . . .'

'James!'

'Well . . .'

'Of course he isn't! He was being nice! What's the country coming to when a priest can't enquire about a young man without some nasty old goat like you deflaming him?'

'*Defaming*. I'm defaming him.'

Elizabeth rolled her eyes and shook her head. Mary noticed again that her father was looking in her direction. Was he doing this deliberately? Being argumentative to see if it annoyed her? Apparently so. Well, she wasn't going to stick around for that sort of carry-on.

'I better get back,' she said, getting up.

'That's very sudden,' her mother said. 'Will you not have another cup of tea?'

'I've had two already.'

Elizabeth slapped James on the forearm. 'Now look what you did. She's going. Nobody wants to sit around listening to you *defaming* people. I hope you're pleased with yourself.'

'I'll give you a lift,' James said.

'It's all right, I'll walk.'

'You're better off walking,' Elizabeth said. 'He's half blind and he won't go to the obstetrician.'

'Optician,' James sighed.

She slapped him again. 'I *know*, eejit. I was only seeing if you were awake.'

Mary looked from one to the other in wonder, said goodbye, and left. She walked home with Paul McCartney crooning plaintively in her head.

23

Tommy 'Helmet' McGuiney was giving Umberto a dirty look as he crossed the school yard. At least, Umberto guessed that the look was pointed in his direction. It could just as easily have been aimed at Dessie Doherty, who was sitting with him on the steps by the science lab. You couldn't tell with Helmet, whose eyes rarely opened more than a millimetre or two.

Umberto had seen him give other people that same look many times before. It was often a prelude to some sort of violence. He hoped it would be so again. He had been thinking hard about Mary and Peter and the possibility of getting the priest involved. Consequently, he was in a very bad mood. Not because he thought that the idea couldn't work. It was, even if he said so himself, a very good idea. He was in a bad mood, in fact, *because* it was a good idea. That meant that he had to follow through, for the sake of his conscience, and get the priest's advice. He tried to console himself with the certainty of the plan's success.

Helmet terminated the dirty-look treatment and nodded

when he arrived in front of them, as if they were all friends. Nothing would have given Umberto greater pleasure than to pound on the top of the wee prick's head, driving him into the ground, like they did in cartoons. Helmet stood five foot nothing and weighed about six stone. It would not only be fun, but easy, even for someone like Umberto who had never deliberately struck another human being in his life.

'Hello, ladies,' Helmet said, planting a foot on the step between Umberto and Dessie. 'Grand weather we've been having.'

Umberto and Dessie muttered longsufferingly in unison, and then both looked away into the middle distance. Dessie was no giant himself, but he wasn't afraid of Helmet either. Thing was, no one was afraid of him, not physically anyway. Everyone knew this but Helmet. He swaggered around the place with his thumbs tucked into the belt loops of his shiny school trousers, showering insults and threats like a Made Man. Many if not most of the jibes Umberto suffered came from his quarter.

Relatively harmless though he was, no one wanted to get on his bad side since he did have his admirers among those rough-hewn students who were all too capable of beating a person up. If he tried to beat someone up himself – as he often did, post dirty look – the wise move was to defend yourself as best you could but not to fight back too hard. A couple of kids had landed good punches on Helmet's bony chin and later found themselves upside down in a hedge somewhere, dazed and bleeding, as the hard half of the football team walked away laughing.

'Maths first thing this afternoon, if I'm not mistaken,' Helmet said.

Umberto said, 'And?'

'What did you make of the homework last night? Hard, very hard, I thought.' He turned his head to spit. Phtoo. 'I had a few problems finishing it. And starting it.'

Umberto shook his head slowly. 'Jesus Christ. What age are you? Still trying to copy people's homework at lunch-time. It's pathetic. Are you going to be like this your whole life, cheating and scrounging?'

Helmet took his foot off the step and looked around him in shock. Umberto guessed that he was looking for a hidden camera, or maybe Jeremy Beadle himself.

'What?' he spluttered.

'Grow up, Thomas,' Umberto said. 'I hate to be the one to break it to you, but you're not in primary school any more. Act your fucking age.'

As a general rule, Umberto tried not to swear. He thought that people who swore all the time tended to sound thick, no matter what they said between the expletives. This was a special occasion, though. And besides, Helmet was one of those people who only really listened when the air was blue. If you didn't swear at him, you might as well be talking to your foot.

'What?' Helmet said again, drawing himself up to his full height, and puffing out his meagre chest.

Umberto squinted at him. See how he liked it. 'I'm not in the humour for you today. Do us a favour and just fuck off.'

Dessie moaned.

'Are you telling me . . .' Helmet grunted. 'What are you telling me again?'

Umberto felt that this would be a good time to fake an exasperated sigh. He did so, with gusto. 'All right, I'll tell you again. But this is the last time. Are you ready? Ears switched on? Here we go: Please . . . fuck . . . off. Go and find some other fool to copy from. We're talking here.'

Helmet seemed finally to understand that there was no hidden camera and that this was not a joke. Someone was actually talking to him this way! And not just any old someone, but Umberto McKeown, the big poofy twat. He raised his right hand and pointed.

'You . . .'

His lips kept moving but there was no follow-up.

'Umberto,' Umberto said. He pointed back at Helmet. 'You Thomas.' Then he pointed at Dessie. 'Him Dessie.'

Dessie chuckled, despite himself. As soon as he did, he put his hand over his mouth, like someone who had burped in polite company.

'You too,' Helmet said, turning slightly to point at Dessie.

Umberto responded immediately. 'Four-piece Irish band, several multi-platinum albums, hits include 'Where the Streets Have No Name' and 'Desire'. Ten points to me. Next question.'

That went right over Helmet's head, as humour often did. He walked away, backwards at first, still pointing.

'Now. Where were we?' Umberto said. He was feeling quite buoyant now and vowed to take it out on Helmet when he felt down in future.

'Special effects,' Dessie said in monotone, staring at Helmet's retreating figure.

'Right. Actually, I was all done with that.'

Before they were interrupted, Umberto had been giving Dessie the benefit of his latest theory, which stated that a person who doesn't want to know how movie special effects are done is more likely to believe in God. The priest had been on his mind, of course, but in truth he often treated Dessie to his philosophical musings. He was a good listener, Dessie. Lots of people were good listeners, Umberto supposed, but there weren't many who were willing to listen to *him*. Not in this school anyway. Maybe that would change if his bad mood and attendant assertiveness persisted.

Dessie cleared his throat. 'I'm not sure I like this, y'know. Helmet.'

'I don't like him either.'

'You know what I mean. He'll be after you now, and me too 'cos you made me laugh, ye cunt.'

Umberto pulled a face. 'So what? I'm sick of that guy. Copying homework . . . we're not children any more.'

'Even so. I'd watch out if I was you. Or me.'

'You are you.'

Dessie ran a nervous hand through his filthy hair. 'Don't remind me,' he said.

It was common knowledge that Mr Devine the maths teacher had been of the physical force tradition in years gone by and greatly resented the trendies in government whose wishy-washy liberalism meant that he could no longer punch an errant pupil in the face. The boys knew this because he told them about it one day, eyes rolling like marbles in his head as he spoke.

Now, with his bite muzzled, he had evidently spent time and energy in the development of a world-class bark. When he shouted, things fell off shelves. And he shouted a lot. Only a fortnight previously he had reduced Noel O'Hanrahan to tears by screaming at him from a distance of two inches for three full minutes. Noel was somewhat dim, Umberto thought, but he wasn't a bad lad. His excuse for having no homework to show – 'I left it at home' – sounded perfectly plausible. People were always leaving things here and there. Why not homework? Mr Devine, known to all as Captain Kirk because of his extremely vague resemblance to same, didn't see it that way. He danced on the spot by Noel's desk, obviously trying to find something to do with his fists while he yelled and spat. He could get carried away by a good shout, Kirk, and once or twice he showed his enthusiasm for the procedure by doing a small jump. Umberto trembled in sympathy for Noel at the time, and wondered what had happened to him that he now wanted the same treatment for Helmet. Stress. That must be it. He was under a lot of stress these days. More than usual even. It was making him vindictive. He'd been kidding himself to think of it as assertiveness.

Captain Kirk beamed down to the class in typical style – at great speed and with little ceremony.

'Shut up,' he said simply as he power-walked through the classroom door. The pre-class babble subsided, but not quickly enough for the captain. He drew breath and turned to face his charges. 'SHUT! UP! NOW!' It was a mild outburst by his standards, barely more than a roar, but the effect was immediate. Umberto looked behind him and to his left to the corner where Helmet sat. He seemed calm enough.

Kirk was the only teacher they had who insisted on checking everyone's homework every single day. He didn't check it for accuracy, or do anything else with it of even the most tenuous educational value. He merely checked that they had done it, ordering the rows up one at a time to shuffle past him flashing their documents like tourists at customs. Some days he did it at the end of the class, some days he did it at the start. Today belonged in the latter category.

'Right, everybody get it out,' he barked. This was his traditional prompt for the homework parade. No one was sure if he was genuinely trying to be funny or just daring some reckless student to laugh. He said it every day. No one ever laughed.

The boys from the first row inside the door creaked their way out of their desks and sloped up to the little stage where Kirk and his colleagues performed. Their turn passed without incident. The second row had been similarly diligent in its preparations, although Spazmo Kelly did get a minor bollocking for using black ink. Kirk insisted on blue. 'Black ink is for deviants,' he told Spazmo, his voice rising considerably in volume on the last word. That was the impressive thing about him. Other teachers shouted only when they lost control. It made them embarrassed and resentful. Kirk could not only shout one sentence and whisper the next, he could shout INDIVIDUAL words in a SENTENCE.

The first student to get a proper scream out of him was in Umberto's row. It was Gregory Daly, an occasional sidekick-stroke-straight-man of Helmet's. He was another character Umberto could live without. The really galling thing about him was that he was one of the smarter people in the class – and this was the smartest class, the top stream. He just seemed to think it was cool to get into small-time trouble. He never did anything serious. He didn't set fires or steal computers or crap on the bonnets of the teachers' cars, like some. But he

193

gave periodic lip and sometimes made farting noises in class. That was the entire extent of his trouble-making repertoire. Not enough to earn him anyone's respect – despite all the arse-licking, even Helmet seemed barely able to tolerate him – but enough to get himself noticed, and hated. Everyone hated him. He was no more entertaining than his boss, but at least Helmet was mildly threatening because of his contacts among the genuine pyros and car-crappers. Gregory Daly was a lackey to a lackey. No class.

'What are these *squiggles*?' Captain Kirk snarled, pointing at Daly's homework. 'Did you do this on a rollercoaster?'

Daly smirked and folded his arms. 'No, sir. I was a bit tipsy though, at the time. Sure you know yourself.'

Now there were some students, Colm McCaffrey, say, who were able to get away with this kind of thing. They were popular to begin with and once in a while could crack a one-liner to the acclaim of both students and teacher. Daly had no such charm. The class, to a man, pretended not to have heard him. Kirk, however, made it immediately obvious that he had heard by getting to his feet in an eyeblink and shoving his puffy face into Daly's. At first, Umberto thought he had dispensed with words altogether and was just making high-pitched noises, not unlike a dentist's drill. Then he caught the word 'clown', and concluded there must be a whole sentence in there somewhere. Daly, the prick, smirked throughout the onslaught, which lasted around thirty seconds. Then he said, 'Yes, sir, sorry, sir,' and returned to his seat, basking in what he seemed to think was the awe of his classmates. Part of his problem was that he didn't know contempt when he saw it. Umberto's own homework was snatched and returned with barely a glance. He always had his homework done. Sometimes he wondered if that made him a bad person.

Helmet's row was last to go. As they rose from their seats, Umberto braced himself for Helmet's excuses and Kirk's wrath. He felt his guts wriggle and was suddenly awash with remorse, as if he had sold an innocent man to his executioner. The innocent man wasn't innocent, of course, and the executioner couldn't actually execute, he could merely yell. Nevertheless, Umberto felt small. His heart began bouncing in his chest. He wanted to put his fingers in his ears. Helmet rose quite calmly from his seat and trooped up with the rest of them, carrying his tattered exercise book. Dessie happened to sit in front of Helmet and so was immediately before him in the Kirk queue. The captain grabbed his homework, flipped through a few pages, and then thrust it back at him. Dessie nodded and moved on, glancing back at Helmet as he went. Helmet stepped forward. Grab, flip, thrust.

The first emotion Umberto felt was relief. There would be no shouting, so he had nothing to feel guilty about. Helmet had obviously taken his advice and found some other fool to copy from. Relief didn't last long, though. It was replaced almost immediately by a mixture of dread and regret. *Fuck*. He'd been in a bad mood and had a rush of blood to the head. Now he was on the shit-list of someone who devoted at least 50 per cent of his waking time to causing other people trouble. And for what? Precisely nothing, that was what. He shifted to the left in his seat and stole a peek behind him.

Helmet winked. Then he pointed at Umberto for the second time that day and mouthed the word 'You'.

24

By the time Peter began his drive home on Thursday evening, he had learned to deal with the whole mess by imagining it as a plain brown paper package tied with blue string. There was a label attached to the string, and on the label were large black letters, printed neatly with a thick marker. The Incident, the letters said. Peter had never tried this sort of visualisation before and, so far, he was delighted with it. Every time an unsavoury memory flashed into his mind – and they'd been flashing all day long with great regularity – he took a deep breath and concentrated on the package. The Incident, all of it, everything that happened, everything that was said, was tied up in there where it could hurt no one. He could leave it out for the bin-men. He could throw it in a lake. He could put it in the boot of the car and forget about it. He was safe.

The Thursday tea-time traffic was awe-inspiring in its density and only got worse as it approached the river. Peter eventually crawled up to a set of traffic lights where the green light that came around once in a while was of no use to anyone; everything had come to a total halt on the other side of the intersection and there was nowhere to go. After a few cycles of the lights, people even stopped honking. He looked around at his neighbours. They all seemed perfectly calm, apparently resigned to the possibility that they might never move again. Some were singing along with the radio, others chatting with their passengers. One neckless taxi-driver was repeatedly poking an index finger into his right nostril like a barman putting a glass up to an optic. Peter tried to maintain his cool, but suddenly trapped with no driving to distract him, he was bombarded by unwelcome images and soundbites again. He reminded himself of the package, so tightly tied, so perfectly banal, and tried to whistle a tune.

While he sat there, his windscreen was washed, or at least attended to, three separate times by a flat-topped lad in what looked like his father's anorak. The windscreen-washer was poorly equipped. He had a single grey-black facecloth, which may have been some other colour entirely to begin with, and a trigger spray-gun of the kind used for watering houseplants. The first time he approached the car, Peter thought he was an assassin. The dark figure advancing from the shadows, the moment of eye contact, then the raised arm and the slow squeeze of the trigger. When the boy merely squirted a few blasts of water on to his windscreen and then gave it two quick wipes with the facecloth, Peter smiled with relief. Unfortunately, Squirty took this as a sign of congratulations on a job well done, and stepped around to the driver's window, hand extended. Peter wound the window down and handed the boy a pound, which he thought fairly generous considering that his windscreen was now dirtier than ever with the two extra black streaks across it. The second time the lad came his way, Peter thought he was taking the piss. But no. Squirt, wipe, hand out at the driver's window. There were a few coins in the pocket by the gear-stick. Peter wound the window down again and handed them over, thinking the boy deserved them for cheek if nothing else. Still, he was pushing his luck with the third approach. He's seen my registration, Peter thought, and he thinks he's got some culchie gobshite here who's never been in the big city before. Well, he's got another think coming. The boy peered in at him, expressionless, as Peter slowly shook his head. Forget about it, he mouthed through the glass even though he could have just as easily have spoken aloud. They stared at each other for ten, twenty seconds. Then the lights changed. Whatever obstruction there had been on the other side of the intersection had finally been cleared and Peter was free to depart. Here we go now, he thought, with the swearing and spitting and maybe stone-throwing. But the boy's face remained blank. They kept their gazes locked until Peter was looking over his shoulder. Mary's been doing that same look lately, he thought. That sort of quietly disappointed look. Oh, *God*.

The package, he told himself. The package, the package, the package.

25

It was Umberto's habit, when faced with an unpleasant task, to organise a small treat for afterwards. A long-dreaded visit to the dentist, for example, might be offset by the promise of a new game for the spare-parts PC that Peter rigged together for him one rainy weekend. No such treat was required to balance out his visit to Father Duff. His reward would take the form of a saved marriage. Some minor pain, then a whole lot of gain.

At least, that was the plan. On the walk to the parochial house after school on Thursday evening, however, he began to have his doubts. What if he had this horribly wrong? What if priests were no longer in the business of marriage-saving? Had they ever been, for that matter? Umberto wasn't sure. He had very little first-hand information on Catholicism, other than the snippets he picked up in school. But it sounded like the sort of thing a priest might get up to. After all, they made couples go through some sort of pre-marriage training course – he remembered Peter and Mary telling his horrified parents about it. And they did the actual marrying, the do-you, will-you bit. Any subsequent problems were partly their responsibility, when you stopped to think about it.

But what about the issue of tact? He couldn't just march up to Father Duff and tell him that his uncle was having an affair. He had no proof for starters, but that didn't bother him as much as the idea of rubbishing Peter behind his back. He deserved a good kick in the hole for behaving this way, but there was no sense in pointing fingers. Damage limitation, that was the name of the game at this stage. He supposed that he would simply have to explain his concerns about their marriage in broad terms, and hope the priest would have some advice. There was no need to mention any names even. But, Jesus, suppose he insisted on getting involved first-hand. Suppose he wanted to know who this poor couple were and where they lived. Suppose he showed up at their house, carrying his marriage-saving kit like your man in *The Exorcist*.

Umberto resolved to stand firm. Barest details only. Need-to-know basis. He approached the gates of the parochial house feeling renewed confidence. It was good to be one of life's problem-solvers.

The woman who answered the door had the most enormous feet Umberto had ever seen. Why he noticed, he wasn't sure. Nerves, possibly. They were bloody huge, though, like frying pans. It put him off his stride for a moment.

'Yes?' she said when he failed to announce his purpose.

'Hello,' he nodded, gathering himself together again. 'Is Father Duff in?'

He was aware that he sounded like a small boy calling for his friend to play conkers and wished he'd thought of a better opening line.

'Who will I say is looking for him?' the woman said. Umberto sneaked another peek at her feet. Jesus. She must have terrible trouble finding shoes.

'My name is Umberto McKeown.'

She leaned on to the door frame. 'It's *what* McKeown?'

'Um-ber-to.'

'What class of a name would that be?'

'It's Italian.'

'Italian for what?'

'It's not Italian for anything, it's just a name. What's your first name?'

'Martha.'

'And that's English for what?'

She said nothing.

'You see my point,' Umberto said, dabbing at his brow. He'd come over all testy again. The stress.

'Come in,' she said, stepping aside. 'I'll tell him you're here. I don't think he's expecting you, is he?'

Umberto shook his head no. She left him alone then in the large hallway. It was unlit and exceptionally warm. There was a picture of some black saint or other on the wall by the telephone table, partially illuminated by a single red candle. He looked like Will Smith to Umberto. He was smiling at that idea when the housekeeper reappeared with Father Duff in tow.

'Well now,' he said. 'This is a pleasant surprise. Have you come to give me a chess lesson, Umberto?'

Oh, *yeah*. Chess. He'd forgotten about that. A status quo. Or was it quid pro quo? Whichever. It was a gift.

'That's right,' Umberto said brightly. 'And then maybe you could give me a quick lesson in return.'

'A lesson? In what?'

Umberto knew better than to show his cards so soon. 'Chess first,' he said.

The priests' sitting room was sparsely furnished. There was a coffee table, two high-backed armchairs and a bookcase. A plain wooden chess board sat on the table. It looked as if a game had recently been in progress. A standard lamp was lit in the corner, but it wasn't very bright. Most of the light in the room came from the fire which was banked high with glowing coal. The heat was considerable.

'Is it warm enough in here?' Umberto said, removing his jacket.

'We don't all have your young blood,' Father Duff said, smiling. 'Do we, Father Grehan?'

A shrunken head carrying a pair of glasses appeared from around the side of an armchair. 'That's right,' it said, and then cackled. Umberto started a scream, but caught himself just in time.

'AGH— Oh, sorry. I didn't know there was anyone sitting there.'

'Heh! I must be uglier than I thought,' the shrunken head said.

'This is Father Grehan,' Father Duff said, gesturing in the appropriate direction. 'And this is Umberto McKeown.'

'Hello,' Father Grehan said.

Umberto nodded a small nod.

'Well, it's been nice frightening you, Umberto, but I have business to attend to. I'll leave yiz to it.'

He hoisted himself out of his chair with some difficulty and made his exit.

'Bye,' Umberto said for want of something better to say.

The retreating Father Grehan was met at the door by an advancing Martha, all smiles now.

'Can I get anyone anything?' she said, folding her hands in front of her. Umberto noticed that she had regular-sized hands. It was a mystery.

'Not for me anyway, Martha,' Father Duff said. 'Umberto? Tea? Coffee? Coke? I think we have Coke, haven't we, Martha?'

'Nothing thanks,' Umberto said.

Martha said, 'All right, so,' and left, closing the door behind her.

'Take a seat,' Father Duff said as he took his own. 'I think . . . what are you smiling at?'

'Nothing,' Umberto said. He managed to straighten his face for a moment but it snapped right back into the same smile like it was made of rubber.

'You're thinking about *Father Ted*, aren't you?'

'Well, I'm sorry but it's hard not to.'

Father Duff leaned forward and whispered, 'I know. I do it too. And about half the people who come here crack some joke to her about "Ah, ye will" or "Go on, go on, go on". She's getting sick of it, I can tell. Ducky's not much of a one for comedy at the best of times.'

'Who's Ducky?' Umberto asked.

Father Duff twitched. 'Oh . . . eh . . .'

'Is that what you call her?'

'You see—'

'Ducky?'

'No, no, it's, eh . . .'

'Is it because of her feet?'

The priest caught a laugh in his hand. 'I really couldn't say.'

Umberto shook his head reflectively. 'Right enough, she's got the biggest feet I've ever seen on anybody, a man or a woman.'

Father Duff dropped the act. 'I didn't start the Ducky thing, now. That was Father Grehan's nickname for her. He's always saying that he'll know his eyesight's gone for good when he can't make out her feet. He's sharp enough, you know, despite appearances. Just not one of life's chess players.'

Umberto looked over the pitiful sight on the board. Black had lost two pawns. White had lost everything except two pawns.

'So I see. You could win this game in a couple of moves from here, you know.'

'Oh, I know. I could have won it any number of times in the past half an hour. I chose not to. You can imagine how much fun this sort of thing is.'

Indeed Umberto could. Probably as much fun as playing his dad. Jeff started trying to teach Umberto to play chess at the age of three, on the off-chance that he had spawned a child prodigy. He hadn't. Umberto couldn't remember much about those lessons, except that the pieces had tasted quite nice. It wasn't until he was twelve that he showed any interest of his own and by then his dad had to be carefully cajoled into

teaching him. He didn't seem to think there was much point
any more, now that the days of true prodigy were gone for
ever, but he relented in the end. Umberto was able to beat him
after a week or so. They still played sour, joyless games once
in a while. In the last of these, Umberto had deliberately played
as badly as possible, total beginner bad, comedy bad. Father
Grehan bad, apparently. His dad didn't notice and gloated for
two full hours about his eventual victory. Umberto observed
his performance with great interest and was only just able to
stop himself from taking notes.

'Father Grehan seems to lack a basic . . .'

He trailed off, not wanting to be unkind, so Father Duff
finished the sentence for him. 'Sense of what's going on? Grasp
of the rules?'

'Could be either. Could be both. It's hard to tell. Will he
not mind if we mess up the board to start a new game?'

'I'm sure he'll learn to live with the pain.'

'All right then. You can be white.'

Father Duff wasn't as bad a player as Umberto imagined he
might be. He lost, of course, but he lost in stages, through
a series of minor errors. Not for him the poorly considered
kamikaze moves that usually characterise the beginner. He
did have a tendency to leave his pawns isolated and exposed,
however.

'Pawns are vital,' Umberto told him. 'They're not much use
on their own, but if you get them working together, that's half
the battle.'

The game itself lasted for twenty minutes and then Umberto
spent another twenty telling his opponent where he had screwed

Damien Owens

up. He managed to come up with a dozen or so general pointers, each of which was greeted with glee on the other side of the coffee table. At one point, Father Duff actually rubbed his hands together like Fagan. Umberto eventually signalled the end of the conversation by folding his arms and saying, 'So that's it. That's everything I know about chess.'

It wasn't even half of what he knew, but he wanted to make it clear that this had been a one-off event which was now over.

'Well, thank you,' Father Duff said. 'That was very educational. Most enjoyable game I ever played too, even if it did mark my first defeat.'

'You're welcome,' Umberto said, and then they both went quiet. He knew it was time to say his piece. He coughed. He sighed. Nothing came out.

'So!' Father Duff said, waiting.

Umberto coughed again but stayed silent.

'Well, out with it, lad. Wasn't there something you wanted me to do for you? Did you want some information about the priesthood, was that it?'

'*No.*'

'No, didn't think so. So what is it then? Are you in trouble? Drugs, is it drugs? Don't tell me it's drugs.'

'No.'

'Drink?'

'No.'

'What then?'

'It's someone else's problem, really.'

Father Duff leaned over to give the fire a poke. A fat wave of heat rolled out. 'Go on,' he said.

208

Umberto sat back, then forward, then back again. 'Before I start,' he said, 'I want you to understand that I'm not going to name any names here, right? This is all strictly confidential.'

'Understood.'

'Right. Now. Are you any good with marriages?'

'Someone wants to get married?'

'No, they are married. I'm saying, are you any good with marriages that are in trouble? Helping the couple out.'

Father Duff shrugged. 'It depends on what kind of trouble they're in. Can you be more specific?'

'Now, I don't want you to make any hasty judgements.'

'I won't.'

'Swear?'

'Swear.' He crossed himself. Umberto was struck by the idea that a treehouse might be a more appropriate location for this kind of thing.

'OK then. Well, the thing is this. One of the people in this couple – it's the man, you might as well know – is having an affair. With another woman. Who is not his wife.'

Father Duff twirled his thumbs around each other. 'I see,' he said.

Umberto nodded gravely. 'So. What can I do?'

'What can *you* do? Why, do you mind me asking, is it anything to do with you in the first place?'

'Never mind that. I'm close to this couple, that's all you need to know.'

'How close?'

Umberto patted his knees. 'All right, I have my own reasons for not wanting to see them splitting up. Let's just say I rely on them and leave it at that.'

'OK. Now, tell me this. How do you know about this alleged affair?'

'I just know.'

'How, but?'

Umberto didn't want to admit that his evidence was entirely circumstantial. He decided to tell a minor fib.

'I overheard a conversation. All right? I overheard a conversation that I wasn't supposed to hear. Now can you help me out or not?'

It wasn't too far from the truth. After all, he had done his level best to overhear a conversation. If his mother and Mary hadn't been whispering that day, he would be telling the full truth.

'What exactly did you hear?' Father Duff asked.

'What happened to your great sense of faith? You'll have to take my word for it.'

'Hmmm,' he said. 'If you don't mind my saying so, Umberto, I think you might be a little bit out of your depth here. There's a Catholic organisation specifically for this kind of thing. They're very good. The couple go along, have a chat, explain their situation.'

'No. That won't work. I can't suggest it.'

'Why not?'

'Because they don't even know that I know. What I want . . . what I want is some sort of advice or help that I can give them without them knowing.'

Father Duff looked sceptical. 'That doesn't sound possible, let alone easy.'

Umberto pouted. 'I'm not going to sit by doing nothing. I have to try.'

This raised a smile from the priest. 'You know what helps me think, Umberto? Chess. We'll go again, and I'll have a ponder.'

'How can you think and play at the same time?'

'Dunno. Just can.'

Umberto's eyes narrowed, almost to Helmet-like dimensions. So this was how it was going to be. 'It's a deal,' he said.

The second game was shorter than its predecessor. Umberto had kept it nice and simple the first time, keeping lots of space on the board, giving his opponent plenty of options. In the second, he was more attacking and quickly gummed up both flanks in diabolically complicated knots that Father Duff was unable to disentangle. Although he ran the risk of giving the impression that he was some sort of chess master who had many more secrets to impart, he thought it was better to get it over with quickly.

'I think you were going easy on me the first time,' Father Duff said after his swift defeat. He wasn't angry – he looked impressed.

'Not really. The only reason I can beat you is you're a beginner. I'm not much good at chess, honestly I'm not.'

This was the truth, but the priest didn't look convinced. 'You could beat me and Father Grehan simultaneously blindfolded like one of those fellas on the telly.'

'No offence to Father Grehan, but I'd say the average horse could probably get a draw out of him. If you taught it a system of clumping its hoof to spell out moves.'

'Well, not the average horse. It would have to be a reasonably bright one.'

211

'Yeah. Right, then – have you had a think?'

Father Duff nodded. 'I have, despite the pressures of the game.'

'And?'

'And I think you'll have to leave it with me.'

Umberto swallowed. 'What?'

'It's a delicate matter, you know. I'll have to take a bit of time to think, maybe have a—'

'*Cheat*.'

'Excuse me?'

'You *cheated*. You promised me a status quo!'

Father Duff's eyebrows crashed together, then separated. 'You've lost me. The band?'

'What? What band? What are you talking about?'

The priest closed his eyes for a moment. 'Start again. What did I promise you?'

'A status quo. Something for something. Or is it—'

'You mean a quid pro quo.'

'I was just going to say that! I knew it was one or the other. Either way, you got another game of chess out of me and now you're trying to wriggle out of helping.'

'I didn't say I'd help, I said I'd think about it, and I will.'

Umberto stood up and grabbed his jacket from the back of the armchair. 'I don't appreciate being lied to.' He headed for the door. Father Duff rose and followed. The hall was even darker now and Umberto bashed his shin against something as he stormed down its length.

'Wait a minute, lad . . .'

He had opened the door and was halfway down the steps

before Father Duff caught up with him, placing a hand on his shoulder.

'Hang on, will you give me a chance. Come back in and we'll talk about it.'

He shrugged him away and continued down the path alone. As he came through the gate, something caught his eye to his left. He turned and saw two figures meandering along the street with cans of cider. The one on the left he didn't recognise. The one on the right was Helmet McGuiney. Helmet and Umberto looked at each other. Then Helmet looked through the railings at Father Duff. Umberto didn't give him time to turn back and wink.

He legged it.

26

It was somewhere around Ardee that the package visualisation method stopped working so well for Peter. He passed a billboard advertising the National Lottery and it set him off again. Mary had a thing about lotteries. She often said they were the perfect example of everything that was wrong with the world, chiefly but not limited to the expectation of reward without effort and the belief that money alone can make you happy. Peter disagreed. What about the charities who benefit, he argued, again and again? What about the poor and disadvantaged whose only hope of ever seeing big money is to win it? She never made much of a response. Then a few weekends ago, they'd been flicking around on the TV and happened on the lottery results. Peter had the remote and stayed on that channel, more or less for badness. That week's winner had won on a random Quick Pick.

'I betcha she feels even more guilty than normal lottery winners,' Mary noted.

'Why?'

Damien Owens

'Because she didn't even pick her own numbers, she let a machine do it for her. She has done literally nothing to deserve this. Not even tick off her kids' birthdays or whatever it is people do. It's even more embarrassing than usual.'

'That's like something Valerie would say,' Peter remarked, because it was. He didn't say it in a nasty tone, and didn't mean it in a nasty way; he thought she'd be pleased, in fact. But she went into the same kind of temper that she was in all the time these days. No shouting or throwing things, but a fierce scowl and as many dirty looks as she could muster.

Peter tried forcing himself to think about the package, but it was no use. The blue string was starting to unravel. The contents were spilling out. He groped around on the passenger seat for his mobile.

'David?'

'Y-ello? Peter?'

'Yeah. Listen . . .'

'Good man. How did it go in Dublin? Tell all.'

'What are you doing tonight?'

'Nothing that I know of. Fiona's out golfing again. I'm a free agent.'

'I want to see you. I have to talk to you about something.'

There was momentary silence on the line. 'What's wrong? You didn't even go to the training, did you? You went shopping and drinking for two days. You cheeky *bastard*.'

'No. I went all right. Lookit, can you meet me or not?'

'Yeah, sure. Pint, I suppose?'

'Fine. I'll be home about seven thirty. McShane's, all right?'

'Yeah. Ooh, I'm all excited. Should I be?'

'Seven thirty,' Peter said and hung up.

216

27

Twelve across was a bitch. Author of *The World According to Garp*. Blank, O, blank, blank, I, blank, blank, I, N, blank. Mary sucked on the end of her Biro and frowned. What the hell was her name? She wrote that book about the cruise ship as well. Damn. Valerie would know this. She was only a phone call away. There was one other unsolved clue. Seventeen down. Capital of Bolivia. L blank P blank blank. She was sure the first blank was an I. Lip something. Lipon or Lipal, maybe. Valerie would probably know that one too. In the end, Mary just filled the blanks with random letters so the crossword looked finished. No one would see it but her, she knew, but that wasn't the point. She cast the paper aside and looked at her watch. Nearly seven. Peter would probably be home soon. She thought about that and waited to see how it made her feel. She felt, ha ha, blank. Was that an improvement? She supposed so.

The card that came with the roses was in the back pocket of her jeans. She fished it out and stared at it. *From a admirer*.

And the phone number. If he was a local then he would have written the card himself, in Self-Raising Flowers probably. Graphology wasn't her thing, but she was willing to have a shot at it. The handwriting was heavily slanted to the right. That could indicate a go-getting, dynamic sort of figure. Someone who knows what he wants and isn't afraid to go after it – one of those people you hear about in American soap operas. A man of action. A doer. The letters were tall and thin. Was he? Probably not. Peter's writing was squat and round, and look at the height of him.

She racked her brain for images of dynamic go-getting men who might conceivably fancy her. There were none. She couldn't even think of any who didn't fancy her. There just weren't that many around. But then maybe she was on the wrong track completely. Never mind the slanted handwriting, sending anonymous flowers wasn't all that go-getty. It was almost childish, in Mary's book. And red roses, too. Hardly original. The choice of someone who has seen women in movies but has no idea what they're like up close. One of the pimply kids who came into the shop, maybe . . . wait a minute. There was a guy called Oliver something who came in almost every weekend. Older than Umberto, but not by much. Leaving Cert age, maybe. He wore a blue beanie and purple John Lennon sunglasses regardless of the weather and always had his Walkman on full blast so everyone around him was treated to that wasp trapped in a tin can sound. He was something of a muso, into a bit of everything, rock, dance, blues. On paper, he was one of her ideal customers, the sort she enjoyed impressing with news she'd gleaned from the magazines or the net. Or trying to impress, rather. Oliver usually knew what she was talking about and finished her sentences for her. He was quite sweet really, in a noncommunicative way. But she often got the sense that he was looking at her from behind his shades. Something to do with the angle of his head. There were times when it didn't seem to be pointing at the rack where his hands were busy flipping. It seemed to be pointing at her. And if she looked back, it dropped ever so slightly.

She smiled to herself, wondering if she had the answer. And if so, was it flattering or embarrassing? Years ago, Valerie told her that being attractive to teenage boys was a matter of simply showing up. There wasn't much glory in it. So long as you remembered to bring your breasts, you couldn't fail. On the other hand, it was nice to be fancied, no matter who was doing the fancying.

She was only human.

Eight o'clock came and went and there was still no sign of Peter. Bad traffic in the city, she guessed. God, how did they put up with it? All that noise and dirt and foul temper. And traffic was the least of the problems with city living. You also had your crime, your drugs, your homelessness. Mary didn't think she could live anywhere that had homeless people. How could you step over another human being on your way back from work, knowing that person would spend the freezing night in a shop doorway that smelled of piss? How could you live with yourself? By being anonymous, she supposed. On a day trip to Dublin, she once happened to look out of the window of a bus as it crept past a glass-fronted building. The reflection was almost perfect, but she couldn't find herself in it. She was just another head and shoulders on the top deck, not an

219

individual. Before they pulled clear of the building, she waved. One of the reflected passengers waved back, two seats behind the one that Mary was looking at. When she shifted around in her seat again, she noticed in the corner of her eye that the two middle-aged women opposite were staring at her and nudging each other. She found that she didn't care, because she would never see them again. As far as she understood it, this was a key concept of city life. You could do what you liked, because no one who knew you was watching. You could step over the homeless if you had to.

When he finally arrived, he would tell her about the course. In detail. That much was a given. There would be things she wanted to hear: what the hotel was like, what the other students were like, that sort of thing. But she would glaze over when he got technical. And he wouldn't notice. Still, she thought, squirming. Her own work stories weren't exactly edge-of-your-seat stuff either, and he never complained.

She looked at the card again. Then she returned it to her pocket and went to make a cup of tea. The phone rang before she made it into the kitchen. It was Fidelma.

'I just had to call,' she said.

'I knew you would,' Mary replied. 'What are you like?'

'So? Did you find anything out in the flower shop?'

'Nope, nothing. Because I didn't try.'

Fidelma sounded crushed. 'Oh,' she said. 'Does that mean you're not going to call the number either?'

'It'd be a bad idea,' Mary continued. 'It's probably just some kid who comes into the shop or something. I'm not going to encourage him.'

'But you must be curious! I know I am . . .'

'No.'

'Not even a wee bit?'

'I'm a married woman,' Mary said, ignoring the question. 'I can't go around chasing after secret admirers. It's insane.'

She paused then to examine what she'd said. It sounded good. She felt reassured. Relieved.

'Is it Peter?' Fidelma said, not giving up. 'Are you worried he'd find out or something?'

Mary thought about it for a moment.

'Because you could always let him in on it,' Fidelma went on. 'You know, treat it like a joke between you and then call. Just to find out. Aren't you *dying* to find out?'

'It's not Peter, Fidelma, it's me. I don't want to find out who it is. I really don't.'

'In case it's someone wonderful?'

'Fidelma!'

'Well . . .'

'Like who? Tom Cruise?'

'I dunno, do I, but someone great. You'd have something to think about then, wouldn't you? It'd be like something out of the movies, even if it wasn't Tom Cruise. God, I'm so jealous. You wouldn't have to *do* anything. Just find out who it is. For the laugh.'

Mary chewed the nail of her index finger. 'No,' she said. 'No, it wouldn't be anyone good. I'm telling you, I bet it's some kid from the shop. Or someone who has me mixed up with Valerie.'

'Are you trying to convince me or yourself?'

'I'm convincing you, Fidelma. Now, let's drop this, OK? It never happened. I'm putting the card in the bin and that'll be the end of it.'

'No, wait! How about this, then? Give me the number. *I'll* call. For the crack. I'll ask who it is and pretend to have the wrong number or something.'

Mary's first instinct was to say no. She heard the word in her head and started to form it with her lips. En-oh, NO. Something went wrong, though.

'All right,' she said, and reached for her back pocket.

28

Peter arrived in McShane's to find David already installed at a corner table. There was someone with him. The third party had his back to the door but it was obviously Andy Sweeney, an old classmate from school. No one else they knew had hair that colour, not so much ginger as luminous orange.

'There's himself,' David said as he arrived.

'David. *Andy*.'

'Slim, how are ye?' Andy said and smiled. Peter wished he hadn't. The smile itself wasn't too bad, but the teeth it revealed still bore the traces of several recent meals.

'Not bad. All right for pints, are we?'

David and Andy mumbled and pointed to almost full glasses. Peter went to the bar to get one for himself. On the way back, he managed to catch David's eye and nod at Andy. The nod meant 'What did you bring him for?' David gave his head the tiniest shake. The shake meant 'I didn't.' Peter had suspected as much. He was all right, Andy, but no one in their right mind would voluntarily go out for a drink with him, not unless the bar was in some exclusive gentlemen's club where there was no possibility that he might bump into women. For bumping into women was Andy's thing. Over the years, Peter and David had speculated endlessly about the Sweeney Method, as they called it. Was it the brainchild of someone who knew no fear, who believed in death or glory? Or did it denote some peculiar mental imbalance, possibly something that required professional treatment?

Andy first espoused the Method at school, claiming to have noticed something peculiar about television romances, namely that they often began with an accidental bump. In a typical example, he lectured, a woman is struggling with shopping, usually American TV shopping, the kind with a French bread sticking out of a brown paper bag. The man is strolling along, not paying attention, and bumps into her. Oops. The shopping goes all over the place. Apples roll away, jars smash. 'You clumsy fool!' she says, getting down to pick up the mess. 'I'm sorry, let me help you,' he says and joins her on the floor. They might knock heads at that stage and they might not, Andy explained. That was optional. But they certainly have meaningful eye contact. The tension evaporates. She smiles. He smiles. Then he gets up, and helps her to her feet. Next thing you know, they're leaving a trail of clothes to the bed and someone has started playing a saxophone.

Andy took this notion and ran with it, launching himself at unsuspecting females in the street or in the pub and sometimes giving them a gentle headbutt for good measure. It almost always failed, of course, the encounter ending with the girl screaming and sometimes punching him. But once in a while, it worked. That was the amazing thing – once in a while, it *worked*. He was still at it today, although by now every woman in the town knew all about it. Quite a few of them crossed streets to avoid him.

'Andy can't stay,' David said. He appeared to be reminding Andy as much as telling Peter.

'I've got kendo,' Andy said.

Peter pulled a face. 'Which one's kendo? Is that the one—'

'Beating the shite out of people with a stick.' Andy nodded. 'Great crack. They do it in the community centre, Mondays and Thursdays. You should give it a go.'

'There's nobody I want to hit with a stick.'

'That's not the point. It's good for you, gets you in touch with . . . well, I forget. But it gets you in touch with something.'

'I hope you're not going to start incorporating it into the Method,' David said. 'We wouldn't want that, would we?'

'No fear,' Andy said, swishing his pint around in its glass. 'The Method is sound, tried and tested. You don't go messing with a winning formula. And anyway, I think those days are behind me.'

Peter and David said, 'Oh?' together.

Andy took an enormous gulp of his pint and nodded. 'Aye. It's getting serious, me and Frances.'

Frances was Frances Reilly, someone Andy had bumped into only a few months previously. In an off-licence. She dropped her vodka, which smashed. Andy bought her another, then followed her to the party she was attending. He told them all about it the last time they met, using several colourful expressions to describe her enthusiasm for the physical act of love. At the time, it hadn't sounded serious.

225

'So, what? Wedding bells?' Peter said. He expected an immediate denial.

Andy said nothing for a moment. Then he drained his pint and said, 'Maybe. Who knows?'

Peter and David looked at each other and then back at Andy.

'Good for you,' David said. 'I hope it all works out. Marriage is a wonderful thing.'

'Hmmm,' Peter said.

Andy pushed his glass away and rose, snatching his jacket from the back of the chair. 'Ta. Right, gotta go. See yiz around, sure.'

They said goodbyes and watched him go.

'Sorry,' David said when the pub door swung shut behind him. 'He was here on his own when I arrived.'

'Never mind,' Peter said.

David sat back and folded his arms. 'So!' he said. 'Tell all.'

Time was against him – he should have been home by now – but Peter took a moment to provide a backdrop for his story. He did his best, but was unable to describe the full horror of the course itself. The best he could do was to ask David to imagine being stuck in a lift with a Jehovah's Witness, an office supplies salesman and an urban district councillor seeking re-election. To his credit, David looked suitably appalled. Then Peter cut to the chase.

'D'ye ever remember me talking about Regina Clarke, from college?'

David scratched his cheek. 'Yeah, I think so. Pain in the ring?'

'That's her. Well, she was there.'

'Taking the course?'

'And the piss, as usual. She hasn't changed a bit. I nearly ran out of the door when I saw her. Anyway, I got stuck with her yesterday, and she wanted to know my whole life story, just so she could tell me where I went wrong.'

He paused to take a drink. David followed suit.

'To cut a long story short, she insisted – insisted, mind – that we go out for dinner together. Just the two of us.'

David pursed his lips.

'So we did,' Peter said. 'Indian. Now, I didn't even want to go; you remember the way I used to go on about her. I'd rather have dinner with a fucking leopard. But she *insisted*.'

David looked at his lap and said, 'Oh-oh.'

'And she doesn't let up, even in the restaurant, making her bitchy remarks, cutting me to the bone every chance she gets. And then . . . then she starts on about Mary.'

David looked up. 'What about Mary?'

'About how weird it is that we're still together. That's her word, now, not mine. Weird. She said people used to talk about us even back in Dundalk. She couldn't believe we're still together.'

'I hope you're not going to tell me you took her seriously. Jesus, Peter, it's not ten minutes since you were telling me about Finbarr frigging Grealey saying you should up your game in the bedroom. What's the matter with you? You listen to *me* and no one else. How many times—'

Peter shook his head firmly. 'I don't give two shites what Regina Clarke thinks. *I* don't think we're weird. We've had that conversation before, Mary and me.'

227

'Well, good.'

'But what if she's having a change of heart? Our anniversary is tomorrow. Maybe it's preying on her mind. Maybe she's wondering how things would be different if—'

'Oh, leave yourself alone. Listen to me now. There's nothing wrong with Mary, from what you've told me anyway. I've told you once and I'm telling you again – show the woman some romance! The anniversary is the perfect opportunity. She'll perk right up, I'm telling you. Never fails with Fiona. Are you listening to me?'

'Yeah, yeah, romance, got it. But, eh . . . that's not the point. That wasn't all that happened at dinner.'

David rested his elbows on the table and rubbed his temples. 'Go on.'

'Well. She wasn't just giving her words of wisdom, she was flirting. She kept touching my hand and cracking jokes about me being a married man and what if someone saw us together, all that sort of thing.'

'And?'

'And we had a couple of bottles of wine with dinner. I don't drink wine normally and I was drunk. I don't mind admitting it, I was *drunk*.'

Now David put his hands over his ears. 'Oh . . . my . . . God.'

'Don't worry, nothing happened. Not what you think anyway. But . . .' He paused to take another drink. 'But it all went . . . wrong. *Titanic* wrong, Millennium Dome wrong.'

'I'm waiting.'

'It was bad enough in the restaurant, all these questions about my marriage, and a lot of touching, big-time eye contact. Then she said we should have a nightcap back at the hotel – *my* hotel, which wasn't her hotel.'

'Did she use the word "nightcap"?'

'Yes. She did. See what I mean?'

'Fair enough. Nightcap is a filthy word.'

'That's what I'm telling you. I was really sick of her at that stage and I was panicking about all the flirting, so I said no.'

'Well, that's something.'

'We're standing on the pavement at this stage, arguing back and forth about it. I say we have to get up for the course in the morning, she says I'm a boring old fart, that sort of thing, back and forth, back and forth. And she had her hands on my elbows the whole time, sort of pulling me towards her.'

'Where are your hands?'

'In my pockets.'

'Right.'

'Right. By then, I thought it was so obvious that she was coming on to me that something needed to be said, you know, to clear the air, set her straight.'

'Sure.'

'But I . . . fucked it up.'

'I'm listening.'

'Well, I'd been getting the impression all night that she's become a bit insecure, Regina, and I didn't want to make her feel bad by rejecting her out of hand. Or maybe she was insecure all along and we just didn't notice. You know? That's the way I was thinking: don't be callous, make her feel that it's nothing to do with her.'

'Get on with it, Peter, I can't stand it. What did you say to her?'

229

'I said, look, I'd love to ask you in for a drink – I didn't say nightcap, now, I said drink – but I'm a married man, a happily married man, and it could lead to . . . complications. I told her I found her very attractive – which was a lie – and that maybe in other circumstances, all that.'

'Well, that's fair enough, isn't it?'

'That's what I thought. I was wrong. She dropped my elbows and jumped back, like she'd had an electric shock. That was my first clue that I might have been mistaken. I got my second clue when she stepped forward again and punched me really, *really* hard in the bollocks.'

'*No!* Punched you? Not kicked?'

'What? What difference does it make?'

David shrugged. 'Well, a kick is more traditional, isn't it?'

'She was wearing a long skirt.'

'Ah. It hasn't been a good week for your groin region, has it?'

'No. It hasn't. She left me plums—' He looked around for eavesdroppers. 'She left me plums sitting in me stomach. It was agony.'

'Did you puke? I came down on the crossbar of my bike once and I puked rings around me.'

'Nearly. I was doubled over for a while and then I sort of collapsed. But that pain passes. What doesn't pass is back pain, as I know all too well. And I nearly broke mine when I landed on my arse. It's still killing me today.'

David shook his head remorsefully. 'You have my sympathies.'

'Hang on. I haven't told you the bad bit yet.'

'The bad bit? What's worse than a punch in the goolies and a broken back?'

'I'll tell you. She goes into this rant, reading me the riot act about how she wouldn't touch me with a bargepole, people like me should be locked up, she had a good mind to call the Guards, all this. I'm seeing stars and trying not to heave, people are staring at us. David, it was a frigging *nightmare*. And then she says she has a good mind to call Mary and tell her.'

'Tell her! Tell her what?'

'That we'd been out for dinner and that it ended up with me trying to get into her pants.'

'But—'

'But nothing. I said I'd been doing no such thing and if anyone was trying to get into someone's pants, it was her into mine.'

'Hang on, what about sparing her feelings and all that?'

'That was all forgotten about. So there we were, me on me arse, back in spasms, balls like oranges, and her standing over me with her hands on her hips, arguing about who was trying to do what with whose pants.'

'Well, she was obviously feeling rejected and took it out on you, trying to save face.'

Peter shook his head. 'Nuh-uh. She really was just being friendly. The way she saw it, she was having a nice meal and a chat and maybe a late drink and then I started going on about how attractive she was and . . . so on.'

'That's ridiculous. She got shot down and she—'

'David, she's a lesbian.'

The word caused David to pause, but he wasn't knocked

off his stride entirely. 'You mean she said she was a lesbian so you—'

'No, I mean she's a real lesbian.'

This time he was properly flummoxed. 'How do you know? Did she whip out some lesbian ID?'

'No, she roared it at me, in a sort of aside. But she sounded serious. I certainly believed her.'

'I suppose so. So how did it end?'

'It ended when she got hoarse from shouting and stormed off. I crawled back into the restaurant and called a taxi to the hotel. But I had to see her all day again today.'

'And?'

'She completely ignored me, apart from dirty looks. I tried to speak to her when the course finished, but she walked past me like I wasn't there.'

'So now what?'

'Exactly. Now what? We're in the phone book. Maybe she meant it. Maybe she's going to lift the phone and tell Mary the whole thing. Oh, Christ . . .'

'All right, all right, calm yourself. For one thing, she's not going to ring. That's all bluster, I'm telling you. What's in it for her? Nothing.'

'Revenge! You didn't see the look in her eyes, David, she was really mad.'

'OK then, supposing she does ring. Laugh it off. Tell Mary what you told me. You didn't do anything wrong, did you?'

'Well, no, not technically. But the humour she's in these days, Mary'd probably believe her. And even if she didn't believe the end bit, I still went out for dinner and didn't even call home to say hello. I was too rattled and it was too late and—'

'You're underestimating her, Peter. Come on, she knows you'd never do anything like that. Look at me and Fiona. I make a point of telling her every time someone flirts with me.'

'What? When do you get flirted with? I thought your flirting days were over.'

'I resent your tone. All the time, that's when, out on jobs, in the supermarket, anywhere. I go home and I tell Fiona and we have a good laugh about it. She knows nothing would ever come of it and that's that.'

'Does she tell you when men flirt with her?'

'Now that you mention it, no. But that's not the point. The point is, you're getting your knickers in a knot about nothing. It was an unpleasant evening that is now over. Just forget about it. And forget about Finbarr and his nonsense and whether or not you're a weird couple and all that other crap you're obsessing about. You'll have a great night tomorrow and everything will be back to normal. Remember, now — flowers, chocolates, candles, a bit of effort. I know what I'm talking about here. You'll see. You've got things organised, haven't you?'

'I haven't had a chance, have I? And whatever I come up with, it won't be that candles bollocks. It'll have to be something special. I'll get it organised tomorrow.'

'Suit yourself, but do something for God's sake. Mark my words, if you let your first anniversary pass by like any other day, she'll make you sorry. Now. Do you want another pint?'

Peter looked at his watch. 'Shit, no, I should get back home. I'm overdue as it is.'

'Fair enough. Before you go: I am reminded of an old joke that might cheer you up.'

'I doubt it. Go on anyway.'

'Two women and a man are standing at a bus stop. The women are talking about pain, what's the worst kind of pain. One of them says migraine is the worst, you can hardly see, it's like your head is stuck in a vice, terrible altogether. Her friend says nothing beats a really bad toothache. You can't rub it or soothe it in any way, it's buried away there in your jaw, throb, throb, throb. Your man listens for a while, shaking his head, and eventually he can be silent no longer. He coughs and says, "Excuse me, I couldn't help but overhear what you were saying and I was just wondering. Have either of you ladies ever taken a good smack in the balls?"'

Peter didn't laugh. But he nodded his head in solemn agreement.

29

'This has all the hallmarks,' Father Grehan said, 'of something you should run a mile from. Take it from me. I know what I'm talking about.'

Father Duff settled into his armchair and waited for the story to begin. All Father Grehan's serious advice was given in anecdotal form. Some of these anecdotes struck Father Duff as being wildly unlikely. One or two had plots he'd seen on TV shows that he and Father Grehan had watched together.

'I'm going back now, oh, twenty years maybe. Lord, it could be more. Anyway, one summer I went home to Athlone for a week or so to pay a visit, you know, to catch up with the family. I was staying with Emma, the sister. Now, Emma had a neighbour she was friendly with, a quiet wee woman name of Helen. They weren't terribly close or anything, but they'd stand and chat in the street, or have the odd cup of tea in the other one's kitchen, that sort of thing. A week or so before I arrived, this Helen had called in to Emma in an awful state, in tears. She said she had no one to turn to, no one you could really call a friend and no family in the town – she was from the north, I think. The problem was her husband, Charlie. He was hitting the bottle very hard. He wasn't a bad man, she said, he had that terrible illness, that was all. He wasn't violent or anything like that, and he wasn't, you know, rolling in the gutters at three in morning. But it was heading that way and she was getting to the end of her tether. They were starting to have money trouble and there were a lot of rows. According to Emma, Helen was talking about upping and leaving him to it. There were no children to worry about and she seemed to be deadly serious.'

'And your sister asked you to help?'

Father Grehan adjusted his glasses on his nose. 'No. She was telling me about it more or less in passing and I volunteered. I know a good bit about alcoholics, sure me best friend in . . . well, I told you all that before. I told Emma I could go and have a word with Charlie. Not to do anything dramatic, just to explain that he could get help. And to tell him that he *better* get it if he loved his wife. I thought it might sound more . . . shocking coming from a total stranger. And he was a religious man by all accounts, so I thought that might work to my advantage.'

That was the thing, Father Duff thought. Umberto's parents weren't even religious. Why would they listen to a priest?

'Emma thought this was a great idea, and so did Helen,' Father Grehan continued. 'So she arranged to be out one evening and I called to the house. Early, before he could make any real headway with the brandy. Normal-looking terraced house, exactly like my sister's, you'd never guess anything was wrong inside. I rang the doorbell and he answered it. Big, big man, he was, heavy-set. Pleasant, though, a smile and a "What can I do for you, Father?" Maybe he assumed I was collecting. So I told him who I was and wondered if I could have a word. What about, he says, all suspicious now. I said I'd rather come in first, if that was all right. He obviously didn't want me to come in, but he stepped back anyway. The place was normal inside too, quite neat and tidy. He sat in one armchair and I sat in the other, the way we're sitting now in fact, by the fire. No, range. It was a range. I got straight to the point. I told him I'd heard that he had a problem and that I wanted to help.'

He adjusted his glasses again and shook his head.

'Looking back, I don't know what I was thinking. No one wants complete strangers showing up on their door telling them that they know all about their innermost secrets and shames. I should have realised that. First thing Charlie wanted to know was who had I been talking to. I told him that his wife had gone to my sister for help, in desperation. He started shaking his head and laughing. "That's a good one," he says. "She's something else." I asked him what he meant and—'

'I think I can guess,' Father Duff said. He knew that Father Grehan didn't like to be interrupted once he got the wind in his sails but he had a thing about listening to stories when he knew where they were going. Jokes, especially. When someone told him a joke he knew, he couldn't fake it, he always had to stop them in mid-flow.

'Go on then,' Father Grehan said, slightly peeved. 'Guess.'

'It turns out that the husband is a teetotaller and the wife is the alcoholic. It's a cry for help. He couldn't or wouldn't help so she had to go elsewhere.'

'Close enough, I suppose. Not exactly right. They were both drinkers. Which of them was the worst at the time, I

237

don't know. Maybe she was, since she was the one looking for help. It doesn't matter. They were lonely, awkward people who never had money or much success of any kind in life and now they were getting towards the wrong end of middle age and they were depressed and terrified. He didn't tell me any of this, now, that's only me talking. He just told me that if either of them had a drink problem it was her and, in any case, it was none of my business or my sister's for that matter and, may God forgive him, would I please get out of his house and not come back.'

There was a pause that Father Duff was reluctant to fill. He didn't want to do anything else that could be construed as interrupting. Father Grehan looked at the fire for a while — hoping to generate more atmosphere, the sole member of his audience suspected — before he continued.

'Well, I didn't know what to do. As far as I was concerned, I was dealing with the set-up you guessed. I gave him all the cry-for-help stuff and told him there were lots of dedicated and sincere people she could turn to, but he'd have to be supportive. He stood up then, not a word out of him, and led me out by the arm, physically escorted me out. I had to leave town again the next day, or maybe it was the day after, but Emma kept me updated. Helen admitted to her that she took a drink herself but laughed at the idea that she needed help. Ridiculous, she said. She insisted that Charlie was the one with the problem. Emma decided that the best thing was to leave them to it, which I can understand.'

'So how did it end up?'

'The last I heard about it was three or four years later. I got a phone call one morning from Emma, saying that Charlie was dead of a heart attack. Could have been drink-related or maybe not. Helen wasn't seen much after that – even less than usual. But she was the real thing by then, full-blown as they say. One of those people that you cross the street to avoid. To be honest, I stopped asking about her after a while. I was too embarrassed.'

'You did nothing wrong, though. You were only trying to do the right thing.'

'So what? I didn't help, did I? I probably made it worse. If I'd stayed out of it, Helen might have eventually gone for proper, professional help. So might Charlie, in the end.'

Father Duff wasn't sure he understood the point being made. 'So you're saying I shouldn't try to help Umberto's parents in case I make it worse?'

'I'm saying you have to be very careful when it comes to giving advice to total strangers. I mean, what do you know about these people? Nothing. You don't even know anything about their son. Maybe he's imagined this whole thing with his father and the other woman. He had no proof, had he? Lord, for all you know, he could be trying to make mischief. He is a teenager, don't forget. Maybe they've done something to annoy him and he's trying to get his own back by embarrassing them.'

This wasn't the worst theory Father Duff had ever heard. If the stigmata incident was anything to go by, then Umberto was something of a practical joker. What if they'd stopped his pocket money or something and his idea of revenge was to get a priest round asking about their marriage? Then again, he'd seemed very earnest when he brought it up earlier. And coming to the priests' house obviously made him uncomfortable. It wasn't the sort of thing he'd do for a laugh. Besides, he hadn't asked for any personal involvement. He said he wanted advice, not intervention. There was no need to mention that to Father Grehan, though. It would be grist to his mill.

'I don't think so. He was definitely worried. And he was extremely upset when I hesitated about helping. Not just my-joke-isn't-working upset, properly upset. I think he's genuinely afraid of trouble ahead, divorce even.'

'Even assuming he's sincere,' Father Grehan said, 'you should still stay out of it. For a start, he could have it all wrong about this alleged affair. What's he basing it on? You don't know, do you? Are you going to stick your nose into someone else's marriage with nothing more to go on but the unproven say-so of a child? I don't care how smart he is. You'd want to be mad in the head. And, all right, let's give him every benefit of every doubt. Suppose he isn't just pulling your leg and suppose he's got the whos and whats right too. The fact remains: it's none of your business. They aren't members of your church. And even if they were, I'd still tread carefully. I'm telling you, forget about it.'

A certain tone had crept into his voice. Father Duff guessed he was disappointed that his anecdote hadn't worked on its own.

'Well, what if your sister had told you about the alcoholic down the road who needed help and you had done nothing?'

'Were you not listening, man? I *do* wish I had done nothing.'

'Do you, though? What if you heard the outcome of the story later, knowing you didn't even try? You'd feel a lot worse.'

It was hard to know when Father Grehan was squinting suspiciously. His eyes were mere dots behind those glasses at the best of times. But it seemed to Father Duff that he was squinting suspiciously now. Something in the topography of his brow had changed. 'What's behind all this, Miles?' he wanted to know. 'Why are you all fired up about this boy? I thought you said he laughed at the idea of the priesthood. You can't force him to be interested, you know.'

It was a fair point, Father Duff thought. And it was certainly true that Umberto no longer struck him as priest material, even if he did appear to have certain qualities. He tried to come up with a plausible answer, one that would satisfy himself as much as Father Grehan. Anything other than 'He's good at chess.'

'I dunno,' he said eventually. 'I just want to help.'

30

Mary had nodded off while lying on the sofa waiting for Peter. She woke up when he tapped her on the shoulder, just as his face homed in on hers to plant a kiss. Her scream wasn't particularly loud but it was unexpected. Peter jumped to his feet from the kneeling position, puffing in pain as he did so.

'Sorry, sorry,' Mary said, sitting up and rubbing her eyes. 'Did you hurt your back?'

He was always hurting his back getting up too quickly. She said the solution was simple: stop getting up too quickly. Peter said that was easier said than done.

'No, I'm fine,' he gasped, lowering himself down beside her on the sofa. 'Slept awkwardly, that's all. So, I'm home. Miss me?'

'Of course,' she said, and hugged his neck, causing him to squeak like a dog's toy. It was a lie, but only a small one. She hadn't missed him because there hadn't really been time. She didn't feel bad about saying it because she knew that she would have done in another day or so.

'I missed you too,' he said. 'Anything strange while I was away?'

Mary swallowed. 'Not a thing. I'll make tea.'

'Stay where you are, you're grand. I'll get it.'

He struggled to his feet and hobbled off towards the kitchen. 'You're still limping,' she said. 'Are you sure you're OK?'

'Getting better all the time,' he called, somewhat unconvincingly Mary thought. For the first time, she found herself wishing she'd witnessed the spectacle at the pitch and putt course. David would have an eyewitness account, and he always told a good yarn. She'd have to get all the details next time she saw him.

'How was it, then?' she asked. 'Was it worth going?'

'Hang on, I'll tell you in a minute.' Tea-making noises followed. When he returned with the tray he said, 'I can't do it justice, I haven't got the vocabulary. I'll tell you this: it made that afternoon with your Uncle Larry feel like a trip in the space shuttle.'

Mary whistled, impressed. The afternoon with Uncle Larry was the benchmark by which they judged discomfort. Larry was her father's brother, a factory manager of some description living in Wicklow. He and James hadn't spoken in nearly twenty years because of a row about their mother's will. One Saturday afternoon not long after Peter and Mary were married he called in unannounced on his way home from some shindig he'd attended in Derry. Mary had met him only two or three times as a child – she had no idea where he got their address – and he was a total stranger to Peter. Nevertheless, he stayed for two full hours, during which time he stared at the carpet and spoke only when spoken to. Even then, his answers were almost entirely monosyllabic. They could hear their own heartbeats. Mary initially guessed that he was working towards some sort of reconciliation with James and the family in general and tried to steer the conversation, such as it was, in that direction. But she was apparently mistaken. He didn't want to visit Valerie and Jeff, and he certainly didn't want to visit James and Elizabeth. He was just 'showing his face'. When informed about the visit later, James shrugged his shoulders and concluded that 'the old bastard was probably just gasping for a cup of tea.'

'At least we could laugh about Uncle Larry afterwards,' Peter said. 'I can't see me ever laughing about that bloody course.'

Mary braced herself for the technical details, but none was forthcoming. She found that she was curiously disappointed.

'What were the other people like?' she asked. 'Any familiar faces?'

'Like who?' Peter said, giving her a strange look.

'Well, I don't know, like anybody. Don't you see the same people over and over again at these things?'

'Oh. No. Most people are smart enough to get out of going to more than one every couple of years. Mind you, they're always the same *sort* of people. Trekkers with dandruff, most of them. Some of them, anyway. You know the type.'

She nodded. She did indeed. 'I thought you might have called last night,' she said.

'I meant to. I really did. But . . . but a few of us went out for a drink after the course, and time got away from me. I was going to call when I got back to the hotel, but—'

'It's all right.'

'I intended to.'

'Forget about it.' She meant it, and smiled to underline the fact.

Later, they watched TV in the semi-dark, Peter stretched out in an armchair, Mary curled up on the sofa. Peter had the remote and was moving around the channels in endless circles, tutting every so often as the same chortling gameshow hosts and mournful talking heads reappeared.

'Face it, there's nothing on,' Mary said, lifting her cheek from her shoulder to make herself heard.

'Looks that way. Will, eh . . . will I nip out and get a video? It's not too late, is it?'

She heard the uncertainty in his voice. He was testing her mood.

'I'll get whatever you want,' he added. 'Anything.'

Mary thought for a moment. 'Let's see now, lemme think. Oh! Fidelma was telling me about this new one she saw, just out the other day. Brilliant, she said. But you wouldn't like it . . .'

'No, go on, anything,' Peter said. 'Whatever you want.' He emphasised the latter phrase.

'Well, it's about this wee boy who gets some rare disease, a skin thing. It isn't life-threatening or anything but he turns a horrible shade of green and all the other kids at school call him names and laugh at him. He's a baseball player or rather, what do they call it, eh, little league. All he wants to do is play little league but he can't any more because he's gone green and it puts the other teams' pitchers off.'

She saw Peter clenching every muscle in his body. 'Sounds all right,' he croaked.

'Fidelma loved it anyway,' Mary said. 'She said it was very

uplifting, all about how this boy triumphs over adversity. I think there was some mention of the family rallying together and realising what's important in life too.'

'Great,' Peter whimpered.

'It's called *The Boy who Turned Green*.'

His voice failed him for a moment. 'Good title,' he eventually gasped.

She should have stopped it there, but she didn't. 'OK,' she said. 'Get that.'

'Right. I will. Wanna come for the spin?'

'Nah. I'll stay here. You go.'

He nodded and slowly withdrew his legs, then raised himself into a standing position, frowning hard as he did so. 'I won't be long,' he said, and left.

As soon as the door closed, Mary took a seat by the front room window and watched him inch his way down the drive with feet splayed, like an arthritic penguin. He opened the car door and lowered himself in with great care, but still managed to bump his head. He was always bumping his head on this or that. Mary raised a hand to her mouth and caught a laugh. That was Peter, that was her husband. Too tall and awkward for his own good. Never out of pain. And desperate to please her. As the car pulled away, she started to sob.

The net curtain made a poor handkerchief but she used it to dab at her nose and eyes anyway. After a while, her breathing began to return to normal and she got to her feet, feeling completely ridiculous. There was a mirror in the hall. She went to it and looked at herself. The puffy eyes and make-up streaks were a rare sight, now presented for the second time in a week. Mary

247

Damien Owens

wasn't a crier, and never had been. It was something she'd prided herself on since childhood. In the days when her friends became hysterical at the merest misfortune like a lost doll or a bruised knee, not even a dead pet could break her down, and she'd had her share of those. Bugs the rabbit, Rover the guinea pig, Fluffy the rabbit, George the dog, Sammy the hamster, Robbie the rabbit, Patches the cat, all came and went, and not a tear was shed. Not by Mary, anyway; her father took it hard when Patches ate something he shouldn't have and then took three days to die a mewling death in his smelly corner of the shed. But then her father had always had a soft spot for Patches, a creature who seemed to have been deliberately designed to inspire sympathy. He earned his name not by being a pleasant patchwork of colours, but by being entirely bald in spots. If feline alopecia had been his only problem, he would have been merely pathetic. What raised him to the level of the genuinely tragic was the litany of other ailments that blighted his sorry life: the comical obesity, the blue-grey cataracts on both eyes, the deep scar on his long white nose, the chronic flatulence, the limp, the bent tail, the half-chewed ear. He looked like a cartoon cat who'd just been caught in a cartoon bomb. When he gurgled his last, Mary limited her response to remarking that he was probably better off.

Her parents seemed to think it strange that she was so unaffected by these and other childhood catastrophes. But Valerie frequently offered her congratulations, assuring Mary that crying was for 'girlies', the semi-mythical frilly doll's-house owners who were her sworn enemy. Mary remembered being pleased, but failing to see what she'd done to earn the praise. What was so terrible about a dead rabbit or dog or cat? What

248

was the big deal? It was sad, that was all. Not the end of the world. They weren't people. People said they 'loved' them, but did they really? Mary hoped not. She had her own vision of love and it was a bigger thing than that.

She stared at her crumpled face for twenty minutes or more, poking around in her mind, until she heard the car outside. And she kept on staring, waiting for his key to turn in the lock.

'What? What is it? What happened?' Peter had her by the shoulders, his video dropped to the floor. 'Mary! You're scaring me. What's wrong?'

The tears had started again, but she was smiling through them. 'I'm sorry,' she said, clapping her hand over her mouth.

'For what? Come on, sit down.'

He led her by the hand into the sitting room and on to the sofa. 'Tell me. Please.'

'Don't look so worried,' she said and sniffed.

'I am. I am worried. What is it? Tell me.'

Mary leaned forward on to her knees and rubbed her forehead with both hands. 'I feel so stupid.'

'Why?'

'For getting so worked up.'

'Don't be silly. Tell me what it is you're worked up about.'

She sniffed again and slapped her knees. 'I'm so sorry. I've been taking it out on you. But it's me. As well. Both of us, I mean.'

'What, Mary? What are you talking about? Tell me.'

She brushed some hair out of her eyes and took a deep breath. 'I've worked it out – what's been bothering me. What's *really* been bothering me. This last while, I think I, you know, with

Damien Owens

the anniversary coming up and all, I started to look around at ev—'

'I knew it! I *knew* it! It's me, isn't it? That row about the video wasn't about the video at all. You're sick of me. I'm disappointing you. Oh, God, I knew it . . .'

Mary thumped him on the thigh, not hard, but not gently either. 'Please – let me explain.'

'Sorry, sorry. Go on.'

'And stop apologising. You've got nothing to apologise for.'

'Sorry.'

'What I'm trying to say is, with the anniversary coming up and all, maybe I got a wee bit . . . you know . . . introspective. Did a bit too much thinking. There's such a thing. It happened to be the anniversary, but I suppose it could have been a birthday or anything.'

She looked at him directly, waiting for him to interrupt. He didn't, but grabbed her hand and squeezed. She continued, wiping her eyes with her free hand.

'I've been sniping at you – and my parents too, I suppose – not because of anything you've done, but because . . . because you remind me of what's wrong with me.'

He didn't seem to take offence and squeezed again. 'Which is?'

'Peter, I'm so *ordinary*. I'm unexotic. Average.'

He leaned closer still. 'Bullshit. You're not ordinary, Mary. You're—'

'Yes, I *am*. I am. And so are you. We're common-or-garden. Look at me, I don't know anything about anything. I've never even heard of Cockstump!'

250

Peter blanched but didn't get a chance to speak.

'I don't go on safaris or read big thick books about the bloody universe. I've never lived anywhere but this tiny town and I've been with the same . . . I've been with the same man more or less since I was a frigging *child*.'

'If that's the—'

'Let me finish. The thing is . . . I don't care. I'm ordinary and I'm always going to be ordinary because I'm *content* with being ordinary. You get what you settle for, don't you? And I seem to have settled.'

Peter squeezed her hand again. 'But that's a good thing! Isn't it? To be content?'

'How can it be? How can it be good to be so unambitious?'

He thought hard before replying. 'Don't think of it as unambitious. Think of it as satisfied. I mean . . . you're telling me that you're unhappy because you're happy.'

'No. I'm telling you I'm unhappy because I've got no . . . I'm never going to . . . well . . .'

'Go on.'

She tucked her hair behind her ear. 'You're right. I know you're right.'

'Of course I'm right. Wanting nothing is most people's *goal* in life. You've done it already.' He smiled and pulled her to his chest, kissed the top of her head. 'All right, so you've got a boring, go-nowhere husband—'

She sat up straight again immediately. 'No, Peter. That's not what I'm trying to say. All right, so I took it out on you. But you haven't done anything wrong.'

'But you've obviously started thinking we're strange again.'

251

'You're not listening to me. It's nothing to do with me and you.'

'You just said as much a minute ago. You said, "I've been with the same—"'

'OK, then. Yes. I do think we're strange. So do you, I bet, if you're honest. But so what? We're lucky to be this strange. Lots of people would give their right arms.'

He nodded. 'See? You're making my argument for me. That's exactly what I was about to tell you.'

'I know, I know. I'm an eejit.'

'Yeah, you are.'

He held her in silence for a while.

'Are you sure you're going to be all right?' he said then. 'Tell me what I can do to help, and I'll do it.'

'I'll be fine.'

'Well, what about a holiday? We could pack up and head off for a couple of weeks. Or a month. Whatever you want.'

'A month? And how would we be paying for this jaunt?'

'How does anybody pay for anything? We'll get a loan.'

'There's no need. I don't *want* to go anywhere. I'll be grand.'

'I should do something. I couldn't even get you the right film.'

'What?'

'*The Boy who Turned Green*. They didn't have it.'

'Jesus, Peter, there's no such film. Sorry. I couldn't resist it. I didn't think you'd actually go.'

Peter silently let go of her hand and went out to the hall. He returned with a video and placed it on her lap. It was *Fargo*.

'Don't worry about it,' he said. 'I got this instead. I think I ruined it for you last time. And it seemed pretty good. Wanna try it again?'

She looked at the tape and then at Peter. He would do the voices again. He wouldn't be able to help himself.

'Nah,' she said. 'Let's have an early night.'

Having an early night was the euphemism they had employed throughout their entire sex life, right from the start. It was the corniness of the phrase that had first appealed to them. They liked the idea of sounding like a bored middle-aged couple when really they were hot young things. Now the phrase had taken on a life of its own, to the extent that Peter sometimes told jokes that started 'This prostitute and her client are having an early night up against a wall . . .' or 'This man goes to the doctor and says, "Doctor, my wife and I were having an early night yesterday afternoon . . ."'

Peter placed his hands in the small of his back. 'The thing is . . .'

Mary looked away. Maybe there was a limit to his willingness to please after all. Then he climbed slowly to his feet.

'On the other hand . . .' he said.

253

31

Umberto slept in on Friday morning. At half past eight, when he should have been closing the door of The Cottage behind him, he was still curled up in bed having a fantastically realistic dream in which Peter and Mary hung by their fingertips from a high wire suspended over a waterfall. Every so often one of them would kick at the other, while from a rowboat below, Umberto begged them to see sense. They were both laughing; he was not. He was having difficulty keeping the boat in one place too, and was in imminent danger of being sucked into the white water. It seemed to go on for hours.

When he woke up – just as he finally began to drown – he peered bleary-eyed at his apparently unset alarm clock and moaned from the pit of his stomach. Normal parents, he fumed, would be up and about by now, reminding him of the time. He gave himself another couple of minutes to consider and then dismiss the possibility of taking a sickie before rolling slowly out of bed, already wondering why he had bothered.

*   *   *

First class of the day was history, which was lucky. It was taught by Noel 'Woody' Allen, a man who tolerated anything short of open brawling among his students. Some put his casual attitude down to reverse psychology; others claimed that he simply didn't give a shit. Either way, he wasn't the sort to get all hot and bothered by a rare display of tardiness from one of his better students. Umberto gave the classroom door a single tap and entered sheepishly, staring at his feet. 'Sorry, slept in,' he mumbled and made his way down to his seat. Woody didn't even seem to notice his arrival. Helmet did, though. He gave Umberto a sly smile and yet another of his moronic winks.

Winker, Umberto thought, slumping into his seat.

Woody may have been a pussycat when it came to discipline, but he knew how to dish out homework. He wanted a thousand words on the fall of Parnell and its immediate implications for Monday's class, no excuses valid.

'That's nearly a fucking book!' someone said in the midst of the general protests.

Woody must have heard, but he pretended he hadn't. 'Have a good weekend, all.' He laughed, and headed for the door. He had only no more than opened it when Helmet started up.

'McKeown! Hai, McKeown! I'm talking to you.'

Umberto turned around. 'What?'

'How's your hole? Is it sore? I'd say it is.'

Umberto said nothing, and turned back.

'Did yiz hear about this, lads?' Helmet said, raising his voice. 'McKeown's got a new boyfriend. He's taken up with a priest. And you know what *they're* like.'

No one laughed. But there was a noticeable decrease in the general babble.

'That's right, isn't it, Umberto? Tell us, what caught your eye? Was it the collar? No? Aw, look, he's gone all shy. But are you not too old for him? I thought priests liked them a bit younger.'

Someone chuckled. Umberto looked over and was not surprised to see that it was Gregory Daly.

'There I was,' Helmet said, 'walking along in front of the priests' house, minding my own business, and who comes running out only your man here, with his fat fucker of a boyfriend tearing after him. There must have been a row, was there, Umberto? A wee lovers' tiff? That's what I thought anyway, the way Father Queer was shouting about how you could work it out and your love will conquer all.'

Daly chuckled again. Although he was still alone in doing so, Umberto could feel a great many eyes on him. He kept his head down and tried to keep his breathing regular.

'Am I lying, Umberto? Was that not the way it went? I have a witness and we can't both be wrong, surely to God. Did you—'

The classroom door slammed shut. Captain Kirk had arrived.

'Shut up,' he said. 'Everybody get it out.'

Friday morning's maths class was a double, and Kirk didn't believe in taking a break halfway. For once, Umberto was glad. There was a respite of sorts after an hour however when the school secretary arrived at the door with a message for the captain. She wasn't the only female in the building, but she was the only one who didn't have a moustache or a beer belly (or

257

Damien Owens

both) and that made her special. A reverent hush descended while she stood in the doorway, whispering whatever it was that she had to whisper. Umberto stared at her along with everyone else, even though she reminded him of Posh Spice, which wasn't a good thing in his book. While he stared, something hit him in the back of the head. It felt like a ball of paper. Umberto stared on. He was hit again almost immediately. To turn around would be to give in, he felt. But to refuse might come across like cowardice. When he was hit a third time, he relented and looked over his shoulder. Helmet had done a drawing and was silently holding it up for inspection, like a proud child. He was no artist and Umberto couldn't quite work out what was depicted. He could guess, though, and turned, shaking his head, to face the front of the class again. Behind him, he heard several groans of disapproval from the other boys, and that gave him heart. Juvenile little shite. He really didn't seem to understand that no one, bar Daly, found him even remotely amusing. It occurred to Umberto that a person could make himself quite popular – or at least less unpopular – by once and for all pounding the fucker to a pulp. The sort of pulp that would think twice about getting its hard friends involved. The sort of pulp that would never open its gob to anyone in future.

It would be an act of public service.

Helmet didn't get a chance to say anything – or exhibit any other works of art – after maths. When Captain Kirk opened the door to leave, his successor, Captain Birdseye, was already waiting outside. The captains nodded briskly (the whole school knew about their mutual loathing) and squeezed past each other in the doorway.

'Excuse me,' they said as one.

There was some half-hearted dissent from the class about the lack of a breather between breakless double maths and religion, but Captain Birdseye was having none of it. 'What do you want me to do?' he asked from behind his fluffy grey beard. 'Stand here doing nothing for five minutes?'

'Aw, would you?' Colm McCaffrey said.

'No,' Birdseye replied. 'I wouldn't.'

Religion was a peculiar subject in more ways than one. There didn't seem to be any particular curriculum and the classes tended to take the form of a freewheeling discussion on whatever topic Birdseye happened to fancy that day. If the issue he chose had some religious dimension, then so much the better. He wasn't fussy. Today he was interested, or was at least pretending to be interested, in charity. Was charity always a good thing? Should it begin at home, and what did that mean anyway? Did people give because they wanted to help or because they wanted to ease their consciences? And if it was just to ease their consciences, did that matter? He asked these and other questions, and when the students responded with stares and yawns, he answered them himself. Umberto invariably had something to say in religion class, but wasn't even listening this time. He was busy wondering if fighting was something that had to be practised. Maybe it was one of those activities that a beginner could excel at straight away. Like everyone else, he'd seen a few scraps in the school yard and outside the chip shop, and he didn't think it looked too difficult. In the movies, yeah. It looked like ballet. In real life, as far as he could tell, the trick was to pull the other guy's jumper over his head and then punch or kick him until he either stopped moving or cried. Umberto was sure that he could manage the jumper part, especially given the height difference between himself and Helmet. But could he do the punching and kicking? He wished he'd had a go in his youth. At least he'd know what to expect. It could be a disgusting feeling for all he knew, all that crunching and yelling. On the other hand, it might be all right. Satisfying, maybe.

'What do you think, Umberto? You've been very quiet today. Tell us where we're going wrong.'

Umberto snapped out of it. Birdseye was leaning against the windowsill, arms folded. 'Well?'

'Eh . . .'

'You weren't listening, were you, laddie? Million miles away.'

'He's in love, sir,' Helmet said.

'Is that so, Thomas? And do you feel the same way about him?'

Birdseye got a reasonable laugh for that one, and Helmet clammed up immediately. The damage was done, however. He had raised a giggle himself this time, and not just from Gregory Daly. Umberto had a single thought: this will only get worse. He felt the anger like a liquid in his stomach, bubbling gently.

'Pay attention from now on, Mr McKeown.'

'Sir.'

St Brendan's had no canteen so students ate their packed lunches at their desks. This meant that the teacher of the last class before the break had to hang around for another fifteen minutes to supervise. Most read a newspaper and never looked up, but some foolishly tried to strike up normal conversation, as though they and the boys were friends who were sometimes obliged to play the silly roles of 'teacher' and 'pupil'. Birdseye belonged in the latter category.

'Anyone see the snooker last night?' he asked as the class rooted around in their bags for squashed sandwiches and flasks of tea. Seconds passed and no one answered, although someone whispered 'Tool' under his breath.

Umberto felt sorry for the man and said, 'No.'

Helmet sniggered. 'You wouldn't have, would you, Umberto? You were out on your hot date.'

Umberto forced himself to swivel slowly round and smile. He thought it might seem menacing.

'You seem very interested in Umberto's love life,' Birdseye said.

'Well, sir, it *is* interesting. Fascinating altogether.'

'Is that right, Umberto? Had your head turned, have you?'

Umberto shook his head. 'No, sir. He's trying to be funny. As usual, he's not doing a very good job.'

Helmet now had a mouth full of crisps but that didn't stop him replying. 'Umberto's feeling sensitive, sir. The path of true love isn't running smooth. They've had a fight.'

'I'll be having another one soon,' Umberto said, turning around yet again, 'if you don't shut it.'

Half the class was listening. There was some nervous laughter and one or two squawks of encouragement.

'Now, now,' Birdseye said. 'Let's keep our hair on. A change of subject, I think. Anyone see that programme about the space station on Wednesday night?'

Someone had, and was even willing to discuss it. Umberto

261

Damien Owens

didn't notice who it was. He and Helmet were locked on each other. 'Listen to the big man,' Helmet seethed.

For no better reason than he knew it would enrage him, Umberto blew him a kiss. It worked a treat. Helmet went a funny colour and drew a finger across his throat. For good measure, he slapped a fist into an open palm. Umberto shook his head in contempt. No subtlety. No refinement.

'No time like the present,' he said.

'What's the matter with you?' Dessie Doherty said. 'Are you *trying* to get killed?'

Umberto said nothing.

'Do you think you're hard all of a sudden, is that it?' Dessie continued. 'Because, no offence . . .' He let the sentence hang unfinished. They had reached the steps by the lab and took their seats. Umberto could see several members of his class and was pleased to notice that they were all looking in his direction.

'He picked a bad week to get on my nerves,' he said. 'That's all.'

'He gets on *everybody's* nerves all the time,' Dessie sighed. 'But people don't go around inviting him to have a go, do they?'

'And why not?'

'You know fine well why not. Why are you acting like this?'

Umberto looked straight ahead. 'I think I could take him.'

Dessie threw his hands in the air. 'Listen to Jackie fucking Chan. That's not the point, is it? He'd get you back eventually, him or his dopey mates. Even if you did win. Which you might not. I'm telling you, you better watch yourself. Some dark night when you're out on your own, not paying attention, he'll follow you, sneaking around behind you and then when you least expect it—'

'Here he comes now.'

'Where?! Oh, fuck! He's coming over! Now lookit, I'll probably get thumped too. Thanks, Umberto. Thanks a fucking million. I don't know why I bother . . .'

Helmet was alone and approaching at speed.

'You can go if you want to,' Umberto told Dessie. There was no reply.

'Well, girls,' Helmet called when he was still twenty feet away. 'Having a nice break?'

He sounded very cheery. 'Yes, thank you,' Umberto replied, equally upbeat. 'And yourself?'

'Shut the fuck up,' Helmet said, arriving in front of them. A half-dozen of their classmates were wandering over now, glancing around them for teachers.

'Well, that's not very nice, is it?' Umberto said. 'And we were getting along so well.'

Helmet shifted from foot to foot then folded and unfolded his arms. 'I don't know what your fucking problem is,' he said. 'But you're really starting to get on my tits.'

'Likewise.'

'I'll fucking likewise you, if you don't watch your fucking manners.'

Umberto looked around the onlookers with a puzzled expression, then back to Helmet. 'You'll *likewise* me? I'm not with you.'

Helmet shook his head. 'Smart answers, McKeown, that's all you've got. No balls.'

Damien Owens

Umberto had been wondering how these things actually started, how it went from talking to hitting. He supposed that someone would have to make a physical gesture. This seemed like as good a time as any. He stood up and stepped forward till his shoes were toe to toe with Helmet's.

'Maybe you're wrong about that,' he said, and stiffened, waiting for the first punch or shove or headbutt, hoping that Helmet was as weak as he looked.

Helmet looked up into his eyes. For a moment, nothing happened. Then he said, 'Is that so?'

The only reply Umberto could think of was 'Yeah.'

'Big tough guy,' Helmet said.

'Maybe,' Umberto said.

'Real hard man.'

'Maybe.'

Jesus, was he ever going to start? Umberto was starting to feel self-conscious. He decided to help things along by giving Helmet a gentle shove in the chest. One hand only, with fingers splayed. He'd seen it done lots of times and it always seemed to light the touchpaper. Helmet wobbled slightly when shoved. He felt sturdier than Umberto expected. Someone watching said, '*Yes*.' Umberto liked the sound of that Yes. Approval. Respect. Admiration, even.

He was still thinking that when Helmet's right fist came from below and hit him on the temple. A very loud gong chimed in his head. Oh, the fight's started, he thought, just as another punch caught him in the solar plexus. That one forced the breath out of him and caused him to double over. He had a half-second in which to realise that bending forward like that was practically inviting Helmet to knee him in the

264

face before Helmet issued a loud shriek and kneed him in the face. He fell to the ground without comment. This is what it's like to be knocked out, he thought, and then realised that he hadn't been. So all was not lost. A bit winded, that was all. The jumper . . . he had to pull Helmet's jumper over his head. Then it would be easy. He sat up and was promptly kicked in the side. The kick felt like it had been pulled, which was something, but nevertheless he collapsed again.

'Hard man, eh?' someone said. Helmet, presumably. He sounded very far away, whoever it was.

Umberto eventually got to his feet, expecting to be kicked again at any moment. He wasn't, which was a good thing. Being kicked was no fun, it turned out. Once upstanding, he couldn't immediately pick Helmet out of the crowd which seemed to have doubled in size in the last thirty seconds. Ah. There he was. Tosser. Thinks he's great. Umberto stumbled over and tried to grab his jumper at the sides before he could launch another punch. Now the tables would turn . . . if he could just get the jumper up . . . if his arms weren't . . .

'Are you trying to get my kit off?' Helmet said. 'Are you going to fuck me too?' He turned to the crowd. 'Is everyone getting all this? Do you see what I'm talking about?'

Umberto stopped tugging at the jumper. Why wasn't he being punched? He was well overdue for one. He looked down into Helmet's eye-slits and started a sentence. 'You're . . .' He paused, unsure what he had intended to say.

Helmet brushed his hands away from his sides. 'Fuck off, McKeown, before you get properly hurt.'

Umberto swayed back and forth, then sat down where he

was. It felt good to be sitting. He closed his eyes for a moment and tried to regain his composure. When he opened them, everyone had gone.

Everyone.

32

Finbarr was forever finding things in his house that he had completely forgotten about. It happened again on Friday afternoon. He was bored with sitting around waiting for the mobile to ring and decided on a game of Solitaire (or Rows as he preferred to call it). In days gone by, Rows had served him well. It wasn't fun, exactly, but it was sort of hypnotic. It made time go away, that was the main thing. Some days there was too much time for Finbarr's liking.

It had been quite a while since he'd played, and he had no idea where the cards were. He looked everywhere, in the kitchen drawers, in the bathroom cabinet, under the sofa, in the fridge. No sign. Then he remembered the suitcase under his bed. His grandfather had bequeathed it to his father, a man who never left the house, let alone the town. Finbarr had never used it for its intended purpose either but periodically threw things into it for safe-keeping. He went to his room, worked his way into a kneeling position, and dragged it out. It was covered with a thick layer of dust, into which he drew a smiley face with his finger. Then he added some cat's whiskers and a second mouth. He gave one of the mouths some fangs and finished the whole thing off with a top hat. Finbarr sometimes wondered if he had missed his vocation as an artist. Oh well. That was life.

There was all kinds of stuff in there. The grey woollen hat that his mother used to wear to mass. His father's glasses, one lens cracked. A ferocious-looking teddy bear that Finbarr had owned as a child. It used to terrify him, that bear, but he somehow became very attached to it. He took it to school every day in fact, hidden at the bottom of his satchel. He had a hazy recollection of a fellow pupil discovering it one day, when he was about thirteen. The details were sketchy.

He rummaged further down. Rosary beads. A Harold Robbins novel. A pocket-watch. A leaflet about decimalisation. A thick black ashtray. Three small statues of the Virgin Mary. A newspaper dated 13 June 1961. A pair of stockings. A half-squeezed tube of toothpaste. A hammer. Some toenail clippings in an envelope. Two cigarette lighters. A voodoo doll . . . *Jesus*. The voodoo doll! How could he have forgotten about this? After all the time and effort he put into it? The mind was a funny thing, if you asked Finbarr.

The doll was an Action Man wearing a scuba diving costume. It looked just as it had when he threw it in there all those years ago. It looked like a younger version of Matt Murphy. God rest him.

There used to be a corner shop at the end of Finbarr's street. It was gone now, replaced by an off-licence. A widower called Matt Murphy ran the place, and had done since Finbarr was in short trousers. Murphy was hated by all. He wouldn't give you the steam of his piss, people said. Not even Finbarr's mother had a good word for him and she claimed she could see Myra Hindley's side of the story. No one was sure if he was born mean or had turned that way after his wife died within three months of their wedding, some time back in the forties. Either way, Finbarr could see no excuse for his behaviour. The only thing you could say in his defence was that he treated everybody the same way. Children, pensioners, the disabled, it made no odds to Murphy. If you looked at him funny – or looked at him at all, some days – he'd give you the worst word in his belly and chase you out into the street with a stick that he kept behind the counter, apparently for no other purpose. The very best a customer could hope for from him, even those who had known him for years, was total silence. That was disturbing in its own way, but it was better than the shouting and the chasing.

Throughout Finbarr's formative years, Murphy had been a considerable bogey-man figure, with his wild hair and unblinking eyes. The ancient scar that ran along his cheek, the result of some childhood mishap, only added to his menace. (It was said in the playground that he had a lucrative business on the side, making dog food from passing orphans.) The two didn't seriously clash, however, until decades later. Their first serious falling-out happened not long after Finbarr's parents died. He'd been tucking into his spaghetti hoops on toast one evening when something caught his eye, near the top of the pile. Something black. He picked it up on the end of his fork and held it up to the light. It was a fly. A very large fly. That was what bothered him – its size. If it had been of regular dimensions, he might have overlooked it. After all, he'd read somewhere that the human stomach was full of bugs of one kind or another, so one more wouldn't have made much odds. This thing, however, was taking the piss. It must have been King of the Flies in its day, a wonder among its contemporaries. It was about the size of Finbarr's thumbnail, despite having been drenched in sticky orange sauce. When he let it slide off the fork on to the kitchen table, it landed with something not unlike a thump.

Finbarr had never been much of a one for his rights and all that nonsense. He'd always suspected that if he started going on about his rights, someone would remind him of his duties, and he didn't want that. But that fly could have choked him. Someone would have to be told. He wrapped the offending insect delicately in a piece of toilet paper and went back down to the shop. Murphy was reading the evening paper and didn't look up when the shop bell tinkled. Finbarr coughed. No response. Finbarr coughed again and then whistled. It came out like a wolf whistle, unfortunately, but it did the trick. Murphy stood up straight, or as straight as he got in those days (old age had given him something of a stoop). He read on for another few seconds, then closed the paper and stared at his customer. Finbarr explained about the King of the Flies, offering the contents of the toilet paper as proof. Murphy laughed and waved him away. Was he expected to open every tin can in his shop checking for flies? It was nothing to do with him, he said. Finbarr said he understood all that, he was merely pointing the problem out, letting Murphy know about his suppliers' shoddy standards. The shopkeeper shook his jowly head and asked how the meal had been prepared. In a pot, Finbarr said. Was this a clean pot, Murphy enquired?

Because he knew how lax Finbarr was in his personal hygiene. Maybe his kitchen wasn't exactly spotless either. While Finbarr fidgeted and frowned and struggled to think of a comeback, Murphy got a fit of the giggles. He stopped laughing long enough to say again that this fly nonsense was nothing to do with him, and that the spaghetti hoop people would no doubt be happy to reimburse Finbarr if he took the trouble to drop them a line. Assuming, he added with a wink, that Finbarr could write. They stared at each other for a while then, like gunslingers before the draw. Finbarr had always considered himself to be a fine starer, but he wasn't used to staring into eyes as dead as these. Eventually, he turned and left, without another word spoken between them. Back at home, his tea had gone cold. He was too angry to heat it up and ate it as it was, checking carefully for more insects as he munched.

If he'd been marginally less lazy, Finbarr might never have darkened Murphy's door again. But the next nearest shop was a supermarket in town, a five-minute walk away. That meant a round trip of almost fifteen minutes, all told. In Finbarr's book, that was too much to ask. You start taking fifteen minutes to get a pint of milk and next thing you know, your life's over. As far as he was concerned, he was stuck with the crotchety old shitehawk. Although his next few visits were uncomfortable, the subject of the flies was never broached again. The incident would no doubt have been forgotten entirely, or at least papered over, if Murphy hadn't short-changed him not three weeks later. That was it for Finbarr. Narrowly avoiding death by choking was one thing, but this was serious. He pointed out the mistake immediately, with no real expectation that it would be rectified. He was correct: Murphy wouldn't even discuss it, claiming with

271

some anger that he'd been paid with a pound note and that he knew what a fucking pound note looked like, thank you very much. Finbarr was certain that he'd handed over a fiver, which was quite a sum in those days, but he didn't press the point. He maintained his dignity and walked out of the shop backwards, wearing what he hoped was an enigmatic smile. The fact was, he'd realised that he would never win with this character. For some reason best known to himself, Murphy now had it in for him. Why he should turn actively malicious after a lifetime of mere surliness was a mystery, but there it was. There seemed to be a lot of it going round. The only comeback Finbarr had left was simple revenge.

He considered several options. The early favourite was vandalism. Nothing serious, just a broken window or maybe a bit of door graffiti. He'd noticed that some ruffian had taken to daubing the word SEX in big white letters on walls around the town, sometimes accompanied by an ejaculating phallus. It didn't strike Finbarr as a particularly clever thing to daub, but it had a certain immediacy. He could copy that design and Murphy would assume it to be the work of the same anonymous wastrel. With any luck, he'd have a heart attack trying to scrub it off. Finbarr was all set to go with that plan when fate intervened in the form of a television documentary about voodoo. It came on late one night while he was slumped on his sofa, half a bottle of whiskey to the good. The programme started with archive footage of dusky Caribbeans casting spells in smoky huts, which wasn't all that impressive. But it quickly moved on to testimony from educated-looking white people who claimed to have seen results in a matter of days. One woman broke down as she told the story of the estate agent she had personally crippled by stabbing a cloth doll in the knees with a hatpin. She seemed genuinely sorry and warned viewers not to mess with mysterious forces they didn't understand. Her warning was lost on Finbarr, who found most things mysterious, 'forces' included.

As far as he could tell, he needed four things: a doll, of course, some pins, something personal of Murphy's, and a whole load of candles. The pins and candles he had at home (candles in case of sudden blackouts and pins for pricking the occasional boil). He thought long and hard about getting his hands on a lock of Murphy's hair or somesuch, but settled in the end for a paint chip from the shop door. It was close enough, he reckoned. As for the doll, that was trickier. He tried stuffing a few socks with cotton wool and then sewing them together in the approximate shape of a man, but quickly realised that he couldn't actually sew. Then he tried cutting a Murphy shape out of the back of a cornflakes packet, but that just didn't feel right. It was cheap-looking for a start, and the nutritional information printed on the back took away from the atmosphere somewhat. He had almost given up on the scheme when he spotted the Action Man in the town centre supermarket where he was now obliged to shop. It was early December at the time and the shelves were groaning with toys. The Action Man caught his eye as he passed by on his way to the butcher's counter. It was the perfect size and looked like it would take a good pinning. Best of all, though – Finbarr's eyes crossed in shock – it had a scar on its cheek. Longer and more pronounced than Murphy's own, maybe, but a scar none the less. It was a sign.

Back at home, Finbarr hastily assembled an altar. He lit

273

his candles and mumbled a quick prayer about mysterious forces and wanting a favour. Then he slipped the paint chip inside Action Man's rubbery scuba jacket. After a moment's reflection, he removed the goggles and flippers. Now. Where to put the pins . . . the groin? The eyes? Yeah. The eyes. The eyes that couldn't tell the difference between a pound and a fiver. The pins went in easily, one in each eye. But nothing actually happened. Finbarr had expected blood to come pouring out or a sudden gust to extinguish his candles, as had happened with the people in the documentary. He took the pins out, addressed the mysterious forces again (this time mentioning his willingness to return the favour at some point) and then reinserted them. There was silence. Lots of it. Fuck this for a haircut, Finbarr thought, and went to bed. The disappointment stayed with him for a long time.

Matt Murphy was killed two years later, hit by a van as he crossed the road to post a letter. The driver was inconsolable. He claimed to have seen Murphy starting out to cross and to have seen Murphy see *him*. He didn't slow down as a consequence and was stunned when the old man stepped out anyway. The impact wasn't all that severe, but Murphy was seventy-eight years of age and in no condition for being hit by moving vehicles, which (Finbarr reflected) is a young man's game. How could you miss an approaching van, people wondered. It was a straight road. It was a clear day. His mind must have been on other things. Or maybe it was his glaucoma. He'd always suffered with glaucoma.

Finbarr knew better. All right, so it had taken a while, but the mysterious forces had come through for him. In a big way. He was elated at first, and then frankly terrified. What if they wanted the favour returned? In a panic, he threw the Action Man into the suitcase and resolved to put the whole episode behind him.

The paint chip was still there. Green. Finbarr balanced it on the end of his index finger and looked at it for a long time, the pack of cards entirely forgotten.

Poor old Matt. He wasn't a bad skin, really. If he hadn't been such a—

Biddle-de-dee, biddle-de-dee. The phone was ringing. And this was no wrong number, this was it. Finbarr felt it in his gut. By the time he hauled himself up off his knees and trotted down to the kitchen, the ringing had stopped. He picked the phone up, tossed it from one hand to the other, and casually dialled his message centre like an old pro.

'Oh, hi,' she said. 'I wasn't expecting a machine. This is . . . never mind. I was just . . . look. Maybe I'll try you again some other day. Bye.'

It wasn't perfect. But it was good enough. Finbarr turned to put the kettle on, marvelling at the way an average, boring day could suddenly turn around for a person.

33

Part of Father Duff's plan to give up smoking involved keeping a packet of twenty on his bedside locker. The idea was to provide himself with a constant reminder of the enemy, in the same way that some boxers keep pictures of forthcoming opponents pasted over their bathroom mirrors. He'd read a few how-to-quit books in his time and noted that they all explicitly advised against such practice. The tortured smoker, they agreed, should dispose of all their fags in a little ceremony as soon as they decided to stop. Since those books had utterly failed to rid him of his addiction, and in one case had actually made smoking seem quite cool, Father Duff thought it wiser to follow his own instincts this time. As well as keeping a packet to hand, he was also walking around the house with unlit cigarettes in his mouth and trying, without much luck, to inhale the smoke of passers-by in the street.

His previous attempts to quit had all collapsed in an ignominious pile of ash within days. Sometimes he failed because the cravings were too strong. Sometimes he failed because it slipped his mind that he had ever stopped. Sometimes it was because he met someone who sucked down sixty a day and decided that smoking his own ten to fifteen was practically taking exercise. Stress had never been a factor, though. Father Duff liked to think of himself as an unflappable figure and the defeated hand that eventually reached for his Silk Cut and lighter had always been rock steady.

Today, however, there was just the slightest tremble. He had been to visit Jackie Flynn, whose wife · had recently been diagnosed with liver cancer. It was well advanced, by all accounts, and she had a matter of weeks. Jackie was a retired librarian, a gentle, old-fashioned character who had something of the dandy about him. He had a weakness for extravagant handkerchiefs and still wore a hat which he tipped at women in the street. If there was a better Christian in the town, Father Duff had yet to meet him. And yet, sitting in his front room between Jackie's daughter and her husband, he had found himself listening to the same old questions. How could God let this happen? Didn't he pay attention to the behaviour of his creations? Paula was a saint. And there would be people laughing in pubs tonight, Jackie whispered hoarsely, who would stagger home and wake their children up to give them black eyes. Where was *their* cancer? Wasn't anybody keeping score?

Father Duff listened and nodded and tried to make himself repeat the party line, that God must have his reasons. But he couldn't. He believed it absolutely. He just couldn't repeat it to the shaking wreck sitting opposite. Instead, he restricted himself to practical questions – Was she in pain? Was the hospital all right? – and promised to pray for them all. He left the Flynn house within half an hour of arriving, certain that he had been of no help whatsoever and wondering if he visited the families of the dying and the dead for their benefit or for his.

Back at the priests' house, he sat on the edge of his bed and took his first hit in almost a week. Driven back to cigarettes by the stress of an encounter with cancer. Nice one. He had to admit it, though – he felt better straight away. He stopped grinding his teeth and the trembling in his fingers disappeared. He looked at his watch. Almost two thirty. If he was going to go, he would have to go soon, before Umberto got back from school. With any luck, he could still be of help to someone before the day was out.

It had gone three by the time he rounded the final bend in the lane and pulled up at The Cottage. There was an enormous Jeep parked outside, so someone was obviously home. Father Duff switched off the ignition and contemplated the pros and cons of having another calming fag. His fingers had started to shake again and his stomach felt like it was half-full of feathers. But on the other hand, he had to think of . . . ah, who was he kidding. He reached into his jacket pocket, wound down the car window and lit up.

The compromise he had reached with himself overnight was this: he would talk to them and tell them that Umberto had overheard something troubling and was worried about them, but there was no way on earth that he was going to mention the alleged infidelity thing. He could only bring trouble on his own head by doing so. Better just to give them the wake-up call and tell them to think of their son. And then leave. He took a long drag on his cigarette and nodded to himself. It

279

was all he could do. It was all he *should* do. If only one of them was there, he might have to—

The door of The Cottage opened and a tall man stepped out. Father Duff swore and jumped like a private eye rumbled during a stake-out. He choked loudly on his smoke as he did so and then went into a hysterical coughing fit, with eyes bulging and tongue protruding. The man locked the front door behind him and then walked in Father Duff's direction with a hand raised in greeting. He was dressed for walking, in a bright yellow hooded jacket and hiking boots.

'Hi there,' he said, pleasantly. When he reached the car he got down on his hunkers and folded his arms on the edge of the car door.

'Hello,' Father Duff said through his wheezes.

The man had a severe crop and a light beard, all silver. Prematurely so. He was tanned and healthy-looking. 'Lost, are ya?' he said, in American.

Father Duff looked over the man's shoulder to The Cottage as he ground his cigarette out in the car's ashtray. 'No, no. I was looking for . . . well, for you, I think. Are you Umberto's dad, by any chance?'

The man's smile vanished. 'Oh, Jesus,' he said. 'What happened? Is he OK?'

'No, no, it's nothing like that. He's fine. I keep forgetting that people don't like to see a priest on the doorstep any more than they like to see the Guards.'

He chortled at his own joke, but he chortled alone.

'My name is Miles Duff,' he said, extending a hand. 'I met your son at his school a while back.'

The man got to his feet and shook hands. 'Jeff Vance,' he said. 'Jeff. So. What can I do for you, Father Duff?'

'Look, can we go inside and talk? Is your wife home?'

Jeff looked back towards the house and sighed. Then he walked around the front of the car and got into the passenger seat. Father Duff tried not to find it impolite.

'Valerie's gone to Belfast for the day. Antique shopping,' Jeff said. 'And I have things to do myself. I don't mean to be rude, but what's this about? No wait, lemme guess. Umberto has caused some catastrophic offence to the Catholic Church and you've come here to chastise us for the manner in which he was raised. Correct?'

Father Duff bit his lip for a moment before answering. 'No. Not correct. It is about Umberto, though. He came to visit me at the parochial house and—'

'Whoa, whoa, he what? He came to visit you? Why?'

'Well, he—'

'Because I have to tell you, I'm not wild about the idea of my boy hanging out with a whole bunch of priests. No offence.'

'None taken,' Father Duff said through gritted teeth. 'May I ask why?'

'I was raised a Catholic, Father Duff, and so was my wife. We know enough about it to know that we don't want our son raised that way. If there was a decent secular school around here, Umberto would be attending it. No offence.'

'Still none taken. But I don't think your son feels the same way. Umberto was visiting me because he was looking for help.'

He didn't see the need to bring chess into the equation. The conversation was on thin enough ice as it was.

'Help? What kind of help? Is he in trouble?'

'Look, Jeff, this isn't easy to say, so I'm just going to come right out and say it. I know that it's none of my business and all that, but I feel I'd be letting the boy down if I didn't speak up.'

'Go on.'

'Well, it seems that Umberto is under the impression that . . . things aren't so rosy between your wife and yourself.'

He lowered his head and waited to be shouted at or possibly punched. But there was silence. He could hear birds twittering in the trees. Seconds passed.

'What did he say *exactly*?'

Father Duff wriggled uncomfortably. 'He wasn't very specific.'

'But he must have been. Unless you're in the habit of interfering in people's lives for no good reason. Which, now I think of it, you probably are, being a priest and all. No offence.'

'Fine then. He told me that he'd overheard something. What, I don't know. But it's making him very anxious and I think you should clear it up with him. Especially if he's got the wrong end of the stick. *Has* he got the wrong end of the stick?'

Jeff turned to stare through the front windscreen. 'Do you do this a lot? Calling on strangers and poking into their personal lives?'

'No. I don't.'

'Huh. Lucky ol' us.'

'Lookit, Jeff, I *know* this is none of my business. I believe I even said as much a minute ago. But the bottom line is, someone came to me and asked for help and I—'

'That's another thing. That doesn't ring true. I think I know my own son pretty well and, lemme tell you, he has no interest in religion. Or the religious. I find it very hard to believe that he would swan into your . . . nest, or whatever it's called and tell you all this. I'm sorry. It doesn't fly. You're not telling me something.'

Father Duff blinked. Nest? 'All right then. The reason Umberto called round in the first place was to give me a game of chess. Which, by the way, was very nice of him. He's a good lad.'

He knew it would sound strange but he was no longer in the Impressing Jeff business.

'Chess?'

'That's right.'

'You're telling me he called over to play chess?'

'Yes.'

'He just knocked on the door and asked if there was anyone home who felt like a game?'

'Well, no—'

'What then?'

'We'd been talking about chess before and—'

'Where? At the school?'

'No, actually, it was here when—'

'Here? You've been out here before? Creeping around after my son?'

Father Duff reached for his cigarettes as he answered. 'No. Hang on a minute. I was not "creeping around" after him, and frankly I'm not sure I like your tone. We had a chat at the school and, if you must know, I got the impression that he might be interested in the priesthood.

283

That's why I was there in the first place and that's why I was here too.'

Jeff whispered 'Unbelievable' under his breath as Father Duff put flame to fag once more.

'But we're getting away from the point. All this other stuff isn't important. Now, I repeat again, and this makes three times by my count: this is none of my business. Maybe I shouldn't have come. But I've done it now, so please. Just tell him he's mistaken and that will be that.'

Jeff exhaled slowly and noisily. 'What exactly does Umberto think he overheard?'

'I really don't—'

'Gimme a break, *please*. Tell me. Or don't you think we have a right to know whatever it is we're being accused of?'

Although he hated to admit it, this struck Father Duff as a fair comment. He took his turn to stare straight ahead and made a mental sign of the cross. So much for his compromise.

'All right. All right, he . . . He said he was sure that you were having an affair.'

There was a noise, a slapping noise. Father Duff turned and saw that Jeff had covered his face with his hands. He stayed behind them for a moment and then punched the dashboard with both fists.

'*Shit*,' he said.

There was a minute or more of silence. Father Duff didn't think it was his place to end it, but eventually he grew too uncomfortable.

'It's true then,' he said.

Jeff didn't reply for a moment. Then he gave his face a brisk rub and said, 'I don't know how he could have found out. There's never been anything to overhear. I've never called her from the house and she's never called me here either. It doesn't make sense.'

'Maybe he saw you together and was too embarrassed to say so.'

'No. Not possible. We've been very careful.'

Father Duff's confidence was returning now that he had been (God forgive him) vindicated. 'How long has it been going on?' he asked. 'Is it serious, I mean?'

'Not long. Six weeks, seven. And no, it isn't serious, it's sex. *Jesus*. I feel sick . . .'

'And your wife doesn't know?'

Jeff barked with contempt. 'No, she knows all about it. Of course she does. I always make a point of telling her about my affairs. It gives us something to talk about, you know? She loves hearing all the little details, where we did it, who was on top. She gets off on it.'

Father Duff knew an attempt to embarrass him when he heard one and refused to bite. 'All right, stupid question.'

'Of course she doesn't know. Jesus – you're not going to tell her, are you?'

'I certainly am not. I thought she already knew, to be honest. I thought the conversation Umberto overheard was you and her arguing about it.'

'No. She has no idea. And that's the way it's going to stay.'

'So what are you going to do? You'll have to talk to Umberto at least.'

'Absolutely not. What the hell for?'

'The whole point—'

'Nuh-uh. No way. I'll talk to Fi— . . . the woman and end it straight away, tonight if possible, but that's all. Umberto has no proof of anything and if he ever brings it up, I'll tell him he's imagining things. This can be made to go away.'

Father Duff drummed his fingers on the steering wheel. 'How will she react when you tell her?'

Jeff smirked in a way that made Father Duff like him even less. 'Don't worry about her. She's no more attached to me than I am to her. She'll find someone else and move on. I'm not her first little fling.'

'She's married as well?'

'Not for much longer, the way things are going. If you're looking for someone to help, I'd start with that husband of hers. Loser that he is.'

Father Duff shook his head and fought the urges to sermonise or throw up.

'Umberto will be home from school soon,' he said, deadpan. 'I have to go.'

'Yeah. Well, I guess I should thank you for the warning. You may have saved my neck here.'

'I have to go,' Father Duff repeated. Jeff said good-bye, got out of the car and waved cheerily at him as he u-turned away.

34

'You know something,' Peter said. 'I think my back feels a bit better. More than a bit, in fact. Much better.'

'There you go,' Mary murmured into his chest. 'All you needed was some exercise.'

'Yeah. I'm knackered now, though. Maybe we should get out of bed for some proper rest.'

Mary's hand left its temporary home on his thigh and crept north.

'Are you sure?' she whispered silkily.

He paused, eyebrow aloft, before answering.

'Yeah. I think it's gone numb.'

It was lunch-time. Peter couldn't remember the last time he'd stayed in bed until lunch-time on his own, let alone with Mary. But they'd still been wide awake when the sun came up and were in no condition for work. Most of their time had been spent talking and laughing, although they did have three and a half early nights. The half came at around five in the morning when

Peter, to his delight and astonishment, managed the hard part (as he breathlessly punned) but then ruined the moment with an impromptu rendition of 'Wind Beneath My Wings'. Mary laughed so hard that he lost momentum and then everything else. Despite that, she was very complimentary about his efforts in general. Peter smiled in the dark and wondered how he could ever have doubted himself. He was the same love machine he'd always been.

At breakfast-time, she was the one to suggest that they stay in bed and possibly even have a nap before lunch, but Peter didn't argue. She phoned Fidelma and, amid much giggling, asked her to fill in at the shop while Peter simply called in sick. Earache, he said, on a whim. Severe earache.

'Hmmm. Anniversary today, isn't it?' Mairéad asked him on the phone.

He admitted that it was.

'Lordy,' she marvelled. 'Is there a position that gives you earache?'

'Sorry,' Peter said. 'I didn't catch that.'

Downstairs, the kitchen was a mess. They'd been in the mood for ice cream, crisps, chocolate digestives and red wine at around four in the morning but had most definitely not been in the mood for clearing up. Mary was doing it when Peter padded into the room scratching his armpit and yawning.

'What were we at?' she asked. 'It looks like some kid had a tenth birthday party.'

'Leave it,' he said, moving in behind her and circling her waist. 'C'mon, we'll calf out on the sofa for the rest of the day. We won't lift a finger. Get something delivered for dinner. Watch crap telly. Snog.'

She paused and then pushed her cloth away. 'You talked me into it,' she said.

They went into the living room and collapsed in a heap. Mary kicked off her Pooh slippers and Peter lay back to provide her with a pillow. They were silent for a long time.

Then Mary said, 'This isn't a bad way to spend your first anniversary, is it?' Her voice was thick and sleepy.

Peter had almost drifted off.

'Yeah,' he mumbled. 'Better than all that flowers and chocolates and candles crap.'

'Yeah.'

He chuckled. 'Just as well I didn't listen to David.'

Mary said, 'Hmmm?'

'Oh. Never mind.'

'What's David got to do with it?' Her voice suddenly sounded less sleepy.

'Nothing,' he said. 'We were talking, and he suggested, you know ... a little romance, flowers and chocolates and whatnot.'

He did his Winning Smile. She looked at him.

'And is that the way you want me? All frilly and girly? What's that got to do with romance?'

He sat up and leaned closer to her. 'It's got nothing to do with romance, I know that. The fact that we're still together, that's romance as far as I'm concerned. I was never going to do his idea. I know you better than that.'

It occurred to him that he hadn't come up with his own 'spectacular' alternative either. God, he really was useless. How did she put up with him?

She played with the drawstring on her tracksuit bottoms

and sighed. 'Yeah, I know. I just don't like the thought of you asking for that kind of help. Especially if this is the kind of solution you end up with.'

'Sorry. Lesson learned.'

She smiled and sat back. 'You're forgiven. Now we better eat something. I fancy some soup.'

'Anything you want,' he said in his Matinée Idol voice. 'And not out of a packet, either. Oh, no. It's canned or nothing for you, my treasure.'

After lunch, they returned to the sofa, switched on the TV, and fell immediately asleep. Peter woke at around four and had a shower. The hot water did wonders for his back, which was starting to complain again. When he came back downstairs, Mary was up and about, tidying the kitchen in earnest. He took over and she went for her own shower, pausing to kiss him on the way.

It was a bright, pleasant evening and they decided to go for a walk into town and back. Not to do anything in particular, just to get out of the house. They stopped at Coffee to a Tea and had large, sticky slices of lemon meringue pie. He told her a joke about three tortoises going on a picnic. He did the voices very well, if he did say so himself, and she almost choked on her pie. They walked back to the house hand in hand, feeling a bit silly doing so, but only a bit.

Twenty minutes after they arrived, the phone rang. Mary went out to the hall to take it.

'Regina?' she said on her return. Peter was on his knees building a fire and only the sticks and coal saw his face go into spasms.

'Oh,' he said. His mind was looping the loop. She did it. She actually made the call. He got to his feet and turned, clapping the dust from his hands. But Mary had only been gone for a few seconds. And she looked OK. Regina mustn't have said anything. She was trying to scare him, that was all. He could still bluff.

'Work . . . thing,' he said, faking annoyance. 'Won't be a second.' He went past Mary on watery legs. The door to the hall was fully open. It would look bad if he closed it. He could face the wall, though. At least she wouldn't be able to see his face even though she could probably hear him.

'Regina,' he said in a neutral voice. The tone he tried to affect was business-like, but cranky – why-am-I-being-disturbed-at home-on-a-sick-day?

'Hi,' she said, cheerily. 'Was that wifey then?'

Words failed him.

'She sounds very nice. Good for you. Listen, I wanted to say thanks for dinner and to apologise for the way things turned out the other night.'

He risked looking back into the other room. Mary wasn't in view. Maybe she'd gone into the kitchen.

'I was out of order, getting aggressive like that. I hope you weren't hurt?'

'No,' he said. 'I wasn't.'

'It's not like me, but I was upset. I broke up with my boyfriend a few weeks ago and—'

He faced the wall again and hissed into the phone. 'You said you were a lesbian!'

'Yeah, I did, didn't I?' Regina said. 'Look, I was upset when you shot me down and it seemed like a good thing to say at the time. I do have a lesbian stalker though, which I'll tell you about some other time. She's *obsessed* with me, poor thing.'

'So you were really . . . I don't believe it. And what is this, revenge?'

'Revenge? What are you on about?'

He took another peek. Still no sign of Mary. 'You threatened to do this. You said you'd call up—'

'But I didn't *mean* it, Peter! What do you take me for? I'm calling to *apologise*. I started feeling just terrible about the whole thing this afternoon. And frankly, I think I'm showing a lot of guts here. I didn't have to call, you know.'

Peter chewed on this.

'If I wanted to get you into trouble with your wife I'd have done it a minute ago, wouldn't I?'

It made a certain amount of sense.

'Suppose.'

'There you go then. Jesus, Peter, you should learn to relax. That's your whole problem.'

He gripped the phone even harder and tried to focus on the practicalities at hand. She was a client with a problem and he'd – slap forehead – stupidly given her his home number. Duh.

'Regina, your apology is accepted. Let's just forget this whole thing ever happened. Now, I'm going back in to my wife before she starts wondering what the hell we're jabbering about.'

'Suspicious type, is she?'

He had to swap phone hands. His right was getting sore. 'No. She isn't. Which is why I'm pissed off that I had to lie to her a minute ago. Now, listen: I said this was a work call.

Please tell me you didn't say anything to the contrary when she answered.'

'Don't sweat, that's what I said too. Christ, aren't you even allowed to get phone calls from women without all this hullabaloo? It's worse than I thought. You really do need help.'

'I'm hanging up, Regina.'

'Now you're being plain rude.'

'Goodbye.'

He hung up.

Mary was out of earshot in the kitchen, as he'd suspected. Result.

'You know what?' she said when he walked in. She was leaning against the counter with a glass of orange juice. He felt his palms go moist in an instant. She couldn't have heard anything, could she . . . ?

'No, what?'

'That walk woke me up a bit. Maybe we should go out for dinner. Seems a shame not to do *something* tonight . . .'

Peter fought the urge to phew. 'Of course! Anywhere in particular?'

'We're not exactly spoiled for choice, are we? There's that new Chinese place, though. Valerie and Jeff were in it the other night.'

'And?'

'She said it was "inoffensive". Which is a compliment, for her.'

'OK. Assuming we can get in. It is a Friday.'

'Yeah. So who's Regina then, new business?'

Damien Owens

Shit. He was beginning to think she wasn't going to mention it.

'Nah. Old business. I networked a few PCs for her a while ago and now all of a sudden she can't see the printer from hers. I shouldn't have given her my home number, but she insisted. Nervy type, you know?'

Mary looked at him, saying nothing.

'It's fixed now anyway. IRQ problem. I talked her through it. Simple.'

She took a swig of orange juice. 'Is that right?'

She wasn't just looking at him now. She was staring. Peter's feet went cold. 'Yeah. I'll give the restaurant—'

'She told me you met in Dublin at the course.'

He answered before his brain had time to register panic. 'Did she?'

'Yes. She said, Hi, my name is Regina, I was talking to your husband at the course, can I have a word.'

'Yeah, that's right. She was there too.'

'Why?'

'Why?'

'Yes, Peter. Why was she at a course for IT people?'

'She . . . works in IT.'

'She works in IT? But she has to get you to fix her printer?'

He felt one of his knees start to shake. 'Well, she isn't very good at it.'

Mary put her drink down. 'You're lying. You're fucking lying to me.'

'What? Don't be so—'

'Who is she? I'm not completely thick, Peter. Who is she?'

294

It was hopeless. He would have to come clean. It might not be so bad. 'OK,' he said. 'I'm lying. But I've got a reason.'

'Oh . . . fuck . . . me.'

'Now, let me speak, Mary. Just listen for a minute. Regina is Regina Clarke from college, you must have heard me giving out about her before. She does work in IT, that bit's true, and she was at the course and—'

'I'm hearing things. Am I hearing things?'

He held his hands up in front of him like a goalkeeper. 'Please, Mary, let me finish. She stuck to me like glue all day and insisted that we go out for dinner together and I didn't want to – I couldn't stand her at college and I can't stand her now – but she went on and on, so I said yes. Now, there's nothing wrong with that, is there?'

'Oh, my God, is this how you hurt your back, like in some *Carry On* movie? Shagging an old flame? I can't frigging bel . . . it's too—'

'Don't be silly. That's just . . . silly. Listen to me, now. We went out and it was hell on earth and I couldn't wait to get away. I'm telling you the truth.'

Mary launched herself away from the counter and brushed past him into the living room with her hands over her mouth. For a moment, he thought she was going to vomit, but she just stood in the centre of the other room, absent-mindedly kicking the leg of the coffee table. He followed her.

'Look, I'm going to be brutally honest. I'm telling you everything here. She tried it on with me. And I turned her down. Mary, are you listening to me? I turned her *down*. I didn't tell you any of this because what would be the point? You have to believe me.'

Damien Owens

Mary stopped kicking the table, which was good, but took a step back and formed fists by her side. That was bad. Her eyes were dampening, too.

'It was horrible,' he said. 'She punched me in the nuts when I said I wasn't having anything to do with her. That's why she called. To apologise.'

Her fists wobbled. She said nothing.

'I'll find out where she works!' Peter yelped. 'You can call her!'

Mary seemed to have been struck dumb.

He threw his hands in the air. 'Ask David then! He knows all this! Go and ring him now, he'll tell you!'

She suddenly found her voice again. 'Jesus Christ! Does anything go on between us that David doesn't get to hear about first?'

'What? He's my *friend*. I wanted to—'

'Brag about it? Did you keep her knickers?'

Peter slumped into an armchair. 'OK. Fine. I give up. If you don't believe me, then there's nothing I can do, is there?'

It wasn't a rhetorical question. He really wanted an answer. But he didn't get one. They were interrupted by a series of tremendous thumps on the front door.

Mary wiped her eyes with the backs of her hands. 'Maybe that's Regina,' she said. 'Sorry, was I supposed to be out?'

Peter ignored her.

'You better answer it,' she said.

'They'll go away in a minute.'

They waited, avoiding each other's gaze. Then the thumping started again, this time with a regular slow beat.

'For fuck's sake,' Peter snarled, getting out of his chair. 'At least use the fucking doorbell.'

He marched past Mary and out into the hall. 'I'll get rid of them,' he said, over his shoulder. He swung the front door open at just the wrong moment and Finbarr Grealey came falling in, carried by the momentum of his unmet thump. For a moment, Peter thought he was seeing things.

'Hello,' Finbarr said, straightening himself up. 'How's the man?'

'Finbarr?'

'Fourth time lucky,' Finbarr said, removing his baseball cap. 'I had to go to three other houses before I found someone who knew which one was yours.'

Peter blinked. 'What the hell do you want?'

His visitor looked offended.

'Sorry,' Peter said. 'But you picked a very bad time. What are you doing here?'

Finbarr's tongue appeared suddenly and moistened his lips. 'I wonder,' he said, 'if we could maybe have a private word. Before the missus gets home.'

'What about? And Mary is home.'

Finbarr's shoulders jumped. He stepped out over the threshold and then leaned back in to whisper in Peter's ear. 'I thought she worked late on Fridays.'

'She usually does,' Peter said. 'Are you going to tell me wh—'

'I wanted to get you on your own. I thought I'd strike while the iron is hot.'

'What frigging iron? What are you talking about?'

297

Finbarr shook his head. 'Never mind. Not now. I'll get you again, sure.'

'What is it? Is it to do with Mary?'

He saw Finbarr's nervous grin freeze and then collapse. He suspected some sort of embolism at first, but then realised that Mary was standing behind him in the hall.

'I heard my name,' she said. Then, '*Finbarr?* What are you doing here?'

'Hello,' Finbarr said. 'Well, I better make tracks. Bye-bye now.'

'Wait,' Peter and Mary said in unison. But he was off, jogging almost.

'What was that about?' Mary asked, in a voice that suggested she suspected Peter was having an affair with Finbarr as well as Regina.

'I don't know,' he said. 'He said he wanted to talk to me but not if you were here.'

'What has he got against me?'

Peter shrugged. They stood in silence watching Finbarr's retreat. He was on the other side of the close now, but was slowing down. Then he stopped. Then he turned around. And then he started back towards them, picking up speed all the time.

'He's coming back!' Peter said.

'I can see that.'

Finbarr had his cap on again. When he was halfway across the grassy area in the centre of the close, it blew off his head and landed behind him. He didn't notice.

'His cap blew off,' Peter said.

'I'm not blind.'

Finbarr was dangerously out of breath when he reached the doorstep. 'I have ... decided,' he wheezed, 'that ... I ... Jesus ...'

'Catch your breath, for God's sake,' Mary said. Peter wondered if they should ask him in, despite everything. He was bright pink. There was a bead of sweat on the end of his nose.

'I'm all right,' Finbarr said. 'Not used to exercise, that's all.'

Peter and Mary nodded. They were standing on the doorstep like bouncers, each perfectly erect with their arms folded.

Finbarr took a few more deep breaths and began. 'Peter,' he said, 'I couldn't call myself your friend if I didn't tell you this.'

'*What?*'

Finbarr reached up to his head and found no cap to remove. He patted his crown four or five times before the truth dawned.

'It fell off,' Mary told him. He didn't look at her but nodded sadly.

'Peter,' he said. 'When you told me last week about your marriage and the sex problems and so on, I—'

Mary made a noise like a window smashing. Finbarr jumped a clear inch off the ground. Then she turned and ran inside. Peter swayed back and forth, rubbing his forehead, trying to wake up from this terrible dream. Mary's howling was audible from the doorstep. Peter leaned over, grabbed Finbarr by the lapels of his jacket and hauled.

'You,' he seethed. '*Inside.*'

*　　*　　*

In the living room, Mary was sitting on the floor with her back against the sofa, her shaking head in her hands. She looked up when Peter came through the door pushing Finbarr in front of him.

'That's right,' she said. 'Take him in. Get David round as well as sure we'll all have a great laugh. You *bastard*. You fucking . . . *bastard*.'

Peter was all business. 'You, sit there,' he said to Finbarr.

'I think I'd rather st—'

'Sit!' Peter bellowed. Finbarr meekly folded himself down on to an armchair.

'I am going to sit here,' Peter said, finding his own armchair, 'and we are going to sort this out.'

He had no sooner spoken than Mary scrambled to her feet and took off. She charged up the stairs and then a door slammed. Peter brought his fists down on the arms of his chair and got up.

'Wait here,' he said to Finbarr.

Upstairs, the bathroom door was the only one shut. Peter slapped it with his palm and said, 'Mary. Come on out. We have to get this cleared up.'

There was no reply, although he could hear sniffling and a running tap.

'Mary. Mary! Come *on*.'

'Cleared up?' she shouted through the door. 'Cleared up?! Fuck off and leave me alone. Go on back down to Dr Ruth.'

'Oh, for God's sake. He's *mad*, Mary. He's delirious, he's imagining things. I never said anything to him about sex, I swear to God.'

He slapped the door again but quickly stopped when he realised how annoying the sound was.

'Mary, please. Come on. If you come down the stairs with me, we'll have it sorted in two minutes. I'm telling you, he's in a world of his own. It's a misunderstanding—'

A bitter laugh crackled on the other side of the door. 'What, like Regina?'

'*Yes.*'

He heard mumbling then but couldn't make out what, if anything, she actually said. He put his hands on his hips and sighed.

'All right. I'm going. If you—'

The lock turned and the bathroom door opened a few inches. Mary looked like she'd been beaten up. Peter said nothing. He was afraid she would disappear inside again.

'Bad enough that you're talking about our . . . life to anyone, but to a . . . a . . . a total stranger . . .' She trailed off into silence, shaking her head in disbelief.

'Mary, listen. I bumped into him in the pub last weekend after we had that . . . falling-out. We had this conversation, a drunken conversation, and he's obviously got the whole thing twisted somehow. If you come down with me now, we'll get to the bottom of it. Come on now. Would I want you talking to him if I had something to hide?'

She looked at the ceiling.

'Of course not,' Peter said. 'We'll talk to him and find out what the hell he thinks he heard and put him straight.'

She dropped her eyes and stared into his for several seconds before answering.

'OK. But I'm asking the questions.'

'Fine, great. Anything you want.'

Mary sat alone on the sofa. Peter returned to the armchair he had vacated a few minutes before. Finbarr had not only stayed in his chair, he seemed to have frozen solid. He was staring hard at the floor, completely immobile.

'Does the name Regina Clarke mean anything to you, Finbarr?'

This was Mary's opener. Peter tried to catch her eye to show her how confident he was looking, but she stared straight at Finbarr.

'Who?' he said, without looking up.

'Regina Clarke,' Mary repeated. 'Peter's girlfriend?'

Peter was about to object, your honour, but thought better of it. Better to let Finbarr clear his name for him.

'Never heard of her,' Finbarr said. Then he glared at Peter. 'I didn't know you had a girlfriend. You'd think you'd have told me.'

'I haven't got a bloody girlfriend. Mary is confused.'

'Don't patronise me,' she snapped.

'You're one to talk anyway,' Finbarr said. He was still apparently transfixed by the carpet.

'Who are you talking to?' Mary said.

'You,' Finbarr said. His eyes darted in her direction for a half-second.

Peter sat forward. 'What does that mean?'

'Yeah,' Mary said. 'What does that mean?'

Finbarr let go of the armrests and put his hands on his knees. 'Isn't that why I'm here? Peter, it breaks my heart to be the one to tell you, but your wife is being unfaithful. She's chasing around after another man.'

Before Peter had time to react, Finbarr looked knowingly at Mary and added another syllable.

'Me,' he said.

35

Umberto had never mitched before and frankly he wasn't all that taken with it. The third-rate thrill of missing school was far outweighed by the anxiety of being on the run. He'd walked out as soon as he felt able to walk (which wasn't that long in fact – Helmet had done no serious damage) and headed into town. There was no plan; he just wanted to get away. It was still lunch-time then and there were lots of school uniforms in the square. He did get some funny looks, however, and the smoky mirror in the public toilets confirmed that his left eye was blackening up. Being hit by a knee didn't agree with it, apparently. Umberto had never had a black eye before either. He was as unimpressed with it as he was with everything else. It wasn't painful, but it made him look like someone who got into fights. Not the image he was after.

He spent the entire afternoon in the cramped and dusty public library, trying not to think too hard. Only one person, an old woman, asked him why he wasn't in school. 'Study break,' Umberto told her. She didn't press the issue, but didn't look too convinced either. He caught her staring at him over the top of her *National Geographic* back issue more than once and eventually found it more comfortable to hide behind a giant atlas. By the time the old woman finally left, he had been around the world four times and had seen nothing.

The temptation to go to see Mary at the shop or Peter at the office was powerful, but he resisted. Both environments were too public. There might be a scene.

Better to get them at home.

36

Mary didn't know whether to laugh or cry. She gave laughing a shot.

'Laugh all you like,' Finbarr said. 'But you've been caught out. You're *nicked*.'

'You better explain yourself,' Peter said to Finbarr. 'And quick.'

'I warn you, Peter, you're not going to like it.'

'Don't worry about me, just explain yourself.'

'This is insane,' Mary said. 'But go on. I can hardly wait.'

Finbarr crossed his legs and cleared his throat. 'In the pub last Saturday, when you told me about the way this one was treating you—'

'*Treating* you?' Mary said.

Peter shook his head. 'All I said was—'

'You've been moaning about me to strangers in pubs?'

'You're getting the wrong picture here, I was only—'

'None of that is important now,' Finbarr interrupted. 'The important thing is that I recognised the symptoms.'

Peter leaned forward and rested his elbows on his knees. 'What symptoms? What are you *talking* about?'

Finbarr got to his feet and began to pace the room like Poirot. 'Adultery! I know the signs, Peter. Oh, I've seen it all on the telly. A good man ruined by a scheming woman.'

Mary caught Peter's eye behind Finbarr's back and twirled a finger at the side of her temple. He gave her a blank look.

'I hope you're not *listening* to this crap,' she said, incredulous. Finbarr spun on his heels and sneered at her.

'Feeling nervous, are we? Guilty secret about to be exposed, hmmm? Well, you should have thought about that earlier. Too late now.'

'Get to the point,' Peter snapped.

'Keep your head,' Finbarr said. 'Don't let her get you rattled.'

'She isn't rattling me, Finbarr. You are. Now if you have something to say, say it.'

Finbarr sat down again and pointed an eye at Mary. 'Get any unexpected gifts this week, dear? Anything unusual?'

'You must be *joking*,' Mary said, putting her hand to her mouth. 'That was *you*?'

'What was? What was him?' Peter said.

'It's nothing. I got a bunch of flowers when you were away. And a note. An anonymous note.'

'What kind of note? You never told me. Why didn't you tell me?'

'Well, I didn't think it was—'

'What? Any of my business.'

Finbarr tut-tutted. 'You see, Peter, this is—'

'And *you*. What the fuck are you doing sending flowers to my wife?'

'Calm down now. I did it for you. To show you.'

'Show me what?'

'The thread you're hanging by. She's no better than the rest of them, Peter. First chance she gets, she'll be off.'

Now Mary jumped to her feet. 'Out!' she shouted. 'Get out of my house now. Get out or I'll get the fucking—'

'Would you like me to play him the message?' Finbarr said. 'Maybe that's the quickest way to clear this up.'

'What message?'

'"What message?"' Finbarr mocked. 'The nerve of her, Peter. You'll thank me for this one day.' He reached into his jacket pocket. Mary knew what he was taking out before he held it up like Exhibit A.

'She couldn't help herself,' Finbarr said sadly. 'She just had to get in touch with her mysterious admirer.'

Mary threw her arms in the air as Finbarr fiddled with the phone. 'I had absolutely no interest in knowing where the bloody flowers came from! If anyone rang you, it was Fidelma. She wanted to know who it was, I didn't *care*. You're not being taken in by this shite, are you, Peter? Are you?'

He wet his lips. 'Let's hear the message.'

'Dial 121,' Finbarr said, and threw the phone to him.

Mary sat down again. 'Fine. Let's hear it. I've got nothing to hide.'

Peter dialled and then held the phone to his right ear, expressionless. 'That's not Mary,' he said to Finbarr. 'That's her friend Fidelma.'

'Let me hear,' Mary said and snatched it from him. She

309

redialled and listened, shaking her head. 'I told you. Fidelma.'

Finbarr seemed to falter. 'A friend of yours, is she?' he asked when he had recovered. 'Well, I take my hat off. That was clever of you, to get her to make the call. Female cunning, you can never underestimate it.'

'You're out of your mind,' Mary said. 'And you're leaving.'

Finbarr looked to Peter. 'I'm sorry, Peter. But it was the only way. There comes a time when a man has to look after his friend's best—'

'Finbarr, I'm going to say this once. You and I are not friends. You and I are never going to be friends. And she's right: you're leaving.'

He nodded. 'OK. I understand. You're upset. This is not what you wanted to hear. You can't see how lucky you—'

'Out. Now. Before I lift you and throw you out.'

'*Well*. There's no need to be threatening. I'm sticking my neck out for you here. This isn't easy for me either, you know.'

Peter stood up very slowly, and then drew himself up to his full height. 'What's *wrong* with you, Finbarr? Do you really think this is how people make friends? Now this is the last time I'm going to ask you nicely. Get. Out.'

'OK, I'm going. But don't come running to me when you get home one day and there's a note on the table telling you she's run off with some—'

'Don't worry, I won't. It would suit me down to the ground if I never laid eyes on you again.'

Finbarr's mouth turned down. Then he nodded sadly, got up

and strolled casually into the hall. Mary followed him, despite Peter's mumbled order to stay put.

'The other day in the shop,' she said to his back. 'You told me you'd never married because you'd never met the right woman.'

He turned and stared deep into her eyes.

She swallowed. 'But you act like you've never met *any* women.'

He closed his eyes slowly. His nostrils flared. For a moment, his face seemed to wilt. Then it hardened again. He snapped his eyes open and smiled at her before turning to open the front door. 'I heard a bunch of young ones talking about your precious shop not so long ago,' he said. 'Standing around outside the pub. They were laughing their bollocks off about it. Pathetic, they said it was. Small-town. Out of date. I interrupted them and stood up for you then, but you know what? They were right. You haven't really got much of a selection, have you? Nothing for the true music fan. I think I'll take my business elsewhere.'

He left.

Mary returned to the living room unsure of where to start. But she didn't get a chance. Peter started for her.

'You've got some cheek,' he said.

'*What?*'

'You had me terrified. I was bricking it about a stupid misunderstanding with loony Regina and all the time you've been cavorting with mysterious admirers on the sly.'

'Cavorting?! Were you not paying attention? It was *Fidelma*. I didn't give a shit. I even threw the flowers in the bin. You're

311

the one sneaking off to Dublin to meet women.'

Peter ignored the last part. 'But then you don't like flowers and all that crap, do you? What if he'd sent you something you like? That wouldn't go in the bin, would it?'

'I'm not going to dignify that with—'

'And you kept it all very quiet, didn't you? I suppose you were having a good laugh about it behind my back, you and her. He could be right for all I know, maybe you did get her to ring, to cover your tracks.'

'I don't believe I'm hearing this. Listen, sunshine, I'm not the one who went boozing with *that* eejit and told him . . . that's another thing. What did you tell him? I never got to hear and you know I'd just *love* to know.'

'I told him the truth! That I was getting plastered because my wife had just flipped out at me for no bloody reason! Rewinding a video, my arse.'

'You total *asshole*. I explained this to you last night; it wasn't for no reason, I'd been feeling—'

'Yeah, yeah. Ordinary and unexotic. Now I know why. One admirer isn't good enough for you.'

Mary took some breaths. She didn't want to say anything that she couldn't take back and they were getting into that territory. 'Don't think I don't see what you're doing. You're trying to flip this on to me. You've been caught out yourself and you think attack is the best form of defence.'

'I've been caught out in *nothing*. I'm telling the truth about Regina and you know it.'

'Oh, I do, do I? I'll tell you what I know, mister. I know that this is no fucking way to— AGGH!'

She was in no state for sudden shocks and this one almost stopped her racing heart. There was a ghost peering in through the living-room window.

37

Umberto had gone around the back of the house out of habit. Almost all his trips to Peter and Mary's started at The Cottage and led him over the fence and up the garden to the back door. He'd felt peculiar approaching from the front.

He heard the shouting before he had even turned the corner. Something started dancing in his stomach. He crept around to the living-room window, praying that the sound was coming from the TV. It wasn't. Peter was on the sofa and Mary was standing over him, pointing at him with both index fingers. It looked bad. Umberto's legs froze. Then Mary noticed him and screamed. He was tempted to run but before he could move he saw her recognise him and then recognise the fact that he'd been in a fight. She was at the back door in a second.

'Jesus, what happened?' she said and took a step towards him. 'Are you all right?'

'I'm OK,' Umberto said and burst into tears.

She ran to him and put her arm around him. 'Who hit you? You're so *pale*.'

Umberto didn't answer at first. He simply could not believe that he was crying again. Twice in one week. He was fourteen, for God's sake. It was absurd. 'Guy at school,' he eventually blubbed. 'I was asking for it.'

Mary rubbed his shoulder. 'I'm sure you weren't. Some people—'

He stamped his foot like a five-year-old and felt even worse for doing so. 'I *was*,' he said. 'I wanted a fight. I wanted an excuse to hit somebody.'

'And did you?' Peter said. Umberto hadn't even noticed him coming out of the house. 'Should I see the other guy?'

'No. The other guy is fine.'

'We'll go in and have a cup of tea,' Mary said, 'and you can tell us why you suddenly want to start hitting people.'

Umberto wriggled out of her embrace. The tears had stopped but he felt far from composed. 'No way. I'm not going in there. You're fighting. I saw you. I heard you.'

Peter and Mary looked at each other.

'We can fight later,' Peter said. 'Come on.'

'There's no steak, but you can have a sausage for your eye,' Mary added. She seemed to forget to smile. Then she rectified her mistake.

'Stop it!' Umberto yelled. 'Stop being so nice!'

Peter and Mary looked at each other again and then back at him.

'Why?' Mary said.

'Because I'll have to get along without this, won't I? The way things are going. I better start getting used to it.'

'What things?' Peter said.

'Your things. You two. You won't be together this time next week at this rate.'

Mary reapplied her arm to his shoulder. 'We're just having a bad night. Couples fight. It's nothing for you to worry about.'

'It's not just a bad night! I know what's going on!'

'There's nothing going on,' Peter said. 'Not on my end anyway.'

Mary gave him a filthy look. 'Mine either.'

Umberto suddenly wanted something to do with his hands. He put them behind his back first but that made him feel like Prince Charles. He abandoned that pose and put them in his pockets. 'Don't treat me like a child. I know there's something going on. I know you were saying something serious to Mom last weekend. About Peter.'

'Is that right?' Peter said, looking at Mary.

Mary stood on her toes and then dropped again. 'What did you hear me say, exactly?'

'Well . . . all right, I didn't hear you say anything specific. But I knew it was something bad.'

Peter puffed in Mary's direction. 'And you're giving out about me talking about you behind your back? You've got some—'

'Don't start,' she said. 'If you must know, I *was* moaning about you but only because . . . look, I explained all this last night. Let him continue.'

Umberto wasn't sure that he knew how to continue. He was beginning to feel less sure about things. 'Hang on. Are you two on the rocks or not?'

'No,' they said together. Then they looked at each other, apparently both surprised.

Umberto shuffled his feet. He was more confused than pleased. 'But Mom said ... well ... I suppose she didn't come right out and say anything but she hinted ... that ... eh ... maybe she didn't hint it either.'

'You're imagining things, Umberto,' Peter said. Then he looked at Mary. 'There's a lot of it going around.'

Umberto felt hope dawn, but still couldn't discount the evidence of his own eyes. 'What the hell were you fighting about tonight then?'

Peter and Mary shrugged in unison. Then they looked at each other's feet.

'Nothing important though, right?'

'Well ...' Mary said.

'Has something important happened or not?'

Neither of them seemed willing, or perhaps able, to answer.

'There have been some ... misunderstandings,' Peter said.

'There sure have,' Mary mumbled.

'Misunderstandings? Is that all? Well, then! One of you apologise. Go on.'

Neither of them responded.

Umberto's patience ran out immediately. 'Peter, you're the man. You go first.'

'Why should I?'

'Go *on*,' Umberto insisted. 'For *my* sake. Please. For *me*.'

Peter thought about it and then kicked at nothing. Dust rose.

'Something small, even,' Umberto said. 'Anything.'

'All right, all right,' Peter said. 'Mary. I'm sorry I rewound the video when you were trying to tell me something. *There*.'

'What?' Umberto said. He was ignored.

'It doesn't matter,' Mary said. 'I suppose.' She stared at her reflection in the living-room window. 'All right then. I'm sorry I bitched about you to Valerie.'

This made more sense to Umberto. It sounded like progress. Peter flapped his hands by his side.

'Well, I shouldn't have said anything to David. Or Finbarr Grealey. Finbarr especially.'

'Who?' Umberto said.

'Bloody right you shouldn't,' Mary said. 'But maybe I could have told you about the flowers.'

Umberto wasn't sure he even wanted to know.

Peter nodded. 'Same goes for the dinner – the *innocent* dinner – in Dublin.'

'Well, OK then,' Mary said. 'Maybe we could call it quits. For Umberto's sake.'

'Yes!' Umberto screeched. 'Call it quits!'

'Fine by me,' Peter said. They all looked over each other's shoulders, uncertain of the next move. Seconds passed.

'Why don't we all go for dinner?' Mary said then. 'Umberto, you come too. You can tell us who you want to hit and why.'

Umberto smiled and gleefully clapped his hands together. 'Never mind that. The urge is leaving me already.'

'Have you even been home yet?' Peter said. 'If you're coming, you better call your mum and dad. They'll be worried.'

'No they won't,' he replied. 'But who cares?'

He told them about Helmet McGuiney as they got into the car.

319

'You meet these people from time to time,' Mary said. 'All you can do is avoid him. Stick with your own crowd.'

'I haven't really got a crowd,' Umberto said.

Mary turned to face him. 'That can be a compliment.'

'Can it?'

'Definitely,' Peter said. 'You'll come into your own some day, Umberto, mark my words. When you get out of this crappy little town.'

Umberto was surprised by this. 'I thought you liked this crappy little town,' he said.

'Oh, we do. But that's because we're . . . ordinary.'

It sounded like a jibe to Umberto, but Mary agreed immediately. 'That's right. You'll get out and you won't look back.'

'Will I?'

'I'd bet the shop.'

He gave it some thought. 'Maybe so. Eh, listen, can we make a stop in town before the restaurant?' Umberto said. 'It'll be quick.'

'Yeah, sure.' Peter nodded. 'Where?'

Umberto coughed. 'You have to promise you won't get mad . . .'

Father Duff didn't look surprised to see Umberto. He looked alarmed.

'Is everything all right?' he asked. They were on the front step. Ducky had asked Umberto to come in, but he declined.

'Yeah,' Umberto said. 'It is. Things are fine. Listen. I want to say sorry for giving you a hard time about not helping. I shouldn't have asked you. You were right to say no, it turns out. I had the facts all wrong anyway. Like you guessed.'

Now Father Duff looked surprised. 'Really?' he said.

'I know, I know, it was a close call. I'm very embarrassed. But they're fine. We're all going out for dinner now.'

He motioned in the direction of the car, parked on the street. Father Duff looked. 'That's not your . . . who is that?'

'That's the couple I told you about. You may as well know now.'

'Is it?'

'Yeah. It's my aunt and uncle. Do you know them?'

The priest shook his head. Then he patted his pockets and withdrew his cigarettes. 'No.'

'Well, keep it that way. They don't need any help. If they ever did. I'm a bit confused about it, to be honest.'

'Right. Right. No problem.'

'Good. I'm off, then.'

Father Duff nodded silently. Umberto turned and walked away. But he stopped halfway down the path. 'You never know your luck,' he said. 'I might give you another game some day. If I can fit you into my busy social schedule. Which I almost certainly can.'

He expected an ecstatic reaction to this news, but Father Duff just nodded dumbly once again. Umberto shrugged and headed for the gate. No pleasing some people.

The Chinese was full. Their enthusiasm for eating out died on the spot. 'We'll get fish and chips,' Peter said. 'And watch that movie. Have you seen *Fargo*, Umberto?'

'Four times. But I could look at it again.'

321

Peter went into the chip shop alone. Mary and Umberto sat outside in the car. 'You've gone all quiet,' he said after a while. 'Are you all right?'

'Yeah,' she said. 'Listen, Umberto, I want to ask you something. Have you ever heard kids talking about the shop? In school or wherever?'

'What shop? Yours?'

She nodded.

'Maybe,' Umberto said.

'And . . . do they like it? Is it . . . never mind.'

'Is it what?'

'Well. Is it considered . . . cool?'

He didn't want to lie. She could usually tell when he was lying. 'It's not bad considering it's in Drumshanagh,' he ventured as a compromise.

'Yeah. That's what I thought. Never mind. That's good enough for me.'

Peter came back holding the greasy bags aloft like a hunter returned from a kill, and they drove off. They hadn't gone thirty yards when he honked the horn and banged on his window.

'There's Fiona,' he said. They all looked to the other side of the street. Fiona Sheridan was walking alone, head down. She didn't seem to see or hear them.

'She doesn't look too chuffed, does she?' Peter said, looking in his rear-view mirror. 'Maybe we should turn around. I've got a new joke, might cheer her up.'

'No,' Mary said, emphatically.

'I wasn't being serious.'

She smiled. 'I know.'

'Tell it to us,' Umberto said.
Peter took his eyes off the road to look at Mary.
'Go on then,' she groaned and put her fingers in her ears.

38

Finbarr sat on a stool at the bar and ordered a double whiskey. The Dead Leg was filling up rapidly, it being Friday and all. When the whiskey arrived, he didn't so much drink it as throw it at his face. Then he caught the barman's eye and nodded. Same again.

Turning slowly on his stool, he took a good look around the room, scouting for a decent seat. There was one in the corner, on a sofa half-occupied by an exhausted-looking man in a crumpled grey suit. Finbarr didn't recognise him. An out-of-towner, probably. He paid for his drinks and made his way over. The man turned and nodded to him as he sat down. His eyes were dark and heavy behind his thick glasses and he wore a serious expression. Finbarr raised his glass. The man nodded again.

Then Finbarr cleared his throat. 'Women trouble,' he said. It wasn't a question. It was a statement.

DAMIEN OWENS

DEAD CAT BOUNCE

'A very funny and sparkling début from a writer who is here to stay' Joseph O'Connor

'It's hilarious . . . everything from existentialist nuns to hard ass girls. Every single man should read it to affirm how sad we really are' Dermot O'Leary

Joe Flood is under no illusions – he knows that the universe isn't fair. He knows that things can and do go wrong. They're generally small things though, and they usually have the decency to go wrong one at a time.

No longer. Joe's various problems have bumped into each other, fallen in love, and apparently started to breed. Now his family is imploding, his job is making him feel ill, and his ideal woman suspects he may be simple.

But there's light at the end of the tunnel. Joe has a plan – and a movie script. If he can keep it together for just a little while longer, Hollywood will surely come calling, with its starlets and its millions.

If he can keep it together . . .

Wisecracking but clueless, caring but confused, Joe is a man determined to do the right thing – just as soon as he works out what the right thing is.

Dead Cat Bounce is the fresh and funny novel from a truly remarkable new voice.

HODDER AND STOUGHTON PAPERBACKS